28 S

the Dog Knew

Friday Poodle

BLACK ROSE
writing™

© 2015 by Friday Poodle

All rights reserved. No part of this book may be reproduced, stored in a retrieval system or transmitted in any form or by any means without the prior written permission of the publishers, except by a reviewer who may quote brief passages in a review to be printed in a newspaper, magazine or journal.

The final approval for this literary material is granted by the author.

First printing

This is a work of fiction. Names, characters, businesses, places, events and incidents are either the products of the author's imagination or used in a fictitious manner. Any resemblance to actual persons, living or dead, or actual events is purely coincidental.

ISBN: 978-1-61296-589-5

PUBLISHED BY BLACK ROSE WRITING

www.blackrosewriting.com

Printed in the United States of America

Suggested retail price $17.95

28 Secrets the Dog Knew is printed in Adobe Garamond Pro

JS Bookshop
Southampton University
Tel : 02380671069
Email : orders.js@johnsmith.co.uk
Follow us : twitter.com/BookshopatSoton

Description	Qty	Cost
9781612965895		
8 Secrets the Dog Knew	1	11.95
Total To Pay:		11.95
Payment: Southampton Entitlem		11.95

A credit note will be issued
for any goods returned within 14 days
if stock is in perfect condition with a
receipt. Thank you for your custom.
VAT : GB 259 5488 08
Receipt No:079382:17/03/16:1444:1605:41

Dedicated to Rose Greenberg

Introduction

First and foremost, I want you to know that I'm a standard poodle and I wrote this book. Yup, me. Throughout this quest novel you will learn that I am the keeper of secrets. People confide in me. I do not know why. Perhaps it's because I have big ears.

Still with me I see. Yet still distrusting? You assume incorrectly that my inability to speak precludes me from being able to write.

My point is this. You are reading the innermost thoughts of a standard poodle. We just agreed that I cannot talk in words, so it stands to reason that I must have somehow written them down. How else can you explain that I know everyone's secrets? Having said that, I suspect that you are still resisting the idea that a seven year old apricot standard poodle could pen a book. Maybe, you would believe it was more possible if I were a ten year old standard poodle. Trust me when I tell you that three more years would not make a difference.

In many ways, our cognitive limits exceed humans'. Did you know your stockbroker asks his basset hound for the stock tips every morning? (Every other canine knows that basset hounds are the world's dumbest dogs.) If you were going to ask a canine for stock tips, and I do not recommend that, at the very least ask a Dachshund/Yorkie cross. Not because they are smart, but because Dorkies are known to pass on insider trading tips. Such gossips.

The primary problem is that you want to anthropomorphize, attribute human characteristics, to what I say. For example, as discussed, when you hear I am a seven year old standard poodle, you want to explain my book writing ability by multiplying by seven. This human age conversion concept is absurd. I am a seven year old standard poodle. I am not acting like a forty-nine year old human male. Have you ever heard me say once that I want to take watercolour classes at NYU and paint artistic masterpieces at my newly renovated loft downtown where I live with my 28 year old girlfriend?

I have translated the conversation in this book into your language to make it easier for you to grasp. No dogs in this book actually talk with exception of Earl, and he only knows how to say one word. Any reference to dog conversations are simply my translations from my canine language of the moving and experienced images that my senses provide into your English language.

I hope that at this point that you are open to the idea of learning more about my canine world. Let's say for example, you and I are on *Jeopardy* and the final Category is Canine Facts. It reads, The Taco Bell Chihuahua. Without hesitation, I write the correct question: Who is Gidget?

It may surprise you to learn that there have been other canine novels. I heard from a reliable source that *Lassie Come Home* was first written as a parenting tool by Lassie's mom. It was originally entitled, *Lassie Come Home and Clean Up Your Crate*. And then I heard, Jack London's *The Call of the Wild* success was largely due to Buck the dog's input. Many people do not know the original working title suggested by Buck was *Don't Buck with Me*. Word around the dog park is that *Old Yeller* is about a poor dog that was chained to a yard post all afternoon. I might be mixing that up with another bestseller called *Shut up You Stupid Cocker Spaniel*. My point is merely, people love dog books.

I have come to understand that every book has three components: a beginning, a middle, and an end. I will follow that format. Please read my book. I pawed my heart into it.

About My Assistant (Co-Author)

Barry Greenberg is an award-winning condominium marketing/sales expert. With over 23 completed projects, resulting in 4,082 condominium sales, he is well known in the Manitoba condominium industry.

Each of the 23 projects required a six page full colour booklet aimed at the Winnipeg, Manitoba condominium target market. Hence, stretching the meaning of the word "author" to the max--he has 23 published works. Then again, so does his nephew Cameron if you count crayon fridge art as published work. Hmm, Cameron did the cover for me.

With January and February Manitoba weather reaching -40 Celsius, he took up writing novels to fill his show home time commitment hours. (He correctly surmised that building more than 44 snowmen could result in his sanity being questioned.)

Wanting to make his mother proud and simultaneously letting his dad know that his parents' investment in Barry's college psychology courses was more than four years of vacation, he began training full service dogs to work on the palliative floors of hospitals. I was one of them. This after hours non-profit venture has a long waiting list of canine owners wanting to enroll. Although there is no charge for his therapy dog training classes, a donation to their favourite animal shelter is encouraged. And, he will accept a Starbucks coffee on a frosty winter training day (no sugar, one cream).

He sees his words as a way to shed light on the canine world, fighting for canines that cannot fight for themselves. Donating all his writing profits to animal shelters, he hopes to leave the planet a little better than how he found it.

28 Secrets
the Dog Knew

Chapter One

My Beginning

My mom's pregnancy lasted 63 days following conception, the exact amount of time it took Moses to locate the Ten Commandments (it would have been longer if he had not had help). According to Rabbinical laws, Moses wandered the desert aimlessly for more than two months, dehydrated. Unable to continue a step further, he tripped over a standard poodle napping on the cool tablets in the midday sun. Legend holds that in return for the great gift, Moses promised the poodle that he would create an eleventh commandment, my people shall love thy poodle above all other canines (evidenced today by the fact that many Jewish people have standard poodles). I know this to be true because I heard it at the dog park from a very reliable border collie mix, SammyFarber.

My Mom's increased appetite ballooned her weight from her normal of 49 pounds to 57. Set on 20 acres northeast of Toronto, Ontario, Canada is where it all happened in Toronto Cantope Orphanage. If you are in the neighbourhood, a purple poodle silhouette marks the entrance of my birthplace. Howling Toronto winds announced my arrival on the eve of March 12, 8:88 p.m. blinking on the digital clock radio.

A few days before she gave birth to me (known as whelping), Mom refused to eat. Noticing this sign of readiness, Peter and Diane, the adoption directors, knew to put her in a whelping box, sufficiently large to accommodate a comfortable stretch for her. It had low sides and was placed in the corner of the spare bedroom in the main house, a warm, dry, draft-free and secluded area. The bottom of the box was lined with soft light green towels. Maybe they were blue? Seems like such a long time ago. So much has happened, so very much.

Shortly before my exit, her body temperature dropped to 98 degrees, three degrees lower than I was used to. It was go time! All eleven of us felt around for the exit. I was so far in the back that I thought I would never get out. By the time I found the birth canal, ten puppies had already exited and were taking their place on her shaved belly, attaching themselves to vacant, swollen nipples.

Finally, I emerged last.

'Hi Mom, I am here. What are your other two wishes?' I mumbled through my own placental membrane. Before I could suffocate, my mother removed it by tearing off and eating the membrane, and then she severed the umbilical cord with her sharp teeth. Tired as she was after ten of these operations, she licked me and refused to stop licking until I started breathing. My Mom knew it was very important for me to suckle soon after emerging from her womb, nosing one of my earlier siblings out of the way. That way I could ingest colostrum, a milk-like substance containing maternal antibodies produced by her mammary glands just after birth. This was the first and only time I dined on my Mom's belly. Mom said that once would be enough to protect me. She was wrong. Dead wrong! Later, when I was less than one year old, I lay in my den unable to move, cursing my Mom's decision. Yeah, I know. It's hard for my mom to know where one set of medical thinking stops and another replaces it. But I think it is around nine p.m. on a Wednesday that it was decided one feeding on Mom was not enough.

Mom's name was Rebecca and her friends called her Reba. She

exuded an aura of elegance, intelligence, and pride. I always thought of her as an active dog. However, I have no facts to base this on except the birthing of eleven of us. Her apricot body was squarely built, and properly proportioned. She had a fairly broad, deep chest with well-sprung ribs, and her loin was stout, broad, and muscular. Strong and smoothly toned, with the blades properly set back defining her shoulders which stood above straight and parallel forelegs. Mom was a confident dog. Her small, oval-shaped feet ended with well-arched toes. Her well-proportioned neck allowed for a prideful head carriage. Her muzzle, although straight and fine, was not as long as the typical standard poodle; her almond shaped eyes, far-set, and darker in color than normal were flanked by her larger than life orange ears that hung close to her head.

My Mom loved to listen to the radio, which might explain her big, droopy ears. And during her pregnancy, it was on 24-7. So, I too learned to love the radio. Her favourite was Bubba the Love Sponge on Howard 101, a daily three-hour show. At first I didn't listen to Bubba, but I gave him a listen and he can be pretty entertaining. If I ever become a sailor, then I will have the language down pat. Scott Ferrell also has a daily show on Howard 101, but his show is a little too sports-oriented for my Mom's tastes. Dad likes to listen to him. Then again, Dad likes Mel Tillis singing *How Come Your Dog Don't Bite Nobody But Me.* The first time I heard country western I knew it was not for me. Yuck! Maybe it's true that I'm just a bug on the windshield of life. But I do not need it sung to me.

My knowledge of the world comes from two sources, talk radio and SammyFarber, who you will meet later. There are people who will argue that music in the womb is a bonding experience, telling you that soft music of string instruments such as sitar, santoor and violin will increase the "peaceable" as well as "courageous" temperament of the puppy. I do not know much about that. But I can tell you that the first time I heard talk radio in the womb, I knew that everything you needed to know about life could be learned from talk radio.

For those who may not know, talk radio is a format containing discussion about topical issues. Most shows are regularly hosted by a single individual, and often feature interviews with a number of different, exciting guests. The best part is that talk radio typically includes an element of listener participation, usually by broadcasting live conversations between the host and listeners who "call in" (usually via telephone) to the show. Most callers are from Iowa. The only nationally-syndicated, politically oriented weekday talk radio show in Canada is Adler on Line, hosted by Charles Adler and heard on eleven stations across the country. As a pup, I listened to Peter Warren, much better than Adler. But I heard he quit and got a better job filling toothpaste containers in Vancouver. My other favourite is the conservative, less-political commentator, Laura Schlessinger aka Dr Laura featuring personal and relationship advice. Did you know that Louis Doberman, a German tax collector, created the Doberman breed in the late 1860s to protect him from his wife? If you do not believe me then call Laura and ask her. And, of course, I never miss Ask the Vet. Dogs are identical in anatomy, with 731 bones and 42 permanent teeth? More importantly, Bingo is the name of the dog on the side of the crackerjack box? See, there is so much to learn from talk radio.

I do not want to comment on her haircut because after all she is my Mom and she was giving birth to me. My dad, Waika Watson (who I called Dad) was refined, elegant, and dignified. He too, like Mom, was apricot. He was even-tempered, and sensitive for a guy, highly intelligent and very comfortable in the company of people. His only flaw, if you consider it a flaw, was that he couldn't stand to be alone for extensive periods of time. He loved and needed to be petted.

With the exception of a slight tinge of dark red around my ears, I am the spitting image of my Mom. But, I have Dad's personality. I need a lot of attention. I suffer from an anxiety disorder characterized by excessive rumination, worrying, uneasiness, apprehension and a fear of future uncertainties either based on real or imagined events, which may affect my physical and psychological health. Based on personal introspection, without help, I am sure I am going to be one of those dogs that bite everyone. Cause no one listens to me except when I fart. I'm afraid of raw carrots and squirrels. Speaking of squirrels, did you know if you change your clothes three times in 15 minutes before you go on a date then you turn into a squirrel. Yup, it is true. How else do you explain all those female squirrels that act like teenagers?

After my initial feeding with Mom I was separated from the pack. This was to be Mom's last litter as she was getting on in years, producing not enough milk to satisfy a large litter, so prompt action was needed. Diane and Peter took on the task of hand rearing me. Having fed once from Mom and now full of precious antibodies, it was goats' milk from here on out. I was fed at regular intervals, every two hours. I would have preferred longer naps.

After each meal Diane would clean and gently rub my genitals with a damp warm cloth to stimulate and encourage me to empty my bladder and bowels. The routine ended with a warm, damp cloth passing over my body. Two hours later it would all start again.

I do not know if was the lack of sleep from my radio addiction or some other factor that caused me to have great concerns over my goats' milk diet. Perhaps it was triggered by the fact that one day in the womb, Mom's ear was glued to the show, Fat Bride - Thin Dress. It was all about, 'you are what you eat.' Mom, who was feeling a bit depressed, changed the channel and before I could say forget the guy and supersize the fries, we were listening to a documentary on goats. I learned that they are blunt, squarish-looking animals with a narrow head upon which slender, black, shiny horns rise in a backward curve to a length of nine to twelve inches. Each time after feeding, I would rub my head on the ground to see if my horns had started to grow. And, if that is not enough proof, I am sure-footed and agile. Last time I checked, (about ten minutes ago) I did not have hooves with cushioned skid-proof pads for grip. But, I am more sure-footed than my siblings, who crash into anything and everything all the time, feet going in four different directions at once.

And, with all this goats' milk I was putting on weight. It would not have surprised me to be a Billie tipping the scales at 250 pounds within a week looking for my Nanny. Yes, I was definitely becoming part goat. Shhh, it's a secret. Do not tell.

I looked over at my siblings: three girls and seven boys in all, ranging from clumsy to extra clumsy, from dull orange to dark red and from chubby to chubbier. Dogs judge objects first by their movements, then by their brightness, and then by their shape. Hence, my siblings are clumsy, dull, and fat. However I am agile, apricot and thin, just like my Mom. I know what you are thinking, there was a fox in the henhouse for there to be all the different pups since my dad is also agile, thin and apricot. Rest assured, in my canine world having children of many colours, sizes, and skills is very common unless your parents are border collies. Then they are all the same. No one has ever found a really good way to tell one border collie from another. And, do not think for one minute that they do not use that fact to their advantage. In my opinion, the world would be a better place if everyone had children all colours of the Crayola box, more tolerance, more understanding. The other solution would be to have only border collies. But then, who would they herd?

Today, like the four weeks before, I sat mesmerized by Mom's radio. Not bragging, I knew from very early on I was different, special. My specialness confirmed to me by a cloth string and a numbered paper tag around my neck and those of my littermates, one to eleven (or as I like to call eleven, onety-one). According to talk radio, most people have only five minutes of fame, and here I was only nine weeks of age and already I had achieved the status of onety-one. My future was unlimited.

With high status comes high responsibility. Being the smallest and smartest male, I suffered. Boy, did I suffer as a puppy. One day after working ten hours in the salt mine, carrying heavy bags of sea salt on my back; I stopped, only for a second, which was not allowed, for a morsel of crusty white bread and a drop of muddy water. I had disobeyed my masters. I was beaten with an oak switch, blood oozing out of every paw till I begged for a swift and painless death.

Okay, that was not true. But times were tough for me. This was my Mom's last litter. Having birthed forty-seven puppies in five previous litters over the years, she could not look after all of us in her retirement litter so I was put in a separate pen and weaned on goats' milk. On the rare occasions I slipped past the guards to access the teat well where this very pushy auburn girl wearing number 3 would nose me away. I would pay number 3 back one day. After awhile I accepted my fate, I was going to grow up to be a goat. Then life intervened when a couple from Winnipeg, needing a pack leader, picked me out of the entire grouping. The fact that I was the last one available had nothing to do with their choice, nothing at all.

Chapter 2

Running with Wolves

Upon hearing the news that her last child had been adopted, my mom licked my face clean like only a mother could, so I would look good for my Dad. Mom was considerate that way.

'Your father wants to talk to you,' she said. 'I will be back soon.'

I expected the typical father-to-puppy advice. I knew him to be less communicative than Mom. I would probably get the "avoid biting when a simple growl will do" or "on hot days, drink lots of water and lie under a shady peach tree" speech. What I wanted to hear from him were words to live by, guiding me through the hard times and warming me during the cold Winnipeg winters.

On this the last day, I knew I was his favourite son. Waiting for his wisdom, I bit my lip to control its shaking. I am a "daddy's boy", always have been, always will be. By "daddy's boy," I mean that I will carry the torch for the family. I am the go-to male puppy. I am fortunate to have been born at Cantope, and had his love and guidance on a daily basis during my first eight weeks of my life. He walked over to me, head down. I thought I detected a thin glaze of water in his eyes. Dad was a very emotional guy. Nuzzling close to him I said, 'Dad, not to worry, your guiding paw on my shoulder will remain with me forever. You can talk to me. I am old enough to understand. I will do the family proud, bearing you many grandpups.'

He looked at me and said, 'Woof.'

'I am about to embark into the cold, hard world and your words of wisdom, make that word of wisdom, to me is Woof ? Are you bleeping kidding me?' At that moment, it occurred to me that he has had 21 sons and I might have to rethink that favourite son thing and the family torchbearer quest. Little did I know that bearing grandpups was a no-no in my contract. We need a better union.

Dad sensed my concern with his word of wisdom. He continued, 'Your new guardians, or Shepherds as us canines like to call them, will receive a pamphlet which will tell them very little about you. However, it will remind them that if you do not fit in then you are to be sent back immediately. That will not happen. The paper will not be followed. I have been here fourteen years and no one has ever come back to this lovely place. If you screw up then your Shepherds will drop you off somewhere in the woods where you will not survive, hungry wolves will have you for lunch. I did not want to tell you this. But, you asked.'

Dad looked up at the sky and counted rain clouds and then back at me before he continued. 'Maybe this adventure will help you. When hunting, I came upon a pack of eight wolves. The smallest was 200 pounds, the largest, grizzly bear size. I ran with them for three days and three nights, matching their every stride. One evening, fending off starvation, I ate one small carrot top. Fearing I would further diminish their food supply, they circled around me and prepared to attack. If not for my lightning speed then I would not be here today. Like me, you too are very fast and agile.'

'And talk radio smart,' I added. 'Smart enough to pay my way,' I promised.

'You cannot find a job that will pay for your room and board. You are a puppy. For now, let them worry about these things; they are your Shepherds and as such it is their cross to bear. You have but one job, it's relatively simple, do not pee in the house. Whatever it takes, whatever sacrifices you have to make, always keep in mind that peeing in the house is forbidden. It is the number one reason why puppies are set loose in the woods to be eaten by wolves.'

'How,' I asked? 'How do I survive,' I said with a furrowed brow as I paced back and forth on wobbly legs. I do not know what to do. 'Should I never pee? If not in the house, then where should I? And when? '

'Although high strung, you are a smart boy, you will figure it out. Every Shepherd's yard is different.'

'How, tell me how? Please tell me? How? How?' I paused, streaming tears from my eyes.

'At first, the new rules, of which there will be many, will seem like a heavy burden. Think of them as a privilege. The new yard will be different than the Cantope acreage and have its own challenges, but think of it as an opportunity. And lastly, perhaps most importantly, you have a benevolent gift that one day will be unlocked. A gift greater than you can ever imagine. You need to find it. Dig until it is uncovered. A great gift,' he repeated. 'Now, I have ten other children to say goodbye to today. Just remember, do not pee in the house. Your mother and I love you. She will come by later to say goodbye.' I knew at that moment why he was called Watson the Thinker. I felt loved. The promise of a great gift that one day I will find. I decided to start digging for it as soon as I arrived at my new farm.

As predicted, my Mom strolled by a little while later. She looked worn and tired.

'Mom, I will be fine. Dad told me what I need to know, no peeing in the house and no carrots,' I said trying to reassure her.

'Not that running with the wolves nonsense, I hope. 'Cause here's what really happened. Peter took all of us hunting one sunny afternoon and your dad zigged when he should have zagged and was lost for a few hours. There were no wolves, only two rabbits that lived on the north fork just outside of our acreage. Their names are Fuzzy and Tail Runner. Fuzzy was pissed off when she found your dad had eaten all of their carrots so she sent him packing. He had eaten so many carrots that his pale orange coat turned bright orange for two days. Some of his offspring, like you, have dark orange ears because of it.'

'Are you sure they were rabbits?' I asked.

'Yes, I am very sure. Tail Runner is a good friend of mine. Your dad watches too much of the Nature Channel on television. Why, did he tell you wolves?'

'No, he never mentioned wolves,' I lied. Sometimes, lying is the right decision.

'There is important stuff that you should know.' She paused to let the whistle of the night air settle.

I moved closer so as not to miss a single word. After what seemed like forever and a day, she spoke, softly and clearly.

'Three things to remember. Firstly, dachshunds, although small, were originally bred to fight badgers so do not argue with them. Secondly, chocolate contains a substance known as theobromine, similar to caffeine, which can and will kill you if you eat it. Avoid it, regardless of the temptation. Lastly, and most importantly, everyone in life needs someone to tell their secrets to,' she said. 'Be that someone and your life will be filled with rainbows.' Walking away, she whispered, 'Think of me often as I will you.'

'Be the holder of someone's secrets,' I repeated over and over, and then I cried. I knew I would never see my parents again. I did not want to go.

As she fed me my last bottle of goats' milk along with some wonderful dry lamb, the kennel owner, Diane her brown eyes brimming laid out the plan. A wonderful journey awaited me the following morning. She told me that both she and her husband Peter would take me to the airport. She reminded me that as Rebecca's last child, I was very special. With my arrival, Mom was officially retired. She kissed me on the head and suggested I get a good night's rest.

Unable to sleep, I counted stars. Now before you start wondering whether or not I can count, I want you to consider that although I cannot count in order, I can most certainly count. I started with twenty - four, onety-one, eighteen, seven, twenty-one, thirty-one and on I went with my counting. Counting takes my mind off my problems.

Later that night, I had a visit from two resident beige poodles that I had become friends with whose call names are Scout and Makala. It was common for them to often stop by my area while they wandered around the acreage. On this particular day, they told me that I would be tested in the morning and offered useful tips. Scout said to limit the prey drive.

'Prey drive?' I asked.

'Stay calm,' he said, bouncing from front paws to back and then again.

Makala offered that no matter what noises I heard in the test; I was not to sharpen my teeth on anyone. 'If you do, you will not be allowed to go,' he said wisely.

I considered this option.

Kids being kids, I stayed up all night listening to the radio. The topic was cats. By the time morning came, my head was filled with advice. There was Marty from San Diego who said he had ace, king suited so he went all in and won. I have no idea what that had to do with cats but he seemed so happy to call in and tell everyone. And, Lynn from Colorado who said, "First I had a cat, then puppies and then kids and then more puppies. Now, I am looking for a cat. Life is a cycle." More advice came from Cheryl in White Rock who said, "I always wanted a three legged cat and now I have one so I am going to India."

I promised myself that I would become a great listener. I knew one day it might change a life (and it did – more on that later, I can`t give it all away up front). I hoped my new home would have a radio, tuned to talk shows 24 hours a day to soothe me as it did on the farm. But, no country western. By the time I was seven weeks old, I could quote the greatest sayings of all time. Bert's classic: "Opinions are like assholes, everyone has one," rolled effortlessly through my mind. And of course, I mouthed the phrase, "We'll be right back after this important commercial message," along with the host every time.

Because I had listened to every word during those seven weeks, often skipping meals and naps, by the time I boarded the plane to Winnipeg I was fluent in three languages: Dog, English and Bleep. Dog was the easiest because there are not many sounds puppies can make. Dog is a language of joined images, not unlike Chinese. English is confusing and even with an avid listener like myself, problems with the multiple usages of English words often occur.

Bleep, my favourite language, is clear and direct. It is most often heard on the late night shows. SammyFarber speaks bleep sometimes. He also has his own language that I call Oy Vey. I wish everyone spoke Oy Vey, a beautiful language, rolling off the tongue, clear and easy to understand, uniting the world, one common language. The thought of a worldwide common language makes my tail wag. You will meet SammyFarber later.

I remember one show, broadcast from 3 to 6 am, where the host suggested that pit bulls and Rottweilers are more vicious than any other breed and should be put to sleep. The callers that night all spoke bleep or mumble. "Are ya outta yer bleeping mind, you bleeping bleep. I'm gonna put you to sleep. I'm getting off this couch and coming down there and beat the bleeping bleep out of you and your bleeping beagle dawg. You bleep." See what I mean? What a melodic, crystal-clear message. Easily understood by everyone.

In the morning, I was so tired from no sleep that I could barely move. I was taken to a secluded area and the test, administered by Diane, was over quickly. I do not remember the test very much except at one point she threw a tennis ball and although I was tempted to run after it, I calmed myself by counting.

"Not a working dog," she said. I did not know what that meant. I assumed it was a good sign. After that, there was a lot of noise, ringing bells and clanging spoons. This was followed by touching in places that I thought was inappropriate. Hmm, I thought, readying to bite. When Diane played with my paws, I relaxed and giggled a bit. Truth be told, I could not bite Diane under any circumstance, even if it meant being allowed to stay. The test was over in a few minutes and I was returned to my area and given a bottle of goats' milk.

Peter carried me in a small crate. Inside was a white blanket and there was a small white stuffed bear off to the left. `Going to Winnipeg? ' I said to the bear, who did not answer. Peter taped something to the top of my traveling kennel; I do not know what it was. Me, the crate, the blanket and the bear were soon in the back of the Cantope van.

After a three-hour car ride, we arrived at the airport; there were many forms to fill out. I did not understand much of it. However, I listened carefully, my ears hanging on each word.

Peter nibbled on a peanut butter sandwich while fighting with the paperwork. Finally, it started to make sense to me. I was going to live with the "Ship To" family.

I was very excited at the thought of living with the "Ship To" family, sailing the ocean blue. (Winnipeg has an ocean? This proved to be incorrect.) Puppies make a lot of incorrect assumptions but we do not care. We find guessing to be a very fun game.

Just before I was loaded on the plane, I remember Peter slipping his fingers into my crate and drugging me. I had heard on late night talk radio about the evils of drugs and how I would be forced into a life of desperation and prostitution. Me, a nine week old puppy, an addict. Try as I might, I did not resist the temptation. At the end of his index finger was the most wonderful smell. It was intoxicating. I had never smelt anything like that before and I was in heaven. Not wanting him to pull his hand away, I bit into the white bread that housed the soft creamy maple coloured substance. I knew at that moment that I would spiral through the stages; constant cravings and preoccupation with obtaining the substance, using more of the substance than necessary to experience the intoxicating effects, and experiencing tolerance then withdrawal symptoms, and decreased motivation for normal puppy activities. I thought the taste would be bitter and I prepared myself with the possibility that I might vomit.

Oddly enough, none of these things happened. Instead, I was pleasantly surprised, to learn the peanut bits were fairly tender and they broke easily as I munched them. The creamed peanut butter blended in nicely with the crunchy peanut bits. At that moment I knew I was addicted to the crunchy peanut butter stuck to the roof of my mouth. This was the first experience I had with the peanut butter drug and it was not to be my last. I shifted back and forth in my crate waiting for the latch to pop open so I could board the plane and snack with the other first class passengers. 'I'll have the duck,' I practiced in my mind, knowing full well that I could not say much more than Woof. The next thing I knew, I was still in that smelly crate. Jammed into the heated cargo hold and told to shut up. I think the exact words were, shut up right now you stupid goat. And then it occurred to me. I was obviously traveling on points.

I am not very good with estimating time. However, I am sure the flight to Winnipeg took four days and seven nights. I was at the airport three hours before flight time, that is the rule for canines.

Having no one else to talk to, I tried to strike up a conversation with my cabin mate who I called 'White Bear'. But, he was not in a chatty mood. So, I rested my head on the soft white blanket and dreamed of days to come. I would like to tell you that I had a nightmare of epic proportions where I was forced to drink goats' milk till I morphed into that horrid creature. I would like to tell you such things that would cause you pause if you ever decided to use drugs.

But alas, I must confess that the only thing that happened from my peanut butter addiction was that I got a bad case of dry mouth and a keen desire for grape jelly. I slept most of the way. It was the first sleep I had in more than 30 hours. The drop in temperature told me that it was time for me to exit the aircraft. I looked around for the birth canal.

Chapter 3

Cleared For Take-off

During the long flight, I pondered two things. Firstly, what my radio call name would be. I ruled out Melchior, Gaspar, and Balthazar, which are great names for Shepherds, not dogs. I gave some thought to Snoopy, Scooby-Doo, or Astro. I think they are all taken.

Dogs want a dog name. Like cars want a car name. I'm Porsche and these are my friends, Lamborghini and Ferrari. If you were a car, would you want to be called Arnold? Trust me, no dog wants to be named Arnold either or any other Shepherd name for that matter. I settled on 'Tuesday the Poodle', talk show call in name, Tuesday.

Secondly and equally important, I wondered about the origin of the word 'dog'. I can hear you snickering as if you would do something more important travelling in a cargo crate. Where was I? Oh yeah, specifically, how I came to be called dog.

According to Ask the Vet, which is on the radio every Sunday morning, the old fashioned, most popular theory is that we evolved from wolves. And to understand the term 'dog', you have to look to the wolf pack. One caller named Stanley, suggested that the wolf pack theory was far too simplistic to have any merit, suggesting instead that we went from wolf to settlement dweller and then to the now common term, dogs. In a high-pitched, tinny voice, he explained that my ancestors, settlement dogs, circled the wagons in search of food, whereby the more brave ones were rewarded, not the fearful wolf types. The human fires warmed the settlement dwelling animals, the closeness protecting them from large predators. Furthermore, a single "lone wolf" social life proved rewarding, you do not need a wolf pack to attack a 7-11 dumpster.

I agree the wolf to dog theory has a lot of holes in it but I am not totally supportive of the wolf to settlement animal theory either, although it makes a lot more sense than the wolf direct to dog tale. No pun intended. During my flight, I remembered a radio story of how I came to be called dog or dawg as SammyFarber would mumble. I will share that story with you now.

As you may know, if you listen to Ask the Vet as much as I do, there is group of dogs who retrieve information and tennis balls. Those dogs are the Chesapeake Bay Retrievers, Golden Retrievers, Labrador Retrievers, Nova Scotia Duck Tolling Retriever, and, of course, mi familia, the Standard Poodle.

Here's the tale: During the great flood, it was our job to convey Noah's message to all the people not on the Ark. (Where it is written, I do not know? Note to librarians everywhere: Stop kicking me out of the library and I will find it one day.) Anyway, back to the story. Due to the incessant, high-pitched, irritating barking of a terrier, Noah sailed without us, leaving behind two standard poodles whose only error was having the misfortune of standing next to a terrier.

This particular troublemaker was sturdy and tough, measuring 15 inches at the shoulder. He was predominantly white in colour (more than fifty-one percent with black and tan markings). This dog was feisty, energetic, clever, brave, and had a low tolerance for other animals, even poodles. He was a dog with an attitude that he was eager to assert. According to the legend while Noah was giving boarding instructions, this dog was always either digging or barking, sometimes barking while he was digging. The hyperactive, digging, barking terrier's name was Jack Russell.

Some people wonder how it is poodles survived if we were not on the Ark like all the other breeds and the answer is simple. My ancestors and Jack Russell traveled by raft to the nearby villages. I should mention that my grandparents did not actually build the raft, standard poodles do not do manual labour. At the time the raft was being built my ancestors were chatting in the midday sun. Jack managed to bark so much that two border collies built it with the thought of putting him on it and setting it adrift with no paddle. Lucky for Jack they were called to the Ark before they could set their plan in motion.

The message from Noah to Jack was a simple one. Since you three like to talk so much, go tell the people to learn to swim. They did it. They delivered the message and were rewarded by the people they saved. They were going to call us Gods, my ancestors liked to say. But, that name too was already taken so they reversed God and got Dog. And that is how I came to be known as a dog. That's my history and I'm sticking to it. That is until I come up with my own theory. Then I'll believe that one hundred percent. It's a poodle thing.

When I arrived in Winnipeg my two Shepherds were waiting for me. I feared that when they learned that I was part goat, a Gopoo that they would send me back, or worse, leave me in the woods like my Dad had warned. Having said that, I make it a point never to prejudge anyone. Living in the present works for me.

When I first met him he did not say, "Hi Tuesday" which further added to my anxiety, confirming he was looking at a goat and not sure of what to call me. Finally, he uttered, "Sit, Sit, SIT". Hence, I named the male Shepherd, the Director, a name that proved to be true. He was more than six feet tall and I guessed his age to be mid-thirties. He was wearing jeans and beige sweater with a black line in the middle.

'Please take that sweater off. You look like a homeless pencil,' I mumbled too soft for anyone to hear.

She, the female Shepherd, on the other hand, made such a fuss, pulling me out of my safe haven by my floppy ears, hugging me tightly (way too tightly). "Puppy, Wuppy, Duppy," she kept repeating. "I love you!" What a production! So, I called the second Shepherd the Producer and still do today. Everything she does with me is such a production. She was five and a half feet tall and dressed in frog green from head to toe.

'Did you know that frogs cannot swallow without blinking. Bet you can't either,' I said. She did not respond.

It was apparent to me that I was going to be called either 'Sit-Sit-SIT', call name SIT or heaven forbid 'Puppy-Wuppy-Duppy' call name Duppy. But the good news was that as long I did not develop a craving for tin cans then my Gopoo secret was safe.

I hoped to spend my entire life with the Director and the Producer, leading a very large pack. 'I am the alpha dog, hear me roar.'

Travelling by car to my home, the Producer's lap was my cushion. Wonderful smells of the spring blossoms filling my nose, lilac my favourite by far. Freed from the pongy crate, my nose hairs tingled with delight. You can take it from me, never again will I travel on a plane with a stuffed bear (they may be quiet travelling companions but they poop at the slightest turbulence). On the winding roads, I learned that the Director was a real estate salesman. However, his passion was fighting fires as a volunteer firefighter. The Producer was a personal trainer. I hoped that I was not in for too much running. As you know, I prefer talk shows about fitness as opposed to actually jogging.

Descending in elevation, the tree-lined roadways gave way to a concrete bridge that spanned a magnificent river below. Peeking out the crack in window, I saw so much water, flowing gently from red clay bank to bank. Personally, I do not swim. (Poodle comes from the German word for 'water splash' not 'scuba diver'.)

Unexpectedly, the car slowed to a crawl. Up ahead, I could a see a yellow sports car with a redwood log crushing the cloth roof. To the left was a flatbed truck in the ditch, sprawling lumber everywhere. It was obvious what had happened. The logs on the flatbed truck had shifted causing the truck to lose control and careen into the oncoming sports car. One of the larger logs had landed on the roof of car before the truck hit the ditch.

"Stay here," commanded the Director. The Producer rubbernecked but did not leave the vehicle. In his haste, the Director had left the driver's door partially open, making it easy for me to follow unnoticed.

When we got to the car I could see that there was a middle age man pinned to his seat by another monster log that had pierced the windshield. Gasoline fumes and smoke filling my nose, I gagged. Looking toward the engine, I saw the source of the smoke. Massive flames, three feet high, were escaping successfully.

"Kill me, please kill me. I cannot stand the pain," pleaded the weak voice of the man trapped in the car.

Grabbing a crow bar from the trunk, the Director held it spear-like, then paused. I looked away fearing that the Director was going to harpoon the trapped driver's head with one mighty steel blow, ending his misery. Instead of braining the driver, he pried at the partially crushed door. It did not budge. Gasping for air, the driver begged once more. "Do it. Please, I beg you!"

"Get back in the car," the Director yelled at me as he high jumped over me. Stunned by fear, I did not move. When the Director returned, he had a small red fire extinguisher in his right hand. Sweat engulfed me as the engine's flames reached new heights. Facing the man through the open car window, the Director leaned in and moaned, "I am sorry. It's going to explode." An angst-ridden struggle crossed the Director's face. Clearly, the decision was agonizing. Discharged foam exploded from the extinguisher into the man's mouth choking off what little air he had left. There was not enough foam in the extinguisher to quell the blazing engine fire. But, it had done its job. It ended the misery.

Suddenly I felt airborne. It all happened so fast. The Director had scooped me up with one hand while running toward our car. Seconds later, I felt the heat from the explosion on my puppy fur. The resulting fireball shredded the vehicle and hurled debris more than 100 metres, with the car's hood suspended high in a tree while the windshield was tossed in our direction.

"This will be our secret," the Director whispered, streaming tears down his cheek.

I nodded. 'Be the keeper of secrets' echoed in my puppy brain. Police sirens filled the soiled air as we sped away in silent prayer.

The story the Director told the Producer on the way home was more or less true, leaving out the part about the fire extinguisher snuffing out the failing man's last breath of life.

Keeping my mouth shut, I knew I had a lot to think about. There was no time to read the manual, assuming there is a manual for this sort of quandary. Playing over and over again in my puppy brain was the right to life every living creature has. Balanced against the request of a dying man in excruciating pain for a merciful action before the car exploded. There is much to learn about these Shepherds. One thing I knew for sure. I would keep the secret. I slept.

Time passed. I was so excited to see my new acreage that I could hardly contain myself, wiggling my butt, trying to free my small frame from the Producer's hardy grasp. Racing from thought to thought, my mind wondered: How many poodles would I bunk with? Big ones, small ones? Silver, white, beige, black and apricots? What would my den look like? Would Scout and Makala visit? Maybe they would catch a ride with Reba and Watson. I pictured a farm like Cantope with streams of blue water and tall oak trees where I could leave messages and catch up on the pack mail.

My eyes strained, studying each house for the familiar purple silhouette poodle that marked the home of every poodle everywhere. Finally, we rolled into a driveway, no poodle sign. Looking down at my feet, I thought while I held back the bile rising in my throat, maybe not.

My feet were wet with goo from the rain soaked leaves.

We were surrounded, giant houses on both sides of our humble abode. I was sick when I saw the tiny city yard. I live in a dump.

'Welcome to Winnipeg. Set your watch back twenty years,' I thought.

The Producer eyed me. "Puppy-Wuppy-Duppy' this is your new home. Don't you just love it?" Extinguish me now is all I could think of. I kept quiet. When we got inside the small, one and half storey, two bedrooms and den, cold chills surrounded my body. I searched in vain from room to room, for my canine roommates, finding none.

When I hit the glazed tile kitchen floor, I slid out of control, careening into the black fridge. I had never been on tile before. The Director joined me, putting a silver bowl with fresh water and an adjoining bowl with dry kibble, a mixture of lamb, rice and flour. Although it was more than passable in flavour, I was not hungry, nibbling before I continued to explore.

The living room had a wood burning fireplace, couches, chairs and a coffee table. Searching on, I found the room I was longing for, my den. I heard on the radio that canines liked dens, adding to their security and sense of calmness. One of those wolf things I guess. The real estate shows, like Flip this House, Love or Leave it, or Decorator to the Stars had explained to me exactly what a den looked like. I found mine off the living room, complete with a state of the art stereo and a big screen television, leather chairs, pool table and books. Things were looking up for me, Tuesday the Poodle. Okay, there was no big screen television, pool table, or stereo. But, there was a radio.

Without warning, the Producer put my airplane crate right in the middle of my den. At first I was very upset and then I reasoned that the den was large enough for both me and the crate. The next few days I would learn to be a city dog. Yuck!

Later that night, peeking through my crate door, I could see the Producer scrubbing her hands in soapy water before adding yellow latex gloves. Encouraging bleeding by pressing lightly on the tissue on either side of the wound on the Director's exposed back with her gloved hand. Then she scrubbed the area around the wound using a nailbrush and disinfectant solution. I could see from the Director's face, that the scrubbing was painful. And then, believe or not, she held a syringe perpendicular to the wound, about 2 to 3 inches above it. The way they baste a turkey on the cooking shows. Angling the syringe and then tilting the wound so that the solution would flood the wound and drain away from the opening. She continued irrigating the wound till she was satisfied it was clean before bandaging up the Director. During this whole process, the Producer constantly suggested that the Director go to the hospital. He refused.

"Why, tell me why? Tell me. Why will you not go to the hospital," she repeated.

"What are you hiding?"

"It's nothing. It will heal," he said.

I could tell her. But, I am the keeper of secrets.

Chapter 4

Rods and Cones

A small experience can produce a large effect on the behaviour of a puppy. So was the case for me. This period of my puppy life was a balancing act between what I call my internal poodle behaviour and what I perceived were the expectations of the Shepherds and their world. Shepherds and canines have more in common than you might think. Did you know that we both have prostates? I did not know this to be true. But later that night it was proven to me.

Here is what happened from my point of view. The sun had already set and I sat comfortably in the living room watching television with the Shepherds.

I function better at night because of the low level of light. My pupils are much larger than the Shepherds, which allows for more light to get in. The trade off is that I have limited depth of field vision. I have rods and cones similar to them. However, it is the abundance of my rods that make it possible for me to see so well in dim light. I only need one quarter the amount of light that a Shepherd needs. This may not seem important to you. If your life depended on getting to a fallen potato chip quickly in dim light then you would feel differently. However, my eyes are not particularly good for television watching. My eye set up evolved in such a way so I could locate and track fast moving predators or potato chips as the case may be. Pekingese never look where they are going. I think the reason for this is that the ancient Chinese carried Pekingese puppies in their robes so there was no need for the Pekingese to develop a sense of direction. To this day, Pekingese owners buy the extra-large housecoats at Bloomingdales.

Not only do I see the world differently than my Shepherds, I see the world differently than say a greyhound. As you may know, the greyhound is a sight dog. Detecting that something has moved and understanding what that something is, based on the pattern of movement and its smell is a very important combination for a hunter like me. It is not that important to a greyhound. All they care about is that it looks tasty. If the greyhounds stopped to smell the track rabbit they would soon learn that it was a mechanical rabbit and stop that foolish running in circles.

I know this because once the Producer asked me if I wanted a hotdog. And like, of course, I said yes. Who does not want a hotdog? So she gave me a big stuffed red and yellow hotdog that I bit into. If you have never had one, trust me when I tell you that it tastes like crap. Had I have smelled the hotdog before sinking my teeth in, then the entire 'stuffing all over the house' episode may have been avoided.

I do not blame the whole racing in circles thing on the greyhounds. To a large degree, I blame their Shepherds. In my opinion, the solution to ending this sport or at least modifying it to an acceptable level is very simple. Get eight or ten very young children, three year olds would be ideal, and put them on a track, being sure to number each child. Then tie a bowl of macaroni and cheese (do not try making it at home, it has to be Kraft Mac and Cheese), to the moving rail and set the kids loose and see who wins. I'm just saying. It is an idea.

Getting back to the TV, I have only two types of cones and therefore see blue and yellow easily. Shepherds have three types of cones, red, blue and yellow. My point is that the colours on the television are very odd to me. There is a misconception that I am colour blind. The fact that I see colours differently does not mean I am colour blind. There are many scientific and anatomical reasons why television does not appeal to most canines. It is more than the fact that the colours appear differently to me. I am here to tell you that the main reason, with the exception of Big Brother for which I'm auditioning next season, is that TV shows suck. The patterns give me a headache. I prefer to face away from the television and listen because of all the blurry lines. And really, who needs to look at Larry King? He never has dogs on his television talk show. How many times can you watch Lassie reruns? In my opinion, the Lassie show went downhill when Timmy arrived as an orphan boy in 1957 and basically took over the storyline. I can tell you that if I fell down a well; all that would be said is that the stupid poodle never looks where he is going. Maybe they should have had an episode called Timmy gets glasses.

I have learned three valuable lessons while watching television. Firstly, if a dog barks on TV, I do not need to suddenly stand up straight when I am lying under the coffee table. Secondly, the doorbell ringing in the TV is not the one for our house. (Why a television has a doorbell I will never know.) The third lesson that surprised me the most, was the living room sofa is not a face towel.

After TV time, I was taken outside by the Producer to pee. No directions provided, just go out and pee somewhere and come back in. I was 16 weeks old and I had little bowel and bladder control. I needed to go out at least once more during the night, usually around 2 am is good. So I thought rather logically (I was proud of myself for this), I'll sleep by the door. But at night, I could not go out and was forced to sleep in a cold, damp coffin. Oh, how I wished for someone to come and save me. Fast! I am located in a large blue crate on the main floor with no food or water. I have no toys. I am parched. Bring yogurt.

Now you are probably wondering how I got into this mess and all I can tell you it is because of books, hundreds of them. One wall of our house is lined with dog books. The Director reads them nonstop and turns into the puppet master, pulling my strings. A warning to any puppies who are out there and reading this, I suggest that you pee on all the dog books. Or better yet rip 'em to shreds.

Even worse, the Director likes to read them to me. Why, I do not know. He reads: Crate training is an effective way to keep your puppy quiet in his crate at night and during the day whenever you are not interacting with him. Avoid all toys because they can induce choking. This is also true of towels and blankets. Lure him into the crate and go upstairs to your warm and comfy king size bed.

I could not believe what I was hearing. Put the puppy (that's me) in a dark, plastic cell with no toys and go upstairs to sleep. My puppet master believed every word of this. I want to know how many nights the writer of that gibberish spent in a crate in the kitchen.

The Director has decided that by nature, I am a den animal and therefore I would enjoy a safe area in the home to call my own during the night. He has put me in the crate with no toys for fear that I might choke, claiming that this crate can provide me with a safe, personal area to enjoy a restful night. Without the crate, the dog book says I may find unsafe areas in the home to curl up in and hurt myself. When was the last time you saw your dog turn on the dryer and jump in? One of the main reasons for using a crate is to confine me without making me feel isolated or banished. The Director thinks I will not pee in my crate because I do not want to soil my home. This is not true. The reason I do not pee in my crate is because I do not want to alert any lions on the prowl as to where I am sleeping soundly, albeit uncomfortably.

Regardless of the reason, the crate was placed in a corner, near a "people" area in the home. He made sure it was free from cold drafts or direct heat.

"The dog should be able to have privacy, yet feel as though he has company when people are home sleeping," he told the Producer. "For this reason, I am putting the crate in kitchen facing the fridge. He likes the fridge. "

I went into the crate without a fuss.

Eight to sixteen week old puppies have very little bowel and bladder control. What this means is that the new puppy, like me will most likely have to be taken outside to potty at least once in the night (preferably 2 am). According to Ask the Vet, on average, cows poop sixteen times a day? All those cows, in the crate, out of the crate. Must drive the farmer nuts.

The solution is simple. Let me sleep in your big bed. If you try it the dog book way then this is what will happen. I will bark till you let me out. After peeing, I will resist going back in the crate by howling for the next two hours. This means that you will be up from 2 to 4am every night. I am nothing if not persistent.

Then after a week of this you will give in. First, I will be allowed on the bed, but only when you invite me, probably on Sunday mornings. Then, provided I do not go under the covers, I will be allowed to sleep on the bed anytime. Then, I will be allowed under the covers only if you invite me. And finally, I will be sleeping horizontally on the bed and you will be in the corner without a blanket for fear of disturbing me. And really, that's the way it should be. Wouldn't it be simpler if we just started that way? You'd lose a whole lot less sleep.

Time passed. I dozed comfortably. Like clockwork, I needed to pee at 2 am. I remembered what my dad said about peeing in the house and being banned to the woods; I decided to let out a small whimper. This, of course, was not heard. So I barked. The Director came down and my tailed wagged like it was about to fall off. I was saved.

He whacked the top of the crate with a phone book and left. Who does this with a phone book? The dog book theory is that he was to sneak up on me without me knowing who was behind the noise and I would quietly go back to sleep for fear of upsetting the thunder gods. What a bunch of horse poop. I could smell the Director from the top of the steps and his pattern of movement. The shuffling of his slippers confirmed it. I did not need to see him to know who had whacked the crate. I was pissed, no pun intended. It was at that moment I knew I had a prostate and the Director was my pain in the ass.

'Under no circumstances should you ever reproduce buddy,' I said lying back down. I did not mean to insult him. But, it was on the list. I scratched the bottom of crate with my paw.

What seemed like forever, probably five minutes, the Director reappeared.

"I, I n-need ta talk ta ya," he stuttered in hushed trembling tone.

'Okey dokey', I said. Tunnelling out of the crate was not working anyway.

Calming himself, he continued. "I know we just met. However, I want you to know that I will always love you and think of you. You are my first canine. But I will probably be gone away longer than your lifespan. I want you to know that I am glad for the little time we had together.

'Going somewhere?'' I asked. 'Does it have a place to pee. My gut is busting? Can I come?'

"Probably 15 to 20 years in jail, I figure. Come morning, I am turning myself in. Robbing a person of their last breath of life regardless of the reason was not right. I am so ashamed."

'Listen pal, I was there. The guy was going to be burnt toast any second. No dog, as death approaches, has ever declared that he wished he had spent more time in a burning car. We all have an expiry date. You don't get to choose how you're going to die. Or when. You can only decide how you're going to live. You did the right thing.'

He put his arm around me and kissed my forehead. "Be brave little apricot poodle puppy", he said, flowing water seeping from his eyes.

'My promise to you is that I will grow big and strong, safeguarding the house and the Producer. I will be by her side when she is sick, licking the tears away when she is sad, and eager to get her outside and running, keeping her in shape.' I cried. And when my eyes had no more water ---- I cried some more. I loved him. I wanted him to be my Alpha Shepherd forever.

After I knew he was in bed resting, I barked and barked and then I barked again till the Producer showed up and took me outside. After I peed, she put me back in my crate and said goodnight.

Unfortunately, I had a bad dream. I dreamt I was auditioning for the role of the dog in the Wizard of Oz when this Cairn Terrier named Toto showed up. He claimed that in addition to knowing the role, he can kill mice that sneak onto the set. It There was just the two of us left when of all things this mouse with a carrot in his mouth walked across room. I screamed and bolted out the door. I am afraid of carrots. Naturally, he was hired. (I would have looked quite good, I think, on the yellow brick road. Such is life.)

I smelt the Director coming and I knew I was in big trouble. Luckily, he did not have the phone book with him. A strange thing happened. He carried the crate upstairs with me still inside and set it next to the bed. For the rest of the night, the Director slept, hand sticking through the crate. Odd as this may have seemed, it comforted me. I knew if I had to pee again or I had a bad dream that all I had to do to get out was bite his hand really hard. I slept well.

To this day, I do not like phone books. I am, however, quite fond of oatmeal raisin cookies. Just sayin'.

I spent that night in the crate. Later, I met SammyFarber.

Chapter 5

Stop Thief!

Time passed quickly. The Director was still with us. So, it was safe to assume he got a full pardon or decided to let sleeping dogs lie as they say. As I mentioned before, puppies make a lot of assumptions. Unfortunately, most of the times they are wrong.

It was morning, I got up, stretched and had breakfast. The Producer was having her breakfast too, which is a very important meal to her. That day she had coffee and oat bran cereal with a ripe, yellow banana cut in.

When a person has great food and you do not, one of things I have learned to do is to drool. Sitting very close, I let the drool fall to the floor, or for maximum effect, like this morning, on her lap. The Producer busied herself with the newspaper, paying no attention to my drooling.

Having no choice, I moved onto step two which is the knock. Timing and pressure is everything with this delicate maneuver. Just as the coffee cup reached her lower lip, I knocked her arm. If you do the knock too hard then it has a different effect than intended.

"Okay, okay. Out you go," she said, not understanding my request for cereal and banana. Winter was setting in. I peed on the few remaining flowers in the yard. Poodles love to pee on flowers. For me, it is the mix of two of my favourite fragrances, lilac and urine. It was a work day for them, not me. When we went back in, she rewarded me with a piece of soggy banana. It did not sit well. Luckily, after looking everywhere, I was able to find one of the few pieces of carpet left in our house, not out in the open, and I proceeded to throw up. It was the green, fluffy bathroom mat. Blah, I felt better.

Work time. So, I was ushered into my mobile home crate that was now back in the kitchen. During the day, when the Shepherds are out, I have to stay in my crate. The Director tunes the radio to country western. I hate country western. "I Don't Know Whether To Kill Myself or Go Bowling," is the name of the radio tune. 'Go bowling,' I bark out. Eat! Pray! Bowl!

Shepherds always wonder if I dream often. Of course, I do. In my dream that morning, I was using long and drawn-out barks at a high pitch, with pauses between each one, communicating to the rabbit that I was alone and needed company in the hope of luring him closer. At least two pounds with varying shades of brown except for his stub tail with a white underside, this rabbit was not going to be an easy target. He was a cottontail. If you ever tried to bag a cottontail, you know they are one of the smarter breeds of rabbits. The trade off is that although harder to catch, they are more tender and juicy than the average wild rabbit meal.

In my world, high-pitched sounds are a friendly gesture when uttered in long and drawn out tones. Low-pitched growls are meant as a warning. Not wanting to scare off my lunch, I tried for a high pitch bark. Unless you are a terrier, this is not an easy task. When I go to hit a high note, I pull in my abdomen, barking from the throat to resonate in the chamber in the back of my mouth.

Unfortunately, I do not speak rabbit. However, the high pitched bark with pauses was drawing the meal closer and closer. Salivating, I knew lunch was soon to be served. I had not eaten in days. Suddenly, the cottontail's eyes grew large as saucers, as it sat frozen inches from my incisors. Then he bolted, looking down I saw what had foiled my plan. There, by my left foot, was a ketchup bottle. A rookie mistake.

Keys dangled in the door awoke me from my dream. Fifteen minutes or so had passed since the Shepherds had left. Baring my teeth, I readied for the fight. This was my home and I was prepared to stand my ground against all prowlers.

Suddenly, the crate door swung open. Leaping to attack, I hit my head on the chair leg. Ouch, that hurt. Clearing the cobwebs, I focused on the intruder. Huh? It was the Producer. Why? Armed with the phone, she dialled.

"This is Anna Rothstein. Is Doctor Gollum in? Yes, I will hold. "

"Doctor Gollum, Anna Rothstein here. Your office said it was urgent I contact you."

"Yes, last week. Red patch on my neck. Eczema, I think?"

" Basal cell carcinoma disease . . . what is that?"

"No, tell me now!"

"Cancer? Is it curable? Cancer," she repeated, knees buckling as she sank into the chair.

"No. Yes? Which is it?"

"Yes, I think so."

I never liked hearing one side of a conversation. You miss so much, I licked my paw in anticipation of more clues.

'Research causes cancer in rats,' I said trying to be helpful.

Beads of sweat formed on the Producer's forehead.

"Yes, I understand. You caught it early. Yes, I understand. Two percent. ." Two percent she repeated harping on the words, two percent.

"Yes, I know. But, what if.. . um, how long do I have to wait?"

"No, of course not . I will be there."

My muscles went tense. An unblinking stare showed the whites of my eyes. Ears back in a sign of submission and fear, slowly I moved next to her.

"Shh, back in your crate. And, do not tell anyone. This is our secret."

Geez, when my mom told me to be a keeper of secrets this was not what I thought my Shepherds would be telling me. I was thinking more along the line of 'when people are mean to me I secretly cut the buttons off their favorite clothes. Certainly not, I killed a man or I am dying of basal cell carcinoma disease. Geez, this was way too much for my little puppy brain. I rested.

Later that day, the brring-brring of the kitchen phone awoke me from my nap. The Director was home and answered. Straining to listen, here again, I heard only half the conversation.

"Oh hi, yes, arrived fine. I just love him," he said. Obviously, he is either talking about me or else a thin crust pepperoni and mushroom pizza.

"No, half an hour late."

It must be the pizza. I thought closing my eyes, pretending to be asleep again. He continued.

"Puppy test? Attached to the crate. No, I didn't know. I will check."

It was not Mom. She cannot call. Our canine language is not compatible with the phone. Text maybe. Let me speak to whoever that is? Is it Diane? I'm awake. I want to explain the tennis ball incident. I really did want to chase it. 'Gimme the phone! Diane got it wrong. I love to play ball. Throw the ball, throw it again. Yup again. It's the most fun thing ever. I never get tired. '

The Director ignored my plea and continued. "Yes Diane, I saw his test," he said. "Not much prey drive."

'Prey drive? Geez, it's a yellow tennis ball. Throw a squirrel and watch what happens,' I added.

Diane from Cantope had sent my puppy test. What a bleep. Did I pass? Why did she bleeping do that? Is tennis ball chasing really a career path? I'm packing. From safety to desperation, the line is so fine. Which way to the woods?

"Yes, we gave him the food you sent. Yes, a little. He is resting in his crate. "

"Yes, oh I see, that is what the pad is for. I wondered."

"Yes, I know he has to take a training course. Been reading up on it all morning. Yes, I will send it when he has completed it," he said, writing it down on piece of scrap paper by the phone.

Training course? What heck is that all about? Training for what? The military? I heard on the nature show that Portuguese Water Dogs are trained to detect enemy swimmers or divers approaching military ships or piers. I wonder if I can wear water wings? I say this because it is widely believed that the closest relatives of the Portuguese Water Dogs are thought to be the Barbet and Standard Poodle, like me. And, we all know there is a sudden shortage of Portuguese Water Dogs for active duty. Now that I think more about it, maybe that show was on sea lions not Portuguese Water Dogs. I always get those two mixed up.

"Yes, register his name with the kennel club. Three names, correct?"

"Last name is Poodle. Middle name, The," said the Director.

At that moment, my heart raced with excitement. I was ecstatic, no Puppy-Wuppy-Duppy or Sit-sit-SIT. I was going to be monikered: Tuesday the Poodle, call name Tuesday. I was staying. It was a done deal.

"Friday," he said. There was a pregnant pause and he continued, "Yes, that is correct, Friday the Poodle. He is Apricot. Thank you for registering him. We will send the training certificate. Bye for now."

No, no, no. I barked, using my low tones. What the heck is a Friday? Don't hang up! My name is Tuesday the Poodle, not Friday the Poodle. Phone landing on the cradle, I sulked.

"Hi Friiiiiiiiiiday," the Producer said, opening my crate door. "Why so sad, my little Friiiiiiiiiiday poodle dootle smootle?"

I wanted to barf. At least get the pronunciation right. Unfreaking real, everyone will be calling me Friday, make that Friiiiiiiiiiday. I'm ill.

My day was only going to get worse.

The Director gripped me by the collar and attached a rope, proceeding to drag me into the yard, kicking and screaming. I did not know what he wanted or where we were going, or why? Passing the floor area covered by newspaper, we walked out the patio door, down the wooden deck steps, onto the lawn area where there were no flowers. He repeated, "Do it now, do it here." Throwing this smelling pad on the ground, he repeated, "Do it now."

All I could think of was, do what now? I had already peed earlier when the Producer snuck home. He kept pointing to that stupid smelly pad. This was not going well. He did not speak dog. "Do it now," echoed in my floppy ears as I was dragged over the smelly pad. I was so upset I peed again. I looked up at the enemy, bracing for the attack. The Director is in his early fifties, six feet two inches tall weighing in at 210 lbs. White running shoes peeked out from his frayed blue jeans. An over sized grey hoody completed the outfit. He was dressed for battle. And, it was going to hurt. Swinging hand approaching, I lowered my back, feet balanced, breath held to absorb the impact. Unfolding fingers gave way to a tasty piece of chicken in it. I took the chicken and chewed, thinking it was my last meal.

"Good boy! Good job Friday," he said, while I munched on the freshly cooked chicken breast.

Since no more chicken was forthcoming, I decided to follow the Director into the house. Still attached to the rope, the Director said in the most annoying high pitched questioning voice, "Today we learn to walk on lead." The Director, having read one too many dog obedience books, was going to train me? What a disaster, I thought.

I raised my upper lip to show my teeth as if to say, no bleeping way.' You go and take that rope with you', I said, curling up to my radio. I wanted to listen to Howard Stern's afternoon radio show. I really like Robin and Artie.

"Enough with the radio, let's go," he said, turning it off.

Deafness is a disease that can affect a dog at any time. I tried to communicate this concept to the Director by refusing to move. He was not listening. I was resigned to at least try this training stuff. The next thing I did, I swear was only an attempt to look good for training class.

The Director and Producer always try to look clean and neat for work. I was doing the same. His response was not what I aimed for.

"Friday, if you ever scootch your butt across the entire front hall carpet on two legs like that again there will be a heavy price to pay. No radio for a month."

It was first and last time I ever tried to clean up my butt for class.

"Training you is going to be my new hobby," he said.

'There is a very fine line between "hobby" and "mental illness",' I replied.

I found myself outside assaulted by the cool spring air, realizing quickly that my super powered sense was running a discriminating program nonstop in my nose. In the first few steps, I had systemically learned hundreds of new fragrances I separated each one into unique identifiable odours, surrounding my new home. It was fascinating to me, all the city smells; so different from the Cantope farm smells I was used to. Adding to the mystery of these wild urban smells was the fact that if I raised or lowered my head, the smells were different.

A city has layered smells. At nose level was car exhaust, pungent and brazen. Lowering my head, I found sweat and body odour that had wafted up from the many runners who had recently passed. The bottom layer was the most interesting. There were scents of grass, flowers, mildew, saliva, and the hearty odour of nicotine (menthol flavoured, I think).

A new smell quite pungent was passing by in the shape of a large blue truck with men on the side got my attention. When they got to our house, the men got off and took our garbage cans.

'Stop them! They are stealing our stuff,' I said to the Director. He did nothing. I pulled toward the curb, ready to fight for what was ours, and he pulled back. Trying to gain the advantage, I bit into the rope and held on with my teeth. My feet were balanced low to secure my position. The Director fell. I pulled him along the ground. Giving up was not an option. They had our stuff and I was prepared to fight to get it back.

"Stop it!" he said in a low tone. "Stop it right now, you idiot poodle." he said in a not so low tone.

So much information for a puppy to absorb. Next I picked up on a scent trail. An animal not known to me had passed this way about an hour ago. I have no idea what it was. It was definitely not a poodle smell. If you think about it fairly then you will see the world from my perspective. Cantope is all poodles, therefore I have never seen or smelt a city dog. I assumed incorrectly that it must be a lion. As I said before, puppies sometimes make wrong assumptions. I am okay with that.

Having learned from the BBC nature show that lions like to roam, I breathed in, holding my breath to let my nasal computer work the floating bacteria that lingered behind. The result was emailed to my brain. It was true; I was stalking a lion, keeping track of its unique smell. That way when it returned to the pride, tired and weak from the chase I could single it out from the group and devour it in one bite. Suddenly, it occurred to me, having only heard lions roar on the three o'clock show that I did not know how large a lion is. I pulled with all my might on the leash just in case the lion was nearby watching and evaluating my performance. The Director was getting more and more frustrated with me.

Then, out of the corner of my eye, I noticed a small dog on the other side of the street without a leash. At that moment, I realized my error. The smell was emanating from this dachshund across the road, not a lion. Dachshunds are ideal dogs for small children because they are born pre-stretched. A child cannot do much harm one way or another by pulling on them.

I politely barked, trying to warn it that this was my block. Obviously, he had taken a wrong turn and invaded my territory by accident. He crossed over to my side anyway, ignoring my warning. Face to face, he told me that he had been living on this block for many years. I knew right then that a stable hierarchy needed to be put in place. That is one in which each individual knows and accepts his rank on my block. And, I was onety-one. I bit the air making sure to miss him. He snapped back barely missing my poodle butt. I had forgotten what Reba had told me, dachshunds, although small, were originally bred to fight badgers so do not argue with them. I did an inhibited bite, which does not hurt the dog. It made my 'back off' message clear. He yelped.

The Director went ballistic, holding onto the taut rope, yelling at me to shut the bleep up and stop fighting. To be fair, I must confess that I may have barked more than once at the dachshund. The number 82 comes to mind. The Director scooped me up in his giant paw before I could give my neighbour dog another friendly reminder on the neck. Carrying me back into the house, I could tell he was not pleased. Once inside, he set me down and went into the bathroom. I followed close behind him so I could apologize for my conduct.

I banged right into him not expecting him to be bending over the green fluffy carpet mat trying to clean it.

"Do you know anything about this?"

I leaned against him. This tactic I have used before. A simple lean can disarm the most aggravated Shepherd. "You know that the police may come in the very near future and take me away. I must make sure you are trained before that even if we have to work night and day, every day. I love you and want you to be strong" he explained.

I lowered my head, tears forming in my large brown eyes. I was not crying because I was soon to be faced with endless training. I cried because I knew the Director loved me and wanted me to succeed before he was carted off to jail. For that and more, I was his dog.

"It is okay that you barfed," he said, sensing my mood. It is important that at this point you realize that the concept of the indoor bathroom is very foreign to me. And, a puppy brain does not stay focused on any one thing for very long. After a few seconds, I had forgotten about apologizing and it occurred to me that playing tug of war with the Director might be a fun way for us to get back on friendly terms.

While he sat on the toilet, I bit into his underwear and pulled as hard as I could, thinking it was fun for him too. It was not. I leaned a few new bleep words that day. Not amused at my game suggestion, he handed me over to the Producer, "You take him, before I kill him. He tried to stop the garbage men from taking the trash. Then, he beat up that half dead 15 year old dachshund who lives across the street. At some point he barfed on the rug. The rest you do not want to know."

The Producer is in her early fifties, five feet eight inches tall, medium build with short brown hair and sparkling greeny-blue eyes. Her pressed jeans were flower embroidered at dog eye level to entertain the canine passersby. How thoughtful is that? Her top was a soft pink sweater with butterflies sewn on it. She was my kind of dresser, bold and adventurous, with a quiet feminine side. She took me out the front door and let me wander wherever I wanted. We had a very nice adventure, stalking imaginary lions together.

During the next few days, I slowly became accustomed to my hovel, the house from hell. The mornings were okay, puppy chow bowl filled to rim, cool tap water next to it for the taking. The Director attached that dreaded rope to my neck, wandering around the house with me in tow. He had read in one of his many dog books that this was an effective house training method. Resistance was not an option, we went where he wanted to go and that was that. I was a chain gang dog and the guard was always in sight.

Every two or three hours, we would go in the yard and the 'do it now' stuff started again. To this day, I do not know what he wanted me to do when he said, "Do it now". But, I took the opportunity to pee and he seemed happy, very strange Shepherd. Not being a big morning eater, I had a small snack around noon. But, I can down a herd of buffalo with a side of fries after sunset.

During midday, the Producer was in charge of me and although I still was dragging that silly rope around there was a difference, no one was attached to it. The Producer was busy answering the phone and fussing with shoes; a different one on each foot. I longed for a pair of Cowboy boots. I followed her around for a while, having nothing better to do when I realized I had to pee. The Director had yelled at me earlier for barking so I sat quietly by door to the yard and waited and waited and waited, bladder expanding.

Finally, relief oozed out from every pour. A river of warm yellow liquid from my loins started meandering across the kitchen floor. Tightly closed eyes peeked open to find the pee had left my shaking body.

Opening my eyes wider, I found myself face to face with the Director, standing over me looking quite puzzled. After a moment, he yells out to the Producer, "Your dog just peed all over the floor." Shepherd ownership is a very confusing concept for me. When I pee at the door the Director tells the Producer that her dog just peed in the house. Conversely, when I bark, the Producer tells the Director that his dog is barking again. I tell you I live in a nuthouse and it was about to get nuttier.

After cleaning up my error in judgment, the Director attached a row of sleigh bells to door. Then he pulled on the cloth, causing the bells to ring and the door flew open, rope yanking me into the yard where the smelly pad was kept. This process repeated five times. Obviously, the bells were the okay to exit signal that I needed. Enough already. I got it! Wait for bells, exit and pee. Stop the bell ringing! I was getting such a friggin' headache.

I went to lie down in den next to my travel crate. I peeked inside and there was white bear still sitting comfortably. The radio on the counter was on so we listened to *Ask the Mechanic* for an hour or two. I am pretty sure given the right tools I could install new brakes and rotors on a mid-size Ford. Personally, I think playing country music would keep other cars away from you if your brakes did not work. Not wanting to miss the spark plug lesson, I rushed over to the snack dish, quickly inhaled it all, following it with water.

Too much water. So much water that I sloshed when I walked back to the den. Now before you go ahead and say "big mistake". Remember, I have options. I have the bells. Minutes later, bladder busting at the seams,

I waddled my way to the back door and there I stared at the bells. And stared. And stared some more. I must have been there a week, a month, maybe less. I am not good with time. No one came. In the pickle jar again, I felt the victim.

Hadn't we just agreed that I would come to the door, listen for bells, exit and pee at the smelly spot. Hadn't we practiced this fifty bleeping times. And now, it was go time. Where was the Director? All I could think of was, 'no barking', wait for the bells and exit.

Finally, the Director showed up. He sure took his sweet time. Time, as you may know, is very different when you are dancing from paw to paw needing to pee. Finally, he opened the door. I sat quietly and waited, bladder bursting.

"Go! Go out and pee near the pad. What is wrong with you?" he asked. He was rather cranky. It was my first time, after all.

Go? I did not know what to do. I leaned. He looked down at me and bit his lower lip. I could feel his pain. And then, miracle of miracles, he understood my concern: he rang the bells. Did we not just go over this? He rings the bell then the door opens and I go out.

With the bells rung, I raced out into the yard, found the smelly pad, and peed enough to fill a kiddie pool. When I came back in the Director was throwing the sleigh bells in the garbage. Go figure? He tells the Producer that her stupid dog will never ring the bells.

I think that was unfair. When did it become my job to ring the bells? Huh? When?

What I am about to tell you I do not expect you to believe. However, every word of it is true. I had to take control of the situation. I had to train my Shepherds or risk being sent away for peeing in the house. Dad had warned me about this.

Later that day, the Producer gave me a taste of vanilla yogurt, cold and delicious. However, it made me sneeze. So I sneezed and then I sneezed some more. Not wanting me to sneeze in the house, the Producer opened the door. Presto, I had trained her. Later on, I tried it with the

Director watching and holey-moley-sister-sally it worked again. I sneezed and he opened the door. Training Shepherds is easier than it looks. Although, I must admit they have very uncanine-like reactions to snot flying out of your nose.

I met SammyFarber the next morning. I was exactly 12 weeks old. It was spring. I was already living with the Director and Producer for a few weeks when he stopped by for a three day nap. I knew that from the moment I saw him that he and I were going to lifelong pals, kindred spirits, if you will. I learned a great deal from SammyFarber and in my own modest way I suspect he may have learned a thing or two from me. At one point in my life, which you will read about later, an error in problem solving might have cost me dearly. However, Sammyfarber came to my rescue, putting me back on track.

But first, the news. And then, you will meet him.

Chapter 6

Today's Top stories

We gathered in the living room to watch the news. The Director lounging in the recliner, tight grip on the remote, while the Producer sprawled out on the couch, hand resting on my back. Me, I was on the floor rug facing away from the television. Although I love to listen to the news, I find the pictures annoying. The Director increased the volume:

Today's Top stories

Winnipeg's newly formed Park and Recreation board met today to discuss the closing of the Haney dog park citing a much needed extension of the Moray bridge project. Park and Recreation executives confirmed that part, if not all, of the off leash dog park will be used for the highway expansion. Dog owners are outraged by the news.

And, now over to Bob Cameron at Police Headquarters.

"Thanks, Each month an unsolved crime is re-enacted in a video and shown on the Winnipeg Police and the Crime Stoppers Web site," said Bob. "Anyone with information about the featured crime can submit a tip online or call the Crime Stoppers Tips Line. In a related story, Winnipeg Police are asking anyone who has knowledge of a Diamond lumber truck which collided with a passenger car on Highway 59, killing 34 year old Jeffrey Camden of Winnipeg to please contact the Winnipeg police tip line. Police believe that the driver of the passenger car was killed by ingesting the chemical, carbon tetrachloride. It is commonly found in older fire extinguishers. Winnipeg Firefighter Association has not commented on the accident at this time. However, our investigators have learned that carbon tetrachloride is not used by the Winnipeg Fire Department.

If you have information to report to police about a crime and want to remain anonymous, contact the Winnipeg Crime Stoppers program at 204-TIP-LINE. Cash awards are paid if the tip leads to the arrest of a person or persons responsible for an unsolved crime You do not have to give your name."

"Sports coming up after the break."

"But first, this off site report just in:

"There was this earth-shattering explosion and I heard some glasses breaking that made me jump out of my bed," said Salman Kabir, who was staying in a highway hotel adjacent to the crash site on Highway 59. "When I looked out I saw the sports car, flames shooting out. Boom! It exploded. The blast threw glass and debris in all directions and even shattered my hotel window three storeys up."

"Did you see anyone leave the scene?" The reporter asked.

"Yes, I saw an apricot poodle running from the scene," he replied.

'Are you friggin' kidding me, Salman Kabir. All you saw was my apricot butt? I hope one day they name a disease after you.' I looked over at the Director. He was holding his breath, palms pressed together, in a praying pose.

Huffs and puffs told me the Director's pulse and breathing were very rapid. Standing to get a glass of water, he exhibited disorientation, walking in a less than straight line. Had he not staggered to the sink and found refreshment, I am sure vomiting would have followed. The Producer's hand on my coat was cold and clammy. A red blotch on her neck was pulsing.

Personally, I was shocked by the news that the dog park, which I had never been to, might be closing.

After the news, the Producer leashed me up and we were off. Typically, the Producer likes to jog which with my little legs is full out run. However, this evening we strolled leisurely. Once we were out of earshot, the flood gates opened, water streamed out of her eyes, then she fell to her knees, then laid in silent prayer on the concrete. I cuddled up close, using my body warmth to comfort her.

I wanted her to know that although the dog park sounded like fun I would be okay without it. Really!!! 'Not to worry so much about me,' I said. What she said startled me. I expected her to tell me about the phone call. Wrong again.

"Little puppy, I have the flu. I am so sorry I cannot run with you this week."

'Huh, what? The flu? No mention of having basal cell carcinoma disease? Whatever that is?'

"Your father, Frank, will take good care of you till I am better. Please do not tell anyone. Your dad is stressed about something? Okay, puppy wuppy. I am so sorry. Don't tell!"

I nodded my head in agreement. Frank, the Director, was going away for a long prison sentence and Anna, the Producer, was hiding her disease from me.

Really, the flu is the best you can come up with? Less than three months old, I wondered if I could find my way back to Cantope. I loved my new family. But I needed my doggy mom and dad. I whimpered. Somehow we found our way back home. I slept.

In the morning, the Director let me out of the crate beside his bed. After peeing outside, I was bored, wandering into the living room I was surprised by what I found. Lying, face toward the couch, was a two hundred and fifty pound black bear. He had come in during the night and would awake soon. Feeling a kinship with black bears, which I will explain later, I went over to say hello to my hibernating relative. Certainly, my bear friend would be aware of the canine mutual sniff and greet ritual.

'Morning, Mr Bear. Sorry to wake you,' I said, politely, pushing my cool and moist nose against his exposed ear. I took in a deep breath in, quickly realized from the smell that it was not a grizzly bear. A delightful mix of nicotine and urine rose up from the couch. There may also have been a hint of Fort Garry dark ale in the mix? Not sure? Reverting back to my "if not A, then B theory on life" I concluded, if not a bear, then an aged Border Collie, perhaps fifteen?

Crease lines from the long hours of sleep on the textured couch, marred his face. I gave him the name, Prozac. Rolling over on his side, he addressed me.

'Piss-ss off, you stupid friggin' dawg.' Prozac mumbled through phelgm. So, I asked for clarification.

'Did you say, "Nice to meet you poodle?" Let's have a snack later.' Not totally sure I had heard right, mumble being a new language to me. I nuzzled his ear again.

' The next time you have something to say shithead, raise your paw, and put it over your mouth. Now, piss off, you stupid, shithead dawg,' he repeated, turning back away from me. 'Is that clear, shithead?'

'Crystal,' I said. Here was a dog, or dawg as he would say it, easy to understand. The word, shithead, speaks volumes. I loved that word. I needed to work shithead into my growing vocabulary. What I did not know is that the word 'shithead' would surface again and save my life.

He turned back over and was soon snoring again.

I think at this point it is important me to clear up a few myths. Dogs are very aware that different dogs have different points of view. This is not a judgment. Simply, an understanding I've reached by watching the action of other Poodles. Although a border collie mix, I found Prozac to be an easy read. He was a clear thinker. Much time and effort has been given to understanding the effect of domestication on the dog. Studying the behaviour of wolves is a common error in trying to understand dogs like Prozac and me. Wolves are not poodles any more than chimpanzees are people. Dogs think and act like dogs.

Poodles are direct descendants of bears. Yes, I said bears. Here is what happened: The Canidae family is divided into the "wolf-like" and "dog-like" animals of the tribe Canini. This is where the idea of the wolf leading to the dog comes from. However, the standard poodle was outside this gene evolution pool and evolved as a direct descendant of the cutting bear. More commonly referred to as the black bear today. I learned all this from a talk radio person who called in from Norfolk County, Massachusetts.. I think his name was Grizzly Adams.

Some people from Iowa also called in and argued that the poodles came from the grizzly bear not the black bear. This is simply not true. Here's a simple test you can use to tell the difference between a black bear and a grizzly. The next time you see a bear, climb a tree; if the bear climbs it and eats you, it's a black bear. But, if the bear knocks the tree down and eats you, it's a grizzly.

Prozac was still sleeping.

Here is more stuff about poodles and black bears that you probably do not want to know either. So what. I will tell you anyway. You need to listen more. Put those cheese doodles down, they turn the pages orange. My ancestors, the black bear, were kind to trees, never knocking them down. Here are a few more comparative points. The coat of black bears is predominantly black, smooth and short haired. However, there exist a variety of colour variations: chocolate brown, silver grey, or cinnamon tending to apricot like me.

You will probably skip this part too. Do not blame me if you encounter a bear and wish you had read this. Anyway, our warning signs are similar. For example, if a black bear walks with its head held below the shoulders it frequently results in a type of aggressive behaviour. The next time a black bear is charging at you be sure to take note of its tail position. Facial and mouth expressions are also used to intimidate other bears. Sounds such as snarling, actions such as opening and closing the mouth rapidly while salivating, baring teeth and making chomping noises often signify an agitated or angered bear. Similarly, if a dog is bugging me then I start with a glare, move to the air bite and then on to the neck chomp, if necessary. Finally, (bet you were waiting for that word) if the dog is still in my face after that, then I would bite it. Luckily, this has never happened to me. (However, I did bite someone that I will tell you about later. I am not proud of it. It was a chilling experience.)

Two hours later, Prozac was still snoring.

Black bears are shy and solitary, they spend their lives seeking food and searching for a better place to live. Like the Producer, I too, spend too much of my most of waking hours trying to locate the perfect cinnamon bun. Recently I was flipping through a magazine with the Director when we saw an upscale Manhattan condo that we both liked. You see the similarity, food and lodging are important both to me and the black bear. My great-great-grandparents were black bears. I am sure of it. Plus, black bears hibernate for between five and seven months each year. My thoughts exactly. I plan to go to San Diego for the winter.

I am not suggesting that everything I do is directly tied to my black bear ancestry. To better understand how I see the world you must also examine your own Shepherd behaviour. Carvings of a breed of dog that resembles a standard poodle, which are one of the oldest breeds of dogs, are found on Roman and Greek coins. Poodles became a recognized breed in 1890, and became the most popular breed of dog in North America on July 4, 1962 at 5:15 in the afternoon. I think it was a Wednesday.

Twenty minutes later, Prozac was still snoring.

Bored to tears waiting for my new friend to awake, I will tell you a few more secrets about canines. If you want to know why I circle around before I settle down, the answer is very simple. I am not trying to stomp down grass to prepare a cozy place like my bear ancestors did. I am doing exactly what you do when you circle a sofa. I too, am looking for hidden cheese doodles. Why do I stick my head out the car window? Obviously, if you are asking that question, then you have never owned a convertible. Not all people can swim. Correct? This is also true of dogs. People who do not know how to swim have bulldogs. They too sink like rocks due to their body mass. Another common question is whether or not dogs that have hair over their eyes can see. Of course not. Neither can teenagers. Why do some dogs howl when they hear a siren? The secret is that they are trying to keep their pack together. The sound of the siren in some way makes them think a pack member is trying to communicate so they join in to unite the pack. This is very common among basset hounds. So is farting at the TV. (Go figure) Basically, it is the same reason you start yelling, "Did Grandpa push his MedicAlert button again?" when you hear a siren. We connect sounds to those we know. And, we want to keep Grandpa in the pack. Do dogs recognize themselves in the mirror? Some puppies do think the mirror is another puppy. Most dogs do not accept the image in the mirror, not unlike fat Shepherds.

By this time, I had eaten lunch and was attached to my rope that I wore in the house. Lucky for me, the Producer was in charge so there was no one at the end of the rope. She was baking oatmeal raisin cookies, ignoring Prozac.

I wandered into the living room and drooled on Prozac's face. He felt my presence and addressed me.

'What? What do you f-ing want?'

'Well,' I said. 'Do you know who I think I am?'

Prozac looked at me and began. 'I am not sure, have you recently been in a Turkish prison?' When I did not respond he said, 'of course I have no freakin' idea who you are. But, my nose knows there is most likely a dog under that weird haircut. I have been coming here for years, living down the street makes it easy. This is my other home. The Producer and Director sort of adopted me. And, I guess in some sort of weird way they are your Shepherds as well. That does not make us related.

My Shepherd is really, really old. Ancient! She loves me very much.

But, sometimes she forgets she has a dog and calls Animal Control. So, I beeline it over here for a snack and a snooze till she remembers. This is your couch when I am not here,' he said smiling, patting my neck with his aged black and white paw.

'We will get along fine,' he said.

Grateful to have a canine to talk to, I opened the floodgates. 'What is with all this retriever stuff? I am not a retriever. I am a standard poodle. In my mind, that means if you threw it, you go get it. And furthermore, I think I should have been consulted on the tattoo issue. If the Producer had taken me to the vet that day instead of the Director then I am sure that I would have had a heart with the word 'Reba', my mom, on my chest instead of numbers tattooed in my ear.

My brain is not a fixed, unchanging structure, but rather a continually growing and revising structure altering based on my experiences and interactions. Unfortunately for me, most of my experiences are with the Director and Producer. In other words, I am screwed. I am living with soon to be cellmate 82519 and a potential organ donor who also has the flu.

'No, I am not being rude. I know what you are thinking. Yes, I do love them. But, I gotta call a spade a spade.' I could tell by his face he was losing interest in my problems.

Yes, I do have more to say. Get over it. By the time I reached eight weeks of age, my tiny brain increased by 25 percent and measured eighty centimetres. At nine months it will reach 100 centimetres, at which time I will be brilliant. For now, I have to use my puppy brain.

Because my litter was seven guys and three girls, I was exposed to high levels of male hormones in the womb. This is why I am more active and more territorial than boys born in balanced gender litters. As you may know, I was very stressed as a puppy due to that whole goats' milk thing. However, as a result of the early stress, there have been some positive effects, changing my brain responses. When complex problem solving is set up for me, I am less likely to have an emotional response and more likely to solve the problem thru intelligence due to my early adaption to stress. The Director likes to set up puzzles for me. He puts treats inside different shaped boxes and I have to figure out how to get the treat out. Sometimes, it a paper towel cylinder and other times a cardboard box. It's a very fun game. Also, sometimes he freezes the treat and we play find the chicken. That's fun too.

However, I get a little stressed when he puts the treat on a chair that is too high for me. I can smell the treat. But it is very hard for me to get to it. My puppy brain cannot explain the frustration to him, however I have found a solution that works for me. When he stresses me out too much by putting the chicken in places I cannot reach, like a barstool, then I wait till he is having dinner and run as fast as I can and then jump on his leg, spring-boarding on to the dining room table. I try to make sure to land close enough to grab the whole chicken in my teeth. Then, I jump off the table and we play hide and seek. I always hide in the same place, under the bed. He can see me but he cannot get to me. Not unlike the chicken on the barstool. He swears and curses at me. Now, we are even. Eventually, he calms down, I come out and life goes on. Smart, eh? I know. I'm a genius poodle.'

'And, there's more.'

'Please, no more! Make it stop!! Someone please, pretty please with sugar on top, turn the Poodle off,' he repeated.

I ignored him. To a large degree, I credit my superior intelligence to the goats' milk stress test and my exposure to talk radio, which opened my eyes to all kinds of worldly problems. Changing the station on the radio is not as difficult as you might think for a puppy. My puppy paws are well suited for the task. At a very early age, I became accustomed to a variety of noises, human voices and styles of music on different stations, always leaning toward talk radio. The other day I was listening to a song that said everything is beautiful in its own way. What a lovely sentiment. A message to live by. Too bad it is a bald -faced lie. The Chinese crested hairless dog is ugly. A hairless dog? Come on, give me break. It looks like a large rat. Not everything is beautiful in its own way.

Even as a newborn, I pondered in-depth math problems. For

example, why is not the number 11 pronounced onety one? There is twenty-one and thirty-one. Why not onety-one?

I'm a thinker. My mind is constantly reeling with new facts and assimilating them is part of the reason I sleep so much. It tires me. This morning, for example, I heard on the radio that deer only sleep five minutes a day. Talk about stressed out and cranky. My theory is that they cannot sleep because they spend all their time looking for those deer crossing signs. It's just a theory but there may be something to it.

'Keep talking. I always yawn when I'm interested,' he said.

And, I did. 'Since I am experiencing growth spurts and some hormonal imbalance, I have taken up a new hobby, practical jokes. Being a puppy I have only one joke and it never gets old for me. It is called, "made you look". I look up really fast three or four times, really, really fast - and then you look up and I laugh. I have variations of this game called "made you come". I go to the door and bark, bark, bark. When you arrive I bust a gut laughing. The Director does not find these new games fun. In fact, he has decided to enrol me in puppy class. The other choice he gave me was the Marine Corps. I'm not sure about the uniforms, so I picked puppy class. Was I right?'

I moved closer to the couch to hear Prozac's solution. Instead, he told me his.

'I don't have the time, or the crayons to explain life to you Mr. Poodle.'

'Yeah but, I want to learn,' I said. 'Can you help me out?'

'I'd like to help you out, which way did you come in?' he asked, adding 'Oy vey, do you ever stop flipping the pancake on the griddle?'

I did not respond, trying to be more quiet.

'Got a smoke? Got any dark ale? A guy needs a cold one and a ciggy once in awhile, he said.'

I remained quiet.

Looking over at my confused face, he said, 'When life gives you lemons, make lemonade. Then find someone that life gave vodka and party.'

'When life gives you melons... you might be dyslexic,' I said, trying to fit in to the conversation.

'I am so thirsty! And I want a freakin' oatmeal raisin cookie!' Prozac said.

'Did you know that the sentence "The quick brown fox jumps over a lazy dog." uses every letter of the alphabet,' I said, not having any cookies to offer him.

With that he got up off the couch and walked to the kitchen. I followed. Maybe, I could have an oatmeal raisin cookie too.

On the way, I gave a lot of thought to what he said. It was not so much what he said but how he said it. It occurred to me that Prozac had a different way of thinking than most poodles.

I knew I had to do something to help my Shepherds. But what could I do? My thought process is based on the sensory images that I am exposed to and this creates my thought patterns. The fact that my senses are different than my Shepherd explains why my image patterns lead me to different conclusions. For example, if I am the Alpha in a pack of five dogs and there is only enough dinner for four of us then my conclusion might be to kill the weakest puppy. This type of thinking is not right or wrong. It is canine. And in my world, that's okay.

At dinnertime, Prozac asked, 'Can I help with dinner?' What he really meant was the same thing I was thinking, 'Why isn't it already in my bowl?' That night we had broiled chicken. There were six strips of chicken, a scoop of mashed potatoes and three honeyed carrots in our dog bowl. Prozac ate four pieces, no potatoes, no carrots, before I could get my muzzle in there. I knew I would have to be faster to the food bowl next time. This type of thinking is not right or wrong. It is Prozac. I knew we would be fur-ever friends.

Having been used to dry kibble, I correctly reasoned that food was always better when Prozac was on the couch. For dessert, we shared a freshly baked oatmeal raisin cookie or two that Prozac had somehow managed to borrow when no one was looking.

Chapter 7

Putz Park

What I understood from talk radio and the Pet Channel is that a dog park is a friendly facility set aside for dogs to exercise and play off-leash in a controlled environment under the supervision of their Shepherds.

Nothing could be further from the truth. If the Shepherds knew what really goes on in a dog park, then they would never have been so upset with the closing.

Here is what happened to me. At 6:30am, the Director came a'knocking. I had become accustomed to my small one bedroom crate with no washroom and no running water. It was at best a modest bungalow but it was mine. With the exception of white bear, I had few overnight visitors. The Director would switch my radio to country western and I would switch it back. Radios have a scan button on them. Since, my paws are not fitted for dials. I scan till I find my show. You can only listen to *Mama Get The Hammer (There's A Fly On Papa's Head)* so many times.

"Time to go to the dog park. Time to go. Rise and shine Friday," he said happily.

My heart thumped. I was so excited. I wondered how many poodles would be there. I envisioned a place not unlike Cantope where there were acres of grass, trees and a variety of toys to play with. I went outside to pee. The cold, damp air chilled me to the bone, while the Shepherd drank his hot coffee. When I came back, we dressed. He in heavy boots, fleece lined winter parka, gloves and mitts. On me he put a blue collar. It hardly seemed fair given the temperature. However, I was glad to be going to the dog park. Nothing would deter me.

Before leaving I checked the sofa. Prozac had gone home during the night. We walked about seven blocks and stopped. Blades of brown winter grass peeked through the uneven snow cover. It was not what I had pictured. It was a barren yard, half a block long, attached to a school. The sounds of rushing snow tires of the cars on the nearby bridge filled the air. I correctly assumed that this must be my neighbourhood dog park. Pulling on the leash, we walked past a gateless fence. In the distance, I could see a group of four dogs in a close-knit pack. Behind me, I heard the rustle of four paws. Not wanting to be rude, I turned and saw a German Shepherd and border collie mix with a hint of terrier sprinkled in, trying to enter the dog park. Oh my god, it was Prozac.

'Prozac, right? Good to see you.' I asked, blocking the entrance. Not waiting for an answer I continued, 'This is the dog park? Right? It is a fabulous place, right? We will play games and then we will have a light snack and then more games and then a nap and then perhaps another snack before we journey home, right? Does this blue collar make me look athletic?'

Looking up at me he said, 'Oy, not you again, another poodle in the park.' He stopped, cleared his throat, and continued. 'I am SammyFarber. You can call me Pops or SammyFarber. But, if you want to see six months old you better stop calling me Prozac. My real name is Rufus. My Shepherd, eighty-one years old at the time, was losing his hearing and more. When asked what time it is he would answer, "Yes, it does look like rain". So, it came as no surprise to me when the Vet asked him my name for the file he said "Sammy Farber" which, of course, was his name. Anyhoo, I have been SammyFarber ever since. I will call you Friday Poodle. I have been coming to this field for twelve years, and it's always different. Sometimes good, sometimes not so good.'

He raised his lips as if he was doing an Elvis Presley impression before he said: 'As you know, my remaining female Shepherd, God bless the dear soul, is too old to bring me here. So, I come myself. The gate latch is old, the collar is old and me, I am old too. Oy, am I thirsty. Every afternoon I have a little nosh, Gefilte Fish.'

Sensing my lack of understanding, he explained. 'It is a tasty mix of congealed fish parts and transparent schmaltz, slime jelly. The only food that is permissible for Jewish dogs like me to refuse. In some families, they may even be allowed to gag, but politely. I like it. But, it has too much salt. Oy, am I thirsty, he repeated. At dinner time I have kugel.'

'Kugel?' I asked with the same puzzled look.

'Yes, kugel. It's a yummy blend of overcooked noodles, raisins, and curds of ripe cheese. Not fun to look at. But when lathered with sour cream it makes an excellent artery hardener. Here again, too much salt. Oy, am I thirsty.'

'How can you tell when sour cream goes bad?' I asked. He did not respond.

'Why don't you say something about the salty kugel?' I asked, pushing on.

'In life, I have learned that troubles with salty kugel are easier than troubles without salty kugel.'

'You came by yourself?' I asked, changing the topic.

'Why? After 12 years ya don't think I know the way? I schlepped back home last night, seeing the coast was clear and no Animal Service officers looking for me, I had a good shloof in my dog bed. I always enjoy sleeping. Your house, my house, it's all good.'

'Okay, SammyFarber. What do we do now,' I asked, bouncing back and forth from front paws to back. 'Huh, huh, what do we do now?'

'You see those four over there,' SammyFarber said, pointing with his nose. 'They run this place now. The Wheaton is the boss dog. His name is Putz.'

Scratching my nose, I ask, 'What are the names of the other three dog pound specials?'

'Putz.'

'All named Putz?' I asked, still scratching my long nose.

'Oy vey, does it matter to you Schmendrick? If you hang around with a Putz then you are a putz, too.'

'I did not know that,' I said shaking my head. 'What's a schmendrick?'

'You are a schmendrick, a puppy. The Wheaton putz, the alpha, has suffered over two dozen concussions from toilet seats falling on his head over the years. Some dogs were dropped on their heads as puppies. Some, like him, were clearly thrown in the air, hit by the ceiling fan, bounced off the wall, and fell out the window of a highrise. They will come after you. All four of them. It is simply a matter of time. They form a loose pack and if none of the Shepherds break them up, there is potential for ka-ka to happen. These dogs will gang up on weaker dogs like you, Friday Poodle, and physically attack you. They are here on a regular basis and always fight as one. The Shepherds spend all their time trying to stay warm by walking in tight circles, and smoking. Oy, the smoking. Welcome to the yellow teeth club. I always take home a few butts. They have no idea what is going on with us. All Shepherds think that they have the smartest dogs ever.'

Before continuing, SammyFarber sniffed the air to see if it would rain. He decided it would not. 'Why just the other day, I was visiting my friend Ozzie-Ozzie the bulldog. His Shepherd tells my Shepherd that Ozzie-Ozzie is the sharpest tool in the shed; more like a sack of hammers if you ask me. Ozzie-Ozzie had just beaten him at chess. Just between you and me, Ozzie-Ozzie is not that smart. Who do you think taught Ozzie-Ozzie to play chess?'

SammyFarber paused to scratch his ear with his back paw. 'I think most middle class people hate telling the housekeeper what to do, right, I mean, truthfully? In my house, the eighty-nine year old Shepherd cleans up before her housekeeper comes once a month. I think a lot of people feel bad about training their dog or being too harsh with the dog. It seems so old-fashioned and kind of mean. It is not. I am not saying all dogs can play chess after a few dog lessons. Some should stick to an easier sport. Horseshoes perhaps? I mean really, lack of training or guidance and you get a putz. When I was a puppy they threw an obedience book in my crate and said read this. Lucky for them I am a quick study.'

'My Shepherd does not smoke,' I said, hoping to win bonus points.

'Yes, but he has other bad habits. He likes country western music and he snores. Did you ever notice, the one who snores the loudest always falls asleep first,' SammyFarber said.

'So, what should I do?'

'Friday Poodle, you have five choices: freeze, fight, flee, avoid or thrash talk. You pick the one that works best for you.'

'Which to pick,' I pondered, shaking in my boots. The four putzes were approaching and they looked mean. The ringleader had a metal collar with prongs facing in.

'Me, I trash talk. They only bully a dog that they perceive to be weaker or more submissive. Plus, I enjoy a little kibbitz now and again. I am too old to fight anymore. SammyFarber said.

'I do not know how to fight. What does avoid mean?' I asked, hoping it was something I could do.'

He paused. He looked up at the sky again, and then responded. 'On my way home I have to pass a house where Mr. Asshole dog lives. Been barking at me from his window for five years. One day, he is in his yard. I guess his Shepherds had enough of the barking, and he comes flying at the chain link fence full force trying to get at me. Lucky for me, the fence was made by a lance man, tough and sturdy. He is an afghan hound, dumb as a post. I made the mistake one day of telling him that I would like to see things from his point of view, too bad, I cannot shove my head that far up my arse. Anyway, this goes on for a month or two, him charging the fence and me safe on the other side making the odd relevant comment. I always give him words of wisdom when I pass. Like once I told him that he should lose all his teeth except one, and that one should ache. I have to go by him cause it is the only way I go home. I am old. Old people do not like change. One day, I am heading home just before noon and there he is. But, this time he is on the outside of the fence. My side. No leash. No collar. I almost pissed my pants right there on the spot. The Yiddish word for an animal that doesn't either run from or fight its enemies is lunch. Like I said, I am too old to run or fight and freezing only makes sense to deer. So, I pretend he is not there and I walk right by, looking at anything and everything except him. And, Holy Moses, it works. That is avoidance.'

Out of the corner of my eye, I saw on the other side of the park two great Danes lumbering along the fence. 'Who are they?'

Without looking up, SammyFarber says, 'Those are not dogs. They are horses. '

At this point, the Director had taken off my leash. He was wandering over to the smokers. "Enjoy the park Friiiiiiiiiiiiday," he said to me.

'Remember the five choices,' SammyFarber added.

In a matter of seconds, the four putzes had me boxed in. Each one was in the corner of an imaginary square, closing in on me. Avoidance was not a possibility. I took a look around, trying to the find the weak link. I was going to attack him. Each of them had the same posture, flattening of the ears and lowering of their heads as they moved in closer and closer. The Wheaton raised his hackles, wrinkled his muzzle and pulled back his lips. The others quickly mimicked his actions. I was dead meat.

I immediately broke eye contact. I slowly turned away from the ringleader Wheaton, I crept in the opposite direction. Yawning, I avoided all eye contact. I wanted to pacify this dog by appearing submissive as soon as possible. I was frozen with fear. I could tell by the air bites all around me that nothing was working. I was moments from being torn to pieces.

All of sudden they stopped advancing. I looked behind me to see the cause. Over my right shoulder was SammyFarber. He had his tail and ears erect, chest puffed out. He looked directly at the dogs, circling and sniffing the ground in front of him, growling if the other dogs move in any closer on me. He looked over at me and winked.

Directly behind SammyFarber was a shadowy figure. I could not see him clearly thru the bushes. All I know was that he is well muscled and the type of dog that does not show teeth, but bites. Hard! Something about his posture told me that he had had a tough life. I hoped he would be on my side.

One of the great lies that dogs want to believe is that "life is fair". In fact, the exact opposite is true. Even though we have the same inherent opportunities, the truth is that chew bones are not always distributed equitably in the canine world. My thoughts were interrupted by SammyFarber.

'Even with my friend standing guard, I do not think they will buy this act much longer Friday Poodle. So, I suggest we run for it while the opportunity is present.'

Lucky for me many of my ancestors were originally bred to assist duck hunters. My grandfather was a skilled hunter and retriever. He spoke French. I also have first cousins that have won honours in dog sports, agility, obedience, tracking, and even herding. My dad once ran with wolves so I know I have the right genes. I took SammyFarber's advice and I started to run. I ran nonstop at full speed for the next hour. I was still running when I heard a familiar voice behind me.

'Shhhhhtop it you stupid, meshugeneh poodle. Oysgemitchet, shhhhtop right now before I upchuck a lung, I am gonna plotz,' SammyFarber gasped. After catching his breath, he continued, 'You can stop running now Friday Poodle. The Wheaton gang left the park thirty minutes ago. They were exhausted. See you tomorrow. '

The Director called me to come. I stopped and wondered what 'come' meant. He ran toward me so I assumed we were to run in that direction. I was the pack leader and this was the route. He starting yelling at me, which I mistakenly assumed was praise. Finally, I was up against the fence and could go no further, the Director grabbed hold of my collar, attached my leash. He said I was to come to him when he called, pointing out that we were the only two left in the park. He said, "You sure had a good time playing tag with those other nice dogs. I thought you would be tired out with all that running. But, it seems not. I guess we need to press on."

Oh my god, my Shepherd is an idiot. I really needed to go home and nap. After another four blocks, we crossed a bridge that spanned a massive river. I could see off to the right, another dog park, rolling hills and lush green grass. A dirt track ran along the top of this field. When we arrived, the Director took off my leash and I started to cry. I could not take anymore. The thought of running full steam for another hour while Wheatons chased me, biting my poodle ass was too much for me. I wanted to go back to Cantope. I wanted my doggy mom. I wanted Reba.

While I was sitting on the ground afraid to look up, a dog walked by me and smiled. She had a plaid collar around her Labrador neck. 'Welcome' she said. In the next five minutes, five more dogs had walked passed, each with a gentle smile, greeting or wave for me. One was called Raindrop, another Lilly Moon. There was Gentle Bob and Merry-Ann and Crash. No one named Putz.

For the next hour, I walked around the field with my new friends. I asked Crash how he got his name. Just as he was about to answer, he walked head first into a tree and laughed. They were a fun group. On our second loop we came upon a Pit Bull resting near a tree. He was staring unkindly at me.

'What's his problem?' I asked Lilly Moon.

'His name is Meeko. Due to his breeding, Pit-Bull dogs such as

Meeko, have evolved with fewer facial expressions and are often misinterpreted by other dogs, which leads to fights,' Lilly Moon explained. 'I would like to tell you that his bark is worst than his bite. But his bite is worse, much worse. You should say hello. He is a very well-travelled guy. He has been everywhere. He looks like he recognizes you.'

'I probably resemble his last meal. I will pass.'

Another hour passed, and it was time to go. I remembered that come meant 'come to me' not 'come lead the way' so when the Director called, I went to him. This seemed to please him. I made a mental note not do this too often, so as not to spoil him too much. It took us another 15 minutes to get home. The Producer was waiting for me with a hug and a bowl of ice water, three ice cubes just the way I like it. Then I slept.

Chapter 8

Underground Canine Protection Program

The Director woke me at 6:30am. Snow gear and coffee completed by 7am, we were off. When we exited the front door, I spotted the mailman. My mortal enemy!!!! Before I could attack, the mailman leaned down and rubbed my belly.

'Did you tell him to do that,' I asked the Director. 'Did you reveal my biggest weakness to my enemy? Huh? Did you?'

"I might have mentioned it. But, he is not your enemy," the Director said.

'Betrayed by my own butler.'

"I am not your butler," the Director responded. "Let's go already."

On the way to the dog park, the Director told me that night at 7pm was my first puppy class. Mixed feelings, fear of the unknown and joy of the unknown clashed. Maybe with some training I could find a good job, perhaps in the medical field. In doggie life you are faced with two choices: guard dog work or daytime television analyst. I had so many questions for SammyFarber about dog class that I pulled all the way to the park. From a block away, I could see him waiting at the gateless entrance. He looked pale and grey. 'Under the weather?' I asked.

'Even the mighty lion has to deal with the flies now and then. I'll be okay. I got to get home and then to the vet. Remember Friday Poodle, if things get tough at the park today, every hardboiled egg is yellow on the inside. Have a good run,' he said.

'Thanks. But, I wish, I wish, I really, really wish that I was a pit-bull or a rotti. Then I would show them putzes.'

SammyFarber pointed to my front left paw. 'In this one put all of your wishes.' He then pointed to my front right paw and said 'I want in this one you should poop. And then, next time you see me, let me know which one filled up faster. Be happy with who you are. Enjoy!'

'Thanks. Not to worry. I am very fast.' He turned to leave but before he did, I asked, 'But, but, I almost forgot, I need to know about puppy class. I start tonight. What do I wear?

'Oy, such a poodle," SammyFarber said. 'In my day, there were no dog training classes. Like I said before, my Shepherd threw a book in my crate and told me to read it. Lucky for him I was a quick study. It was called *Everything a Jewish Dog Needs to Know*. At school you will start with the 's' words: sit, shlep, and schmooze. You will do very well at schmoozing, it is your calling. He stopped to scratch his moist nose. 'I almost forgot, the chapter on tax law is a bit confusing at first. You earn a bisel and then another bisel and then eventually you have a shisel, and then you pay tax and then you have bupkes. You'll do fine. And remember, crying or whining at dog class doesn't help anything. Try your luck with violent mood swings if things derail. '

He turned toward the exit and yelled over his shoulder. 'And Schmendrik, if you see a pinch collar, metal prongs on the inside, run! It is a bad thing.'

I spent the next hour hoofing it. Still running long after the putzes had left the park, the Director called me. I guess I like running.

On the way to the second park, I fretted over the pinch collar. I should have asked SammyFarber more about it. Then again, I was positive that the Producer and the Director would never subject me to torture. (Boy, was I wrong.)

We got to the second park in record time. I found Meeko sitting under an old elm tree, frowning his usual frown, his muscled frame resting easy on his strong limbs. As I sprinted over to him, I decided that if I was going to walk on thin ice then I might as well dance. 'Hey Meeko, was that you in the bushes at the other park yesterday? You saved my butt! '

'Yeah, what about it? I was at Putz Park. I go to lots of parks. You got a problem with that?'

'Nothing, Meeko. Nothing, nothing at all. ' I backed off so as not to challenge him further.

'Whatever!' he said. ' I was there to see SammyFarber. I saw you too. You are very fast, very fast indeed. Any friend of SammyFarber's is a friend of mine. He likes you. Me and SammyFarber go way back. I met him five years ago when he was twelve and I was two. '

'Where?' I asked.

'I had recently moved into the neighbourhood and I did not know how to act at the dog park. Anyway, day one, this bull mastiff, like comes up to me and places his paws on my shoulder to show me his high social ranking in the park. Like he was a four year old, light brown male about 27 inches at the withers and 130lbs, good fighting weight. I did not know anything about social park ranking which I have learned is a non-violent posturing. All I knew is that this bully dog was pushing hard on my shoulders, trying to force me to lie down. So, like I do what they do where I come from, I beat the snot out of him. If SammyFarber had not broken it up I would have like killed him. At that time in my life, I was not nice,' he explained with a logic I couldn't argue with.

Not knowing what to say to that, I said the first thing that popped in my head. 'Dalmatians are completely white at birth.' And then I wondered why my mouth does not have an on and off switch. 'How old is SammyFarber? Yesterday, he told me he was twelve,' I continued.'

'Like I know, like he tells that to everyone. He has been twelve for a lot of years. He is much older, much much older. He took me under his wing even back then. I had a troubled childhood, crack house, all that.'

'What happened?'

'I will tell you but you must promise to never tell anyone. I do not want to ever go back there.'

'I promise, I really promise,' I said. I seem to be collecting more secrets.

He continued.' Like I was adopted from the no kill shelter by these people. They put on quite the good guy act. When I got to their house, I was chained to a boarded up doghouse outside and like it was my job to bark and growl and bite if anyone in a uniform came too close. '

'Any toys?' I asked.

'My toys consisted of cigarette butts, beer cans and empty glue tubes in paper bags. Condom wrappers, blowing around, getting caught in the dry weeds and pavement cracks nearby where I was chained. I was fed like scraps and drank muddy rainwater. I was getting weaker everyday, too frail to run away. My sun-bleached white coat slid tautly over my panting ribcage. I was so thin like, my species was hard to determine, but the tiger striped brindle in the dark patch around my eye said pit-bull, so like people and dogs backed off. Once, I pulled so hard on the chain my thin head slipped thru the collar. Almost lost an ear,' he said as only a survivor can.

'Tell me everything so I can put it in my book? And, if you buy a copy of my book and you do not like it then you can unbind it and make a paper cowboy hat.'

'Shut up poodle and I will tell you. Later, I was caught and I was returned to the shelter where they read my ear tattoo and called the people to pick me up. When they got me home they beat me pretty bad with bats and cracked two of my ribs. I stopped trying to run away after that. My ears were infected and I had tapeworm. I spend like two years at that job, working day and night, mostly at night. I could catch a few hours' sleep from 6am till 10am, those were the slow hours. Rarely did anyone come by then. If it had not been for a country lady about 40 years old with strong hands who goes by the name of Auntie cutting my chain with bolt cutters in the early morning then I would still be there. She whispered something to me that made me trust her and then shoved me in a van filled with border collies. Her and her pack of border collies took to me to her farm and then the vet came.'

I wanted desperately to know what she had whispered to him. Why did he not attack her? But I did not want to interrupt more so I kept quiet.

He continued. 'Re-tattooed my ear numbers and cleaned me up. She changed my name from Killer to Meeko. I had somehow been drafted into the underground canine protection program. I lived with her pack for a few months till I was normal again. She placed me with a great family where I work afternoons at their attached daycare. Me, a killer, a welcome mat for preschoolers. It is my job to show the little sweetums that dogs are friendly. I am very good at my job. Who would have thunk it?' he said wistfully.

'How did you first meet SammyFarber?'

'One day while I was working at the crackhouse he walked by. I growled at him but he did not flinch. He looked me straight in the eye and said, 'Onions should grow out from your belly button!'

I said 'Come a little closer, trying to bait him, readying for the kill.' SammyFarber said, 'Listen schmuck, I came by your lovely neighbourhood to visit with a white Yorkiepoo puppy named Precious. She usually has a shotgun with her. Seen her?' The truth is that he had taken the wrong turn on the way home from the park and he was dog tired and lost. Getting lost was a more frequent occurrence for him lately and he feared it would only get worse. 'I told him he was quite the smartass, digging in my heels. This is the toughest crack house on the block with very dangerous people inside and wise cracks can get you killed. If you come closer I will rip you to pieces.' He smiled at me and said, 'Kish Mein Toches. Surrounding yourself with dwarfs does not make you a giant.'

'I did not know what Kish Mein Toches meant. If I had known then that it meant, kiss my ass, then things may have ended different. But, it made me laugh the way he said it, trash talking all tough-like. I knew we would be friends. The next day he came back and brought me some kugel to eat and told me not to worry. He had a plan. And, he did.' Meeko stopped to scratch his nose.

'When Auntie came at daybreak that next morning, I growled at her, readying to bite. Like it was my job. How was I to know she was there to help? Like she got real close, close enough for me to bite her so I leaned back so as to get a good spring forward and then she said something that made me understand she was there to help me. She said...' he paused dramatically for effect.

Unable to contain my poodle brain a moment longer, I finished the sentence for Meeko. 'And then she whispered something that changed your life forever. I know. I know what it was she said.' I was busting at the seams. She said 'There Are Some Things Money Can't Buy. For Everything Else, There's MasterCard.'

Meeko, lifted his upper lip, snarled.

'No, no, that was wrong. This time I got it. This time I know for sure. She said: There's a lot of joy in Chips Ahoy. And then she gave you one. Right? Right? Huh? Right?' I asked. One look from Meeko and I knew that nine out of 10 dogs who finish other dogs' sentences are wrong the second time too.

'If you shut your trap I will tell you.'

I bit my lip. 'Sorry, sometimes, I stop to think and I forget to start again.'

Meeko continued. 'At the exact moment that I was about to bite her, she leaned in real close and said, 'SammyFarber wants to know if there is too much salt in the kugel? And, the rest of the story you know.'

'Amazing,' I said. 'By the way, I saw SammyFarber today. But, he had to go home, he was not feeling well.'

'I am sad to hear that. I went by his house yesterday afternoon. He told me a secret.'

'SammyFarber told you a secret. My mom said that most importantly, everyone in life needs someone to tell their secrets. Yup, that's what Mom said. Be that someone and your life will be filled with riches. You are so lucky Meeko. What was SammyFarber's secret? Huh? What was it? Huh? Tell me? I said not totally grasping the concept of a secret.'

'SammyFarber told me not to tell. All will be revealed when the time is right. Now, is not that time.' With that, Meeko walked away.

I yelled after him.' But, I want to know the secret. It is very important to me. Tell me, please. I know secrets. I am the keeper of secrets. It is my job.'

Meeko stopped, looking at me with his steel faced glare. 'You know mine. Be sure to keep it that way.'

I gulped. I was starting to understand what Reba meant. Secret keeping was not a task to be taken lightly. It had rules attached. Some canines waltz to a different drummer and some tango.

The rest of morning was very enjoyable. I was the keeper of Meeko's secret. I was so proud. There were bowls of fresh water for the taking. And Lilly Moon's Sheppard gave me a delicious homemade liver and oatmeal cookie. This was my kind of dog park.

Upon arriving home, I spent the rest of day napping and listening to Oprah. I ate some of my dry kibble and tried not think too much about dog class.

But I couldn`t stop thinking about SammyFarber`s secret. I wondered about SammyFarber's secret and what it was. Would I find out? And when?

I thought back on the secrets I already knew. Some of them were: the Director had gotten a letter from the bank the other day. It tasted important. And, he had mercy killed a man with fire extinguisher foam.

The Producer was dying of Basal cell carcinoma disease. Meeko was really 'Killer'. There were crackhouse dealers looking to put him back to work. Plus, I opened the kitchen the cupboard and ate a whole box of cheezy hound rounds. Whoops, I did not mean to mention that one. Don't tell!

Puppyhood was not what I had expected. There were too many secrets to deal with. And, little did I know, I did not yet have the biggest secret of them all.

Chapter 9

Psycho Bitch

The doorbell rang in the early evening. Barking wildly, I ran to the door. 'Cause, that is what I do. Door opened wide revealing a very fat unattractive woman. She said her name was Grace. She lumbered into our house, knocking over everything in her path. (Which only proves that your name does not dictate your actions.)

Our training class took place in our dark and musty basement. Poodles do not normally go in basements. The Producer and Director joined us and class began. Well, sort of. Grace launched into a forty minute speech on train the trainer. Meanwhile, I sat there the whole time with nothing to do. So I counted...18, 12, 27, 4. Her whole point was that whether or not the Director or Producer were intentionally teaching me, I was always learning, and this is especially true not just for puppies, she read from a piece of paper. "If you do not teach your pet your rules, he will invent his own." She continued, "Positive training enhances the bond between dog and owner, and helps ensure that your dog will respond happily to your instructions."

Now, if she actually believed or understood what she was reading off the paper then all would have been good. But, she did not. She was the trainer from hell. Dumb as a sack of hammers. We walked over to a bathroom door and naturally I thought I should go in so I did. She banged the door into my nose. It hurt like hell. "See," she said, "now the dog knows not to go out the door ahead of you." What Grace does not know is that what I learned is that Grace is a shithead.

Next we learned walking on lead. For fear of having my nose bashed again, I refused to move even when she pulled on my collar. Grace had a solution. She removed my blue cloth buckle collar and put on a metal pinch collar. It was the same one the alpha Wheaton putz had on. This time when she pulled on the leash the prongs dug into my neck and you bet your ass that I moved. I did everything that psycho bitch wanted. At one point, I could see that the Producer and the Director were not happy with the methods. They were however, impressed with the results. I was walking without pulling for the first time.

Let me tell you pinch or prong collars are not appropriate for puppies. If they're not put on exactly right they can cause serious damage to the trachea. Mine hurt like hell.

On the radio, I heard that it has become commonplace in many current circles of the dog industry to utilize force and compulsion. The choke chain, the pinch collar, and electric collars are popular. My greatest fear, the pinch collar that SammyFarber had warned me about, was around my neck.

Grace did what every dim, incompetent trainer does with a pinch collar. She put it around the Director's arm first before putting it on me - not his neck, his arm - and told him to pull hard. It was her attempt to show him it wouldn't hurt me. If I was doing the test, I would have put it around his neck and waited till he was not looking and pulled really hard and then we might have had a fair test. But, whether or not they hurt is not the issue.

Trainers who always use pinch collars on their dogs simply do not understand the canine thought process. The ones who say their dogs have double coats so it is okay are by far the stupidest. They want a quick fix so much they make up brainless excuses. What most people do not realize is that with all of the yanking of the pinch collar, the dog actually begins to work out of fear of reprisal.

I can tell you from having one on, that I did not understand this device. And I am smart. Possibly, some people have made the decision to use these collars because they feel the presence of all of this hardware makes them (not necessarily the dog) look good. These people either have low self-esteem or a small penis or both. Everyone knows a dog owner who claims "my dog has to wear this because my dog is part wolf". What shitheads! Wolves are more pack animals than most dogs. If anything, a part wolf dog would never need a pinch. I am a pack animal and am dependent upon the Director and the Producer within my pack, and the hierarchy of this pack dictates desired or undesired behaviour, not some bleeping pinch collar. Furthermore, I have never seen a wolf with a pinch collar.

Follow me here. I know my Shepherds would never hit me with an open or closed hand. Every dog can sense who might strike them, just like we know which dogs bite. However, many of those same people who would never hit their dog still put pinch collars on their dogs. They correctly believe that hitting the dog actually creates an environment of confusion and conflict. So, they do not hit the dog. Are you at least considering the idea that a pinch collar creates an environment of confusion and conflict?

In my canine world, if I am hit, I have experienced a violent act, one that has brought pain upon my body, and my Shepherd has caused this pain. However, I cannot truly make the correlation of corrective action as the Shepherd perceives it, since this is not a natural activity or trait within my normal pack environment. I may cower and though this may even be the result the Shepherd desired, this cowering posture is primarily out of confusion. It stems from not understanding the pain that now emanates from an activity like petting that is supposed to be pleasing, and the conflict of why the Shepherd (Alpha) has turned it against me. All I can do is cry or cower or both.

Now that you understand why the dog cannot understand being struck as a form of correction, let's talk pinch collar. In your world, if one Shepherd were to place a corrective device such as a pinch collar upon another Shepherd then the recipient of such device understands and can comprehend not only who has placed the device on them, but also why. This Shepherd also understands as well the subsequent corrective measures that may come about through the use of these devices as a result of exhibiting undesired behaviour, even though they may be unaware at the time of what those specific undesired behaviours may be. According to a show I heard on talk radio, this is also the basis of your penal system.

Here's what really pisses me off. Shepherds actually hold seminars to teach other Shepherds how to properly use these pinch collars! WOW! Wait a friggin' second, you actually live in a society where it is socially acceptable to teach others how to be inhumane to animals, to deal with them on a level they do not understand? You can learn this with only five easy payments. Operators are standing by. Have your credit card ready. Comes with free steak knives.

My last point that I want other canines reading this to understand is that if you see Grace at the top of a long staircase it is okay to get under her feet and cause her to fall. (Did I say that out loud? Whoops!)

You need to understand what a dog does when he is annoyed by another dog and cannot walk away. First, we send a signal, a level one warning that tells the other dog we do not want to fight. If that does not work, then we step in the direction of the challenger and bite the air, making sure to miss him. This is a level two warning. And then if that does not work we go in closer and do an inhibited bite that does not hurt the dog (it is the same sensation that a dog gets from a pinch collar). Then, if there is still no respect, of course, we bite the bitch and run.

When a dog wearing a pinch moves forward to greet another dog for play, the pinch tells him that it is level three warning. The dog with the pinch on becomes confused and it will be extremely difficult in the future to socialize that dog. I guarantee you that most dogs who don't get along with other unfamiliar dogs in a park setting had a pinch collar on for a long time.

Just to be perfectly clear, I do believe that one or two in a thousand dogs probably should have a pinch, choke, shock collar, muzzle or whatever it takes to save them from themselves. There are always extremes. And yes, I know I talk too much about pinch collars. Get over it and stop using them.

Over the next two weeks, I endured four more classes from shithead Grace. Each one was dumber than the last. There was this one class where she rolled me over on my back to show her dominance. She said it was a method used by Monks known as the alpha roll over. It was more of that wolf bullshit. What she did not know, was that the wolf when submitting rolled over on his own, never pushed by another wolf. All she accomplished by doing this to me was ruining what little was left of our relationship. So, take it from me, unless you want a neurotic and freaked out dog, stay away from the alpha roll over. Try sharing an apple turnover instead.

Oddly enough, I heard on the radio the next morning that the Monks had retracted this method of training German Shepherds and offered a very sincere apology to dogs everywhere. They are amazing people with good hearts. Perhaps, they should call Grace. If I ever see her again, I will bite her dumb ass.

Finally, I got my certificate and the Producer mailed a copy to Cantope to show I had passed and could stay with them. The next morning, the Producer threw the certificate from Grace and the pinch collar in the garbage. I knew the Producer loved me very much as I did her. That morning, I pledged that if she ever needed me to do anything I was her boy and I would do it! Had I have known then, what one day she would ask of me; I would never ever have made that pledge. Because, as you probably know, a pledge made by a poodle puppy to his Shepherd can never be broken. No matter what!

Chapter 10

Collectibles

Tuesday morning, the Director and I went directly to dog park two, skipping Putz park. I had not been to Putz park for two weeks. Arriving at park two, the atmosphere was ice and chalk, cold and uninviting. Only one dog braved this frigid morning. I hoped others would be crawling out of their warm beds shortly.

'Hey you. Now!'

Without turning around, I knew it was Meeko.

'Two a.m.! Your houseyard! Important!' He barked out each command.

Before I commit 100 percent to anything, I like to ask the important questions. Looking him in his cold grey eyes, I asked, 'Will there be snacks?'

'Kugel,' he mumbled, walking away.

Regaining my thought process, I asked. 'Wuzzup,' trying to sound cool.

''You wanna know SammyFarber's secret or not? Be there!'

'Okay. Two a.m. Definitely be on time. My yard. Count on me,

Meeko,' I said without thinking. As you know, my mouth engages before my brain. How on earth was I going to friggin' do this? Two burning issues raced through my mind. Firstly, I do not even know when two in the morning is. And secondly, and more importantly, how was I going to get out of the house? Turning back to restate my position, I paused to scratch my head. But, Meeko was gone.

After an hour in the park, we headed home. I pulled toward Putz park, wanting to talk to SammyFarber. Pulling back, the Director routed us home.

The day crawled by slowly. Scanning the radio back from country western, I found the Martha Stewart show. Today's topics were fashion designer Lynn Barker shares some must have looks for fall, and a personal recipe for grilled eggplant parmesan using reduced fat mozzarella and fat free ricotta. Plus, top gardening tools and a shoe umbrella to keep your feet dry. I settled down on the rug and listened. With the exception of the grilled eggplant parmesan nothing really impressed me. I slept through most of the gardening tools, woke up to hear the story of the Lesche soil knife. This versatile knife will cut, dig, and slice almost anything in the garden (according to Shaun, Martha's gardener, who uses it mainly for weeding) as its long blade can get deep into the soil to find the end of the longest weed roots, Martha added. The commercial claimed Lesche diggers are well known throughout the metal detecting hobby as one of the best. Don't get caught in the field with a faulty digger! The announcer warned. The Lesche digger comes with a corduroy sheath for $19.95 plus shipping and handling. Order yours today and we will send you knee pads free of charge, normally a $10 value, he said. It sounded like a good deal to me. I went back to sleep.

After dinner, the Director and the Producer took me for a walk, stopping often to practice our sit, down and stay. As usual, I had to do all the work. But, I did not care. It took my mind off my secrets.

Later that night, I woke up, certain it was two in the morning. This is not an uncommon time for me since I usually have to go out for a pee in the middle of night. 'Puppy bladder half full,' I barked. Jumping up, the hazy eyed Producer looked for the source of the noise. I smiled sorrowfully from within my crate, tilting head adding to the effect. After opening my escape hatch, we journeyed downstairs together.

Once out, the cold night air made we want to pee. I resisted, hopping from foot to foot, holding my breath. I tried counting...8, 22, 7, 9, and on from there. Finally, she gave up and went back to sleep. Our arrangement is that whoever lets me out in the middle of the night can go back to sleep provided that they waited at least twenty minutes for me to 'do it now'. The Producer waits approximately thirty seconds but I never tell on her. I keep her secret. After all that is what I do, keep secrets. Then the other person, in this case the loud snoring Director would have to let me back in when I barked. The system worked well in the past.

"Wisdom is knowing what to do next, skill is doing it," I heard that on Oprah today. I was becoming an avid listener. All I had to do was have the skill to do nothing. I could wait and go with Meeko then come back and then bark and then be let in. It was a simple plan. The skill part was sitting there in the freezing cold till Meeko came to get me.

Minute by minute, it was becoming more and more difficult and barking to gain entrance to my warm bed was tempting me. I waited and I waited some more. It was so arctic and I was so tired. Light rain was drizzling down, making the cold air even colder. I was on the verge of becoming a penguin. Lying close to the closed door, I sucked in the small amount of warm air that wafted out under the rubber doorstop.

I had misgauged the time by three hours. Three very long hours. Fearing that my ears had snapped off, I raised my paw to my head. Relieved to find them, I wiped the frozen goo from my eyes.

Finally, at two a.m., three hours into my transformation into a penguin, I heard a very high-pitched squeaking. Think of nails on a chalkboard, except higher pitched and way more irritating. I was not worried about being caught. On Ask the Vet I had learned a Shepherd can hear sounds up to 20,000 Hz. I pegged the current obnoxious shriek at 60,000 Hz. I knew it would not awake my sleeping Shepherds.

Gang of vacuums, I reasoned. I had heard that vacuums roam the streets at night. I was scared, ears bursting. If a Shepherd ever really heard what a vacuum cleaner sounds like to a canine, they would never use one again. And do not get me started on those high-speed power drills. Paws clasped over my ears, I could stand it no longer. I growled.

"Shut up, stupid poodle," it was Meeko, staring at me through the chain link fence.

'How did you find me? How did you know where I live?'

He did not answer. From out of the shadows emerged two of the scariest dogs I have ever seen. Scars of many battles, both won and lost, marred their faces. 'This is Silent Bob. He's the lookout. Lost his voice when he drank antifreeze. The toxic ingredient in the antifreeze is its major component, ethylene glycol. Like, it makes up 95% of the product, ' Meeko said. 'Like, it only takes a small sip of antifreeze to poison a medium size dog. And, according to Silent Bob it tastes quite good so dogs are attracted to it. Me, I drink rum. The good news is he can screech in a very high tone, an important requirement of a lookout. We're gonna get you out of there.'

Silent Bob was an unusual mix. At best, he was Doberman and Belgian Tervuren all mixed into one. One of his eyes was so scarred it barely opened. You would think two good eyes would be the basic requirement for a lookout. But, as discussed before, sight is not our number one resource. His tail, if you could call it that, looked like it had been in a blender. He upper leg muscled protruded like a racehorse. He spent on a lot of time on the run. And, he was not afraid of a fight. I am not fighter. However, if I am backed into a corner by a spider web, I turn into a karate master slicing my way out. Why are you smirking? Are you telling me that you do not do that when you walk in to a spider web by accident?

The other one, who Meeko called Lefty, was a lot more agile. He was rake thin except for his very big head. I suspect he was part Basset

Hound, Beagle and Ridgeback. His distinguishing feature was the ridge of hair running along his back in the opposite direction from the rest of his coat. As everyone knows, or everyone who listens to Ask the Vet 24-7 knows, the English word "hound" originated from the German word for dog, which is "hund." While hund is a word used to define all dogs, hound in English has come to mean a type of dog used for hunting. The hound group of dogs is divided into scent hounds (commonly called nose hounds), which hunt by scent, and sight hounds, which hunt by sight. This guy was definitely a scent hound, which might explain how they found my house.

Lefty was covered in dirt and tar. Meeko explained that he was the canine equivalent of a cat burglar, finding a way into where he wanted to go. And, as you probably have guessed, had a built in GPS. Silent Bob was his lookout. They had been working together for years.

On Meeko's nod, the three of them started to dig. Dirt was flying out behind them at a rapid pace. Realizing the plan, I started to dig on my side. I am not a digger. I have rather small and oval-shaped paws. My toes are well arched and close with webbing. My pads are thick and firm. My nails are short, but not excessively short, I know because I click when I walk on hardwood floors. My front feet may turn out slightly and my rear feet turn neither in or out. Try as I may, this digging plan was not working on my side.

'Will there be any huskies or malamutes with shovels coming soon?' I asked politely.

'Shut up and dig, poodle,' Meeko said. At this point, the three of them had dug deep enough on their side to have their own swimming pool. The problem was that my side looked like someone how scratched the frozen ground surface with a teaspoon. Then it hit me, I raced into the garage and there it was, a brand new unused Lesche knife sitting next to an unused pair of kneepads. Not wanting to push my luck with three street thugs, I decided to remove only the knife. If I had come out wearing the kneepads there is no doubt that at some point they would have kicked my poodle ass.

I rushed back to the gate and using my two front paws and the Lesche knife, I dug. The hole was not getting deeper. Without warning, Silent Bob, up and walked back to the sidewalk. I thought he had given up. And then he came racing at the gate full speed, springing from his mighty legs he was up and over the hole on their side and the fence. The increase in rain had softened the ground and, without warning, Silent Bob landed softly inches from my head.

At his point, SammyFarber showed his face. He looked over at me as I set the Lesche knife down.

'I see Poodle that you've set aside this special time to humiliate yourself in public,' he said before **w**alking up to the fence and undoing the latch.

'Let's go. Lefty, you lead the way.' Meeko said to no one in particular.

Lefty held his nose higher than I would have suspected. He smelled the air at chest level. A scent trail is a snapshot of the past. Remember earlier when I said we communicate in learned pictures? You were paying attention, correct? A scent trail is a similar technique for us. Lefty could determine the identity of the direction of any scent. In this case, he was locked onto Silent Bob's scent, which was pungent. He was, if you will, backtracking, retracing the direction he had come from. They had been to our final destination before they came and got me. Now, they were simply backtracking. Lefty would take three or four seconds to sniff and then confidently lead us in the right direction, tracking from strong to weak.

What I noticed was that the scent of Silent Bob was very strong and then grew very gradually weaker as we walked. It made sense that it was strongest where he had just been. It was easier than I thought, once I knew the secret.

In addition, Lefty stopped to pee every few blocks. He always picked a stationary object and often peed more than two times, making sure the stain was well placed above the other stains, and vertical. He did this by tilting his body so the urine jet spray was focused higher. At that time, I did not know why.

The weather had been drizzly but this had little effect on Lefty. His pace would have been quicker, but Meeko was dragging a toy wagon behind him that made our journey less swift. From time to time, the wagon would flip over and we would all have to use our noses to lift it up. Lefty knew that cars could be extremely dangerous so he gave them respect. At a busy intersection, Lefty would stand with his head low, eyes narrowed and ears pulled back. At the precise right moment, dash across the street with the three of us right behind. Lucky for us, Meeko's wagon stayed upright. Whenever possible Lefty would cross at the middle of the street so as to limit the number of cars that could come at us. His eyes never left the street ahead, but the nearer he got to an intersection or crossing point the more active his ears became. By doing this, he was able to hear any approaching cars. But, more importantly, he was able to gauge the speed of the vehicle and plot its position on the street.

Lefty and Silent Bob would accelerate without notice. They were quick. I am fast, very fast indeed, but I had to stay on my toes ready to dart in order to keep up with them. At one point, it became obvious to me that Meeko was not going to be able to make it with the extra burden of the wagon. And, SammyFarber was at his side. Safe on the other side, we waited. After a few minutes, Silent Bob let out an ear splitting cry. Hearing, Meeko took off and crossed the street, wagon and SammyFarber trailing behind. They did not look, listen or hesitate. They went on Bob's signal, knowing it would be safe. And, it was.

On the way, I had the opportunity to talk to SammyFarber. I learned that his Shepherd was not financially prepared for a life of hundred years, and was running out of funds quickly. To offset her meagre pension, she held a garage sale every year, liquidating the few prized possessions she had left. To augment the diminishing supply of saleable goods, SammyFarber borrowed items from nearby garages and added them to the sale contents. His Shepherd was old, very old. She did not notice the increase in saleable product. Once a month, SammyFarber and his crew went on 'borrowing expeditions', loading the wagon to the top.

They would find a house and SammyFarber would work the garage door till it opened. Silent Bob would stand guard while Lefty picked it clean. After Lefty had gathered a few things, we moved on to the next garage, not wanting to take too much from any one homeowner. After five garages, inventory of the wagon showed: comic books, sports trading cards, vinyl albums, Miss Piggy lunch box, Beanie baby, snow globe, Hot Wheels and a vintage movie poster.

'Snack,' I asked, feeling a tad hungry.

SammyFarber pulled back the tin foil on a casserole dish tucked in the corner of the wagon to expose the kugel. For some reason, I expected it to be made of noodles. However, this kugel was made of bread and flour that made it more savoury then sweet. There were eggs incorporated into the recipe. The addition of cottage cheese and milk created a custard-like consistency. In my poodle opinion, the addition of raisins and cinnamon to the top was not necessary. I am just sayin'. It is not like I ever had kugel before. I liked it. It seemed to be the unanimous consensus.

During dinner SammyFarber explained to me that they had been doing this for five years, helping his Shepherd financially to stay in her home. I felt honoured to be included.

'You open the doors. Silent Bob stands guard. Lefty does the grunt work. But, what's Meeko's role in all this,' I asked.

'He is the insurance policy.'

'Huh?'

'Couple years back we ran into a little michegoss. An alter cocker, shovel swinging. Then, Meeko snuck up behind him and showed his teeth. Oye gavault, I thought he was going to plotz. That my little poodle buddy is insurance.'

Although, I did not understand all the words, the meaning was clear. If you hear rustling in your garage at night, stay in the house. Mission accomplished, Lefty followed the pee trail back to SammyFarber's home where we unloaded. Much to my surprise, SammyFarber lived three doors down from me. Go figure.

It explained how it was that he came and went on my couch. My Shepherds must have recognized him from the neighbourhood and knew that his Shepherd was old, no longer able to care for him. Arriving home, the door swung open and interrupted my thoughts.

"Friday, I am so sorry, I did not hear you bark. You have been out here all night. Please come in and rest. I feel terrible. Will you ever forgive me? "

I wagged my tail and went inside and slept. An hour or so later, I awoke in my dog bed, considering the idea that none of the adventure had really happened. It was most likely a dream. And yes, we do dream about more than chasing rabbits. Maybe, just maybe, the concept of dogs organising themselves and breaking into garages to borrow items is far too absurd. It seemed unimaginable to me that any dog, including SammyFarber, could put together such an inventive plan to help save his Shepherd and his doggie home.

Whether or not you believe it happened or it was a dream I leave up to you. I have decided it happened because I envision a better world for all animals. Maybe a world where chickens can cross the road, without being questioned about their motives.

Chapter 11

Right to Remain Rilent

The next day we arrived at Putz park a few minutes later than usual. Once unleashed, I joined the party, wondering what the crowd was all about. For a brief second I considered that my gang of thieves may have been found out by the police, who were searching the park.

SammyFarber took his place at centre stage. There were a few cats, rabbits and hundreds of dogs of all shapes and sizes. The crowd softened when they saw SammyFarber. He began. 'To my feline friends I can tell you this, thousands of years ago cats were worshipped as gods. That was then and this is now, get over it. You jackrabbits back by the fence, not so close. I see a few putzes out there with less than good intentions.' SammyFarber let the nervous feet shuffling stop before he continued. 'Yesterday, I was a mutt. Today, I am a mutt. And, god willing, tomorrow I will be a mutt.' SammyFarber stopped again, licking front paw, he sighed heavily. 'Oy vey, no chance of being a purebred.'

'But seriously, I want to thank all of you for coming to my twelfth birthday party. I know some of you have travelled great distances'. He looked up at the rain clouds. 'Those of you who mentored me as a puppy and now look down from above and smile. Those of you here today that I have mentored and everyone in between, I thank you from the bottom of my heart for being a part of my life. For me, there has been no greater joy in the world than to be a member of the canine community. Your friendship has enriched my life more than any gold!'

'Speaking of gold, this twelfth birthday party is different than my other twelfth birthday parties. This year, I need your help even more. My Shepherd is very deprived. Me, I have all the money I'll ever need, if I die by 4:00 p.m. today. Anyway, she invested in 'glow in the dark' dog collars, which was my idea and lost a bundle. The 'glow in the dark' paint is safe unless, of course, you eat it. However, I should have realized that some of you chew on your collars and leashes. Whoops, total product recall two years ago, my bad. Had to sell the condo in Florida. When you are rich you are handsome, wise and you sing well

My Shepherd father died a few years back and my Shepherd mother remained a widow. She is ninety-three. As you may know, Jewish mothers are like canines, they love unconditionally and mine likes to remind me that she was both mother and father to me for the last five years, so you can imagine the guilt. Anyway, they had no children so my Shepherd mom was going to leave everything to me. Like I need two thousand eight hundred and twelve neon 'glow in the dark' green collars. This one is fine,' he said rubbing his neck. 'A little tattered on the edges, but fine. I'll make do. So bring your Shepherds to our garage sale next month, we need the cash. Please come! For now, enjoy the park.'

'Is this a legal dog park?' I asked Pageant Patti, the eight pound, champagne coloured, Havanese standing next to me.

'A legal off-leash dog park? It's a vacant field attached to a closed school, you dim wit poodle.'

I explained about park two, wondering if it was a legal dog park.

'Nope, not that one. Although the dogs are nice,' she said. 'Haven't you ever been to a real dog park?' she asked.

'Obviously not,' I said and added further to her already bad mood when I added, 'Should you be out alone in this place?

'I am not fragile, you sheep dog wannabe. I am rather robust, muscular and very athletic with good stamina. I will have you know that I am a watchdog and a herder of poultry. I am recognized by the American Rare Breeds Association as well as the American and Canadian Kennel Clubs. I go to bed late, after the Letterman show. Some consider me royalty. You should too. I am outstanding.'

'And modest.' I said. I hoped to change the subject and the mood by asking her, 'Who are those three wild animals over there by the oak tree?'

Coyly turning her head to the left, she responded. 'The big, strong, longhaired German Shepherd is Alex the Great. The lab cross is Max the Magnificent and the third one, the bull terrier chasing his tail, is Ivan the Stupid.'

'Why is he doing that?' I asked.

'Because he's Ivan the Stupid, and because he can. After a few whirls, he'll get dizzy and fall over.'

As predicted, Ivan the Stupid fell over. I know I shouldn't laugh But it was very funny to watch.

'So, please eat and enjoy,' SammyFarber continued. 'There is plenty of food. Try the kugel. Eat. My Shepherd says it is now made with real cheese.'

What the heck was she using before? I pondered.

With that the party started, dogs of all shapes and sizes played together while SammyFarber worked the crowd. He said hello to each and every animal. When he came to me he said, 'Schmendrick, I mean Friday the Poodle, thank you for coming.' He looked at my mud and dirt covered body. 'Would it have been too much trouble for you to take a bath first? Please nosh. Try the kreplach. You know, a new green neon collar will impress the ladies.' And then, he winked at me before walking away to greet another.

I walked over to the buffet with my new friend, Pageant Patti. Crisp fried potato latkes, chopped liver and much more awaited us.

'Stay away from the kreplach, kishka, and knishes, too much cholesterol,' Pageant Patti warned. 'Try the Turners, half sour pickles, before they are all gone. Did you know Cleopatra claimed pickles made her beautiful.'

'Who is that?' I asked, pointing to an old beagle eating pickle after pickle. 'It's not working for him.'

He had a smooth, somewhat domed skull with a medium-length, square-cut muzzle and a black gumdrop nose. His jaw was strong and the teeth scissord together with the upper teeth fitting perfectly over the lower teeth and both sets aligned square to the jaw. They did not look real to me. He was in good shape for such an old geezer. Large hazel eyes gave way to his mild hound-like pleading look. Long, soft and low-set, ears turned toward me. I lowered my voice.

'SammyFarber says his name is Alder Kocker,' Pageant Patti whispered, knowing he was listening in. 'I have never formally met him. Shows up at every function, invited or not, eats all the Turner pickles.' I settled on a toasted bagel with a salmon shmear. The kugel was too salty for my taste. Here's a secret. Bagels are unsweetened doughnuts that have passed the expiry date. It was delicious. I was having so much fun that I did not hear my Shepherd calling.

'Hey Poodle, your chauffeur is calling,' Meeko said.

Stomach busting, I ran over to the Director. It was go time. He put on my leash and we were off.

On the way, the Director talked. I listened. Hearing him retell the story of the night of the accident, I was saddened. Not only for the victim, but more so for my Shepherd. He was a good man, better than I had thought. In the canine world where you have successfully gotten away with stealing a cookie the last thing you do is confess. It's bad for digestion.

However, for the Director, he had become so overwhelmed with guilt that I feared in the end he would turn himself in anyways. FYI, dogs do not have the guilt gene. I may feel I owe you for your kindness. But, I ain't gonna pick you up at the airport no matter how indebted you make me feel. The voluntary action of turning himself into the authorities would bring him closure. It was a way to right the wrong that he committed.

I needed to think more about that as we walked. Selfishly, I wanted him to 'get over it'. My fear being that I would be abandoned for at least five years. I found this very scary. Did he not have an obligation to me? Am I being too selfish? What about the Producer? If he knew she had cancer would his decision be different? Did he not want to spend her last few months with her? Somehow, I should tell him at this juncture, keeping secrets was at the heart of my dilemma.

However, at the center of his idea to turn himself was the concept that justice cannot be done without some form of punishment. Thus turning himself in was essentially to accept justice as restorative. I learned that on Oprah as well. Around the next corner, he reiterated. "So I'm thinking, maybe if I just turn myself in, confess my crime, maybe the police will be kind to me, and not give my name out to the media. Maybe, Anna will be spared the shame that I feel. Maybe they will only send one police officer to collect me? It would be a first offense, so maybe I would get a minimal sentence as well?

"Friday, stop pulling," he said suddenly. Without realizing, I was pulling him back home. I wanted him to rethink the plan. There were too many 'maybes' and 'what ifs' That is not part of the canine world. Eventually we got home and Anna, the Producer, had gone out. After filling my water dish, he dialled the phone.

After forever and a day, he relayed the story again to his lawyer. And then he said," So you are saying that I have no legal obligation to turn myself in? It **is** perfectly legal to do nothing until the police come for me. In fact, it is my right to remain silent and not the assist the police investigation. Correct?"

I could not hear what the lawyer said. However, based on the Director's next comment I could only assume that the answer was 'yes'.

"Well, isn't that preventing the course of justice?' he asked?

"Let me get this straight. Preventing the course of justice is when I take active steps in hindering a police investigation, which includes disposing of evidence or lying to the police about what happened. So, as long as I do not prevent justice then I am not doing anything wrong, correct?" With a pensive expression on his face, he hung up the phone.

"Friday, stop pacing. Go sit down. Now!"

It was not over, my OCD Director called back again. Are you getting some idea what my training life is like with this guy. Geez, Shepherds think OCD means Obsessive Compulsive Disorder. Take it from me, it stands for, "Over Controlled Dog."

"Sorry, me again. What is reasonable doubt?" the Director asked.

The speaker phoned blared: "If there is a real doubt, based upon reason and common sense after careful and impartial consideration of all the evidence, or lack of evidence, in a case, then the level of proof has not been met."

He went on. I was fascinated. "Proof beyond a reasonable doubt, therefore, is proof of such a convincing character that you would be willing to rely and act upon it without hesitation in the most important of your own affairs. Keep in mind, it does not mean an absolute certainty. The standard that must be met by the prosecution's evidence in a criminal prosecution is that no other logical explanation can be derived from the facts except that the defendant committed the crime, thereby overcoming the presumption that a person is innocent unless and until proven guilty. Let me repeat that because I want to be perfectly clear, no other logical explanation can be derived from the facts except that the defendant committed the crime. Are you getting what I am saying?"

Phone call over, he summoned me to come and sit. Being a good dog, I came and laid down. Close enough I thought. I am not a big fan of this sitting thing.

"Friday, here's the bottom line," he said. "Sitting back and letting the police come to me is simply letting nature take its course, the police are there to investigate crimes, so let them investigate. It's not my obligation to help them, as long as I don't hinder them."

"I feel better now," he said.

'Me too,' I nodded. I replayed what I heard and understood. 'The evidence had to disappear.' Key words, evidence gone. I pondered.

We were not out of the weeds yet. Five minutes later and a lot of nervous pacing; the Director called the lawyer back, asking about warrants to search the house. The phone was still set to speaker.

The lawyer replied, "The information the authorities have would have to rise to the level of probable cause, a reasonable belief that criminal activity may be going on and that they may be likely to find evidence relating to that activity if they could wiretap and/or search your home. Once they think that they have that, they then present that information to a judge. If the judge believes that the evidence presented justifies the kind of intrusion that the authorities are asking for, they will sign the warrant. If the judge believes that there isn't sufficient probable cause to do this they won't. I would suggest if you need to remove something from your car then do not destroy it. Simply, store in a not so obvious place if you know what I mean?" After a pause, the lawyer continued. "Having said that, my experience has been that judges do not rubber stamp requests for warrants, particularly of the sort you're discussing. But is what you're asking impossible? No. And, we never had this conversation."

Desperately, I wanted to write down my plan. I wished someone would take a hot, steamy bath. I usually write my best thoughts on the foggy bathroom mirror. Don't you?

The Director thanked him and hung up the phone. He then went out to the garage and removed the used fire extinguisher from the car trunk, placing it in the corner of the garage behind a vinyl record, titled Elvis' Christmas Album. It was the King's very first of two Christmas albums released in 1957 featuring a specialty red vinyl record. Although in very bad shape, the Director thought it had value. In order to keep the record upright, hence hiding the fire extinguisher, he braced a vintage metal dome 1968 Snoopy Lunch box against it. Both the record and the Snoopy lunch box were purchased at swap meets. I am not a big fan of Snoop, favouring Charlie B. Barkin, that main character in the 1989 animation "All Dogs Go To Heaven". I could watch that a hundred times.

Chapter 12

Platelets

Since my puppy bladder was full, at two a.m. I was let out to pee. Having watched SammyFarber open gates, I decided to give it a try. Easier than I thought, the latch was not secure and with a little giggle and a gaggle the door swung open. Meekly, I advanced, into the garage man door where I managed to nose a few items into a gym bag. .

Knowing my destination was closer to the river, I decided to navigate toward the flowing scent. I lifted my nose above my shoulders to tell the direction.

The name Winnipeg is a transcription of the western Cree word, wi-nipe-k, meaning, 'muddy waters.' I lifted my nose again to find the familiar scent of the sediments. My snout is so sensitive to smell that I can separate the silt into quartz and feldspar. The clay, sand and gravel each have their own smells as well. Quickening my pace, I realized I knew the way to the river.

Here is my secret, I can wiggle my nostrils independently, which is how I determine which direction a scent is coming from. Once I know the direction then I push my muzzle in that direction and I stop breathing. I take in a big sniff and it gets trapped in the upper chamber of my nose and that is where I figure out what the scent is. I break it down to its smallest part. The only exception is when I meet another dog and we sidle around each other to get a whiff of the other's butt. This tells me if I am interacting with a dominant or submissive dog, male or female, healthy or sick. My advice, if you are looking for a suitable mate, take a whiff before the romance goes too far.

Looking up, I realized I was there. Gate unlocked, I entered and emptied the gym bag. So far! So good! I peed to mark the spot in case I got lost and needed to backtrack home from here. Which, of course, did happen.

A herd of vacuums were approaching me. The sound was deafening. I bolted down the back lane. I like the Larry King show because he tackles the tough questions like what is with those blasted street cleaning machines and why do they wake people up in the middle of the friggin' night?

According to Larry's guest, street cleaning studies have found that ninety-seven percent of street debris lies within forty inches of the curb. The accumulation of debris at the curb is caused by the design of the street and vehicular movement. Streets like mine are designed with a crown in the middle sloping toward the sides. And that is why the friggin' machine drives by so close to my den.

I had never seen a street cleaning machine before this, only heard it. I was scared. I thought back to my option list and this time I picked flight. I ran around the same block over and over again, till I could not run anymore. By circling, I managed to evade the attack sweeper. But, I was tired, and a little scared. I walked slowly trying to regain my confidence.

Suddenly, I was face-to-face with a Shepherd about three feet tall, standing in front of me. Eyes the colour of charcoal, thin arms, almost stick like, and his nose was long and reddened from the cold night air. A light blue scarf with orange tassels wrapped tight around his neck and a black wool cap covered his head. It was hard to tell his age. By his size, I assumed he was an eight or nine year old male child. I growled. He did not look away. I bit the air in front of him and eventually locked my teeth on his neck as a further warning. His neck was frigid. Frostbite might have already set in. He looked like he had been outside for a long time. He would not stop starring at me with those charcoal black eyes challenging me. I had tried flight and freeze and this I time I decided on fight. It was a decision I will regret my entire life.

In my defence, I had given him every chance to roll over. He refused. Frustrated, as a final, final warning, I bit hard into his neck and the most gruesome thing imaginable happened. His head separated from his neck and rolled down the cement sidewalk. Needless to say, I did what I had to do and got the hell out of his front yard.

The next time I dared to look up I was in front of my house. I opened the gate. And now, safe in my yard, I puked till I could puke no more. Cottage cheese, sour cream, raisins, cinnamon and sweet farmer's cheese lay in disgusting heap at my feet. I was sick, sick about what I had done to that poor boy.

"Where have you been," the Director asked. "I have been standing at this door forever. I could not see you in the yard."

'I was at a Tibetan monastery learning Kung Fu.'

"I was just about to put up posters of you on the street lamps," he said.

'Can I have the reward,' I asked, entering the warm house.

Shepherds think they know how they will act when their life is threatened. Take it from me, you do not know till it happens. I gained a rare insight into what the Director must have felt when he extinguished the guy in the car. Thoughts flooded my puppy brain. The most salient one, was there another option. Was I certain that my life was in perilous danger. I barely slept, convinced I would be sharing a jail cell with the Director.

The next morning, we left at eight instead of seven. I was grateful for the extra hour, having gone through such an eventful night. Morning thoughts ran through my head. The most disturbing was the headless nine year old boy. Again I pondered, was I too quick to judge that he wanted to harm me, reacting to what I saw and how he refused to submit. The smell of his blue scarf, old and musty, threatened me somehow. That orange evil carrot protruding from his face. The taste of his ice cold neck chilled me to the bone. If I misjudged the boy's intent, and I probably did, then, for my whole life, I would have to live with that knowledge that I killed him unnecessarily. My heart was heavy and saddened, my fate unknown.

The Producer came with us this morning. The mood was quiet, the temperature below normal. It was approaching zero degrees and howling winds added to the wind chill temperature. We were on our way to park two when we stopped suddenly in front of SammyFarber's house.

"Look at that! What a crying shame. What kind of sick person would destroy a snowman?" The Producer said, picking up one of the charcoal eyes that had rolled on to the sidewalk. " It looks like the head has been bitten off. I'm ill. Mrs. Farber must have worked hard on that. She always builds one in the winter near her garage. "

'Snowman?' I wondered. 'Tell me more.'

"You want to try and put it back together," the Director asked. "There's his scarf over there, and here's his hat. It should not be too hard to figure out what he looked like."

'Hmm, I could tell you.' I said to myself.

The Producer put the little snowman's head back on while the Director tied the light blue scarf with orange tassels around his neck. Popping the charcoal eyes back in was easy, the holes already formed. Except for the fact that his carrot nose was shorter than before, he was good as new. I felt much better, and more than a little stupid.

"That looks my gym bag over there. That's odd." the Director said.

"Check when you get home. They look alike," the Producer added.

Arriving at the park, the Director and Producer walked around the outer ring. I followed close behind. At one point, the Producer looked back and asked if I was okay. I thought I was. I thought I was just tired. I was not. I was very sick, and no one knew.

That afternoon we drove out to the country. I was going to puppy class again. This time, I had a plan. I would pretend to be friendly. When Grace got close, I would bite her outreached hand. Then I would be sent home. It would all be over in a matter of minutes and I could rest.

When we got there, seven puppies (three large and four small) were already on the long driveway. A woman walked over to me who smelled of the great outdoors. Even in my very tired state, I was ready, willing and planning to bite her but I put on my friendly dog act, luring her into my waiting jaw. She was not buying it. She made a soft clicking noise with her tongue to get my attention. Approaching very slowly, shoulder turned toward me, she stopped a few feet in front of me, encouraging me to come closer. She was looking to one side of me as opposed to staring me down. Her hands were not visible to me. When I got close in she let me know I had two choices, get the snot beat out of me or change my plan. She told me this with her posture. I understood her pictures. She spoke dog! I picked B, change the plan. No biting.

The first exercise was 'pass the puppy'. It was a very fun game. The Shepherds formed a circle and each puppy was passed around the circle from Shepherd to Shepherd. The next game, even more fun, was called run like a crazy dog. All the small dogs, weighing less than ten pounds, ran first. Then the big dogs, like me, ran next. The long driveway was surrounded by acres of land and we could run anywhere we wanted when it was our group's turn.

Next, we had lure training where the Director held a piece of turkey over my head that caused me to sit. Then the Producer moved a piece of turkey toward my gut that forced me to lie down to get it. I was training and I did not even know it. In no time, I could sit and down on command.

Most of the puppies were doing well except for one beagle whose Shepherd kept saying 'sit-down' followed by 'sit-sit-sit-down' as if they were one thing. The instructor went over and helped him out.

Then we played run like a crazy dog again. But, this time the Shepherds were throwing tennis balls and rope toys everywhere. Not wanting to flunk, I chased everything. I had so many toys in my mouth I could hardly breathe. I think this is where I first developed my love of playing ball.

At the end of the class, we did capture training. In this exercise the Shepherd waits till you do something right and then rewards you. In this case, I had to step on the green fluffy bath mat he had brought from home. I had no idea what I was doing or what I was supposed to do. Wanting to lie down and rest, I smelled my way over to my mat, and like magic, I got a piece of turkey.

The Director quickly figured out what capture training was all about and he asked me to wave. I was fatigued, batting my paw at him, trying to get him to leave me alone. You guessed it, I got another piece of turkey. "Good wave, Friday" he said to me. By the end of class, I could sit, down, go to my mat and wave. It was so much fun.

The instructor came over to see me at the end of class. "I am glad you decided to give it a try," she said. "You did excellent, Friday. You can come and visit me anytime. My name is Auntie Sharon."

You are Auntie? Ohmigod, Meeko's saviour and friend to SammyFarber. I had so many questions for her. And to think, I almost bit her. Shame on me. Bad poodle.

"Come on, Friday. Class is over. You will come back next week," the Director said, pulling my leash. "Let's go home now. You look worn out."

I slept all the way home. I have never been so tired. I knew something was wrong, very wrong.

After an hour, we arrived back home. I collapsed in the doorway. I could not hold up my own body weight.

"Maybe he is just tired. Let him sleep," the Producer said. "It was a hard class."

Later that night, the Director put my dinner out. I tried but I could not eat a thing. By this time, I was unable to walk more than three steps without falling over. My clouded over eyes, pale colour and lack of mobility were symptomatic of the unknown.

"What's wrong with him?" the Producer asked.

"He's tired," the Director said. "Let him sleep. Leave him alone."

"No, no way. There is something seriously wrong. I know it," the Producer said. "Come and look. He looks odd."

The Director looked in my eyes. A dog's eyes are protected by upper and lower eyelids, a third eyelid or haw, and tears. The eyelids are lubricated by a thin layer of mucous to avoid irritation of the surface of the cornea. If the third eye is clearly visible for prolonged periods of time then it indicates extremely stress or deathly ill.

"His third eye is showing. He is very sick. We've got to get him to the vet right now," the Director barked.

That was the last time I ever bashed him for having so many dog books.

"He has three eyes?" the Producer asked, somewhat alarmed at this new information.

"Let's go. Let's go now," the barking Director said, scooping me up and running to the car. On the way, the Director talked about nictitating membranes. I did not understand a word of it. The Producer cried.

At 10:22 that night, the Producer and Director arrived with me at the emergency dog hospital where I was given intravenous fluids and a general injection to reduce swelling. (I do not know what the injection was.) I was misdiagnosed. They wanted to keep me overnight. But, the Producer said that I if I was to die that it would be in her loving arms. I was sent home without a glimmer of hope. The Producer and Director took turns staying up with me all night.

I remember the Director talking to me, very quietly. He said that he was very sorry for leaving me out all night, blaming himself for my current condition. I wanted to tell him that it was not his fault. He apologized for Grace. Saying, he knew it was wrong. He should have gotten rid of her dumb ass sooner. He told me he knew all about the Putz dogs and that is why he stopped taking me to Putz park. I was surprised he knew about the Putz dogs. He told me that he was glad SammyFarber had been in my life. I was too. He said SammyFarber would be waiting for me at heaven's gate one day. He explained that there would be a bright light showing the path. If the pain got too much I was to follow the light and I would be fine. He told me that he understood if I wanted to give up at anytime. He said he loved me and would miss me. I was the best dog ever.

The Producer came to sit with me next. She said I would survive. She knew it. She massaged me for hours, never leaving my side. Through tear-filled eyes, she told me that things have a way of working out, never give up. We would go shopping together real soon. She tried to stay strong but I could see the tears. She loved me very much. I would miss her.

Miracle of miracles, I made it through the night. At the break of dawn, the Producer called Auntie and told her what was happening. She told the Producer to take me to Dr. Spice. I visited Manitoba's top animal vet, Dr. Spice, that morning. Perplexed by my symptoms, or lack thereof, Dr. Spice ordered a complete blood workup. I was once again sent home to rest and wait.

Navigating through tear-filled eyes, they took turns cradling me in their arms. Finally, they laid me down in my favourite spot in our den, next to the radio. It was the place where I thought I would most likely breath my last breathe. Over the next five hours, my Shepherds watched me sleep without knowing my ultimate fate. I cannot begin to tell you the myriad of thoughts that must have raced through their minds as they guessed at the test results and causes. Unfortunately, since there was no way to focus on a solution, they replayed every minute of my short life looking for a clue to my disease. The hum of the fans set up to lower my body temperature, was their only background music. Wanting me to sleep, the radio was turned off.

After some time, I started to wake. There it was, the bright light that the Director had spoken of. I could see it clearly. Looking toward the end of it, trying to catch a glimpse of heaven's gate, I knew the end was nearing. I had a choice to make, to live or die. I remembered what my dad, Thinker, had said, ' Lastly, perhaps most importantly, you have a benevolent gift that one day will be unlocked. A gift greater than you can ever imagine.' I needed to know what that gift was? I did not want to give up.

Knowing that it might not be in my control, I listened to the voice coming from the light for direction. I thought I heard the voice of God calling me. It was not.

"Put that flashlight down," The Producer said.

"Why? I'm just checking for pupil movement," the Director replied, shining the flashlight in my eyes again.

I did not know if I should laugh or cry. While I was deciding, the phone rang. It was Dr. Spice. He requested that I be immediately transported to the hospital. He had diagnosed me with immune-mediated thrombocytopenia. Thrombocytopenia means a reduction in platelets (thrombocytes). Platelets (one of the cell types in the blood) play an important role in the clotting process; thus the main result of a decrease in platelets is increased bleeding, for example, nosebleeds. A sudden bump causing bleeding or airborne disease could have ended my life.

In immune-mediated thrombocytopenia (IMT), the reduction happens because there is increased destruction of platelets by the poodle's own immune system, at a rate faster than they are produced in the bone marrow. Simply put, my body was killing off the very thing I needed to survive. IMT may be secondary to some other process (such as an infection, tumour, or drug reaction) or it may be primary, meaning that no other causative factor can be found. In my case it was primary. It is more common in certain canine breeds, suggesting there is an inherited component.

When we got there, the Director asked about the diagnosis. Dr. Spice explained, "With signs of increased bleeding, we do a CBC (complete blood count), which will show a dramatic drop in platelet numbers. Bleeding does not automatically occur until the platelet count is below 30,000 per cubic millimeter of blood. (50,000 or less is critical. Normal levels are above 200,000 in Poodles. "

"What is his platelet count Doctor," the Producer asked.

"Approximately 34,000. He is critical!"

"Why did you order a complete workup when there were no signs of bleeding?" the Director questioned.

"Just a hunch," Dr. Spice, the 35-year expert replied calmly.

"Will he live?" the Director asked.

Dr. Spice did not answer. He said there is nothing to do but to wait for the test results.

Hour 19 to 36

Over the next 36 hours, I was given prednisone wrapped in peanut butter every 8 hours with hope that it would stop my body from destroying the platelets that I need to survive. My puppy body was confused. During this period, I was on amoxicillin too, also peanut butter wrapped, in order to prevent any outside bacteria from taking over my body during my weakened state. At hour 30, although I was still tired, I bought white bear over to my Shepherds.

'You need to look after him. He is very helpless. I fear I will not be able,' I said, falling back to sleep. An hour later I woke, looking curiously at my leash. The Producer reached for it. Once again, I fall back to sleep a minute later.

When I woke later that night the Director was at my side, reading one of his many dog magazines. On this particular page was a girl taking a bubble bath, above and to the right was a large white cat. The girl's wrist, dangling out of the white porcelain tub, had a very beautiful watch on it. At the bottom of the page were five different bands that allowed the watch wearer to change the colour of the band to match any outfit or collar as the case may be. A wonderful idea I thought. I smacked at the page, knocking it from the Director's hand.

"You want that," he asked, picking it up and showing me the page again. "Really?

Are you sure? Really sure?"

I smacked at it again to confirm yes. It would be a reason to live for, my own watch. I like blue because it's a male color. Also, yellow. Both appear very bright to me, vibrant. This watch had both.

Sensing my joy, the Director promised to get one for me when I was better. I was thrilled. My very own watch. My fascination with having a watch may seem odd to you. As discussed, puppies make wrong assumptions some time. This was one of them. My ideas come from sensory images that I see. It is the root of my language and how I think. If I see a Shepherd spin the wheel on a watch and then announce it is dinner time then it is logical for me to think one created the other, not unlike the chicken created the egg.

Because timers are often set in my house during cooking, I assumed that by spinning the watch dial, time changed. For example, if I wanted it to be snack time then I would spin the egg timer. I knew this would be a daunting task for my web-like paws. Tuning the radio is still an arduous task for me. Once, I spun the radio dial so hard I got Bison Bill's Weird West Show. I would have to practice if I was planning on having snack time often.

Four days later

I was given another blood test. The Producer asked for the bandage to be blue. She knows it makes me feel better. The nurse obliged. We left with fingers crossed. (Them not me.)

Three hours later

Dr. Spice called to say that his lab's blood work machine was not working. However, he did a manual count and he thought it was around 125,000. I do not even begin to understand what he meant by a manual count. (He must like counting as much as I do. Maybe more?)

He suggested that we do nothing till 4:00 p.m. when he would have the outside lab report. Anything over 80,000 is not life threatening, he reminded my Shepherds.

That evening, Dr. Spice confirmed that my platelet count was indeed 125,000 and I was on the road to recovery. My medication would be cut back for the next seven days. At that point, I would receive another blood test. The expectation was that my platelet count would rise to a very respectable 200,000. If so, I would be weaned off the medication (and the peanut butter) and resume my normal life as a poodle.

A week later, feeling better, I went by the Shepherds' bedroom to retrieve my white bear. He seemed fine except he was showing signs of age, white cotton stuffing coming out from his seams.

At that moment, I wanted to express my appreciation to my Shepherds. It is not unreasonable to state, in fact, that the single most important requirement for my canine emotional health and happiness is to feel loved. My soul requires feeling loved in just as real a way as my body requires air and food and cookies. It's so easy to think about love, to talk about love and to wish for love but it's not always easy to recognize love, even when we hold it in our paws. I knew at that moment how deeply I loved my Shepherds. The misconception about canine unconditional love is that it is one sided. That night I learned it was not. With all that was going on in their lives, they showered me with unconditional love. It filled my puppy heart. I would do anything for them. I would give up my life if they asked.

I realized that sometimes, in order to become emotionally and mentally strong, you have to be broken down to your weakest point in order to build yourself back up. Not only broken down, but ripped to pieces in order to realize that life is not that fairy tale of running for my ball in a field. The Producer taught me that being a strong dog is not about ignoring my emotions and fighting my feelings. Putting on a brave face does not make me brave. Why was it not the same for them? The Producer and the Director hide their true feelings, not wanting to scare me with the truth. So, at that moment I had a special interest in knowing what the Produce and the Director think and who they are and what's hiding behind those eyes. Seeing white bear on the floor, I left with him in my mouth because he needed to go back in his crate.

Over the next fourteen days, I made a full recovery, except I had developed a nagging addiction to peanut butter. I went to the living room sofa to check on SammyFarber. He was not there. I had not seen him for weeks. I feared the worst. Maybe, I was contagious and he got it too. I needed to tell him about the peanut butter cure.

Chapter 13

Delphinium

I missed the end of my puppy class lessons due to illness so I was enrolled in two catch-up classes: Adult Obedience and Canine Good Citizen. Normally, a non-graduate of puppy class would not be allowed in these classes, especially one right after the other. But, as you know, the Director is not normal. He got me in. Lucky for me with my malleable puppy brain, adult obedience was doable, mostly nap time, something I excel at.

First, we did sit-stay, than stand-stay and finally down-stay...which should be called sleep-stay. Calendar clear, nowhere urgent to go, I stayed put in the different positions. Next task on deck was walking properly on lead.

As I walked slowly in one direction, I was thinking I was doing good as I cruised along. I was having fun as the only puppy at Adult Obedience. My head was down as I counted the concrete squares, 82, 15, 7, 91,when Auntie barked.

"Don't let him get away with that crap. Make him work," she said, grapping my leash from the Director. "Strut," she said abruptly and off she went. Her pace was quicker than I was used to. I trotted! (Perhaps, a bit too much trot.) When I pulled ahead, she turned and walked back the opposite way, clotheslining me.

To be fair, I was given warning before the abrupt turn. I was so engrossed in counting the squares, I did not hear the warning.

We tried again. I slowed down and focused. Little movements by the leash holder, when I am paying attention, have a dramatic effect on me. I know the visual signals of my canine species and my Shepherds. The Director always leads with his left foot, heel hitting first, while the Producer alternates, depending on her footwear. (Cowboy boots, right foot first. Runners, left foot.)

This was a relative stranger to me. She tapped her left knee. (Clue or a mosquito bite?) Correctly, I guessed clue. Eyeballing that left knee, each razor sharp turn revealed itself, and zigzagging all over the walkway, we were inseparable.

"Yes, yes," she said, throwing in an about-turn. I was not fooled, although at one point she said, "Hurry, hurry!" because I was a split second behind on my timing.

The strong odour of garlic enticed my wiggling nose. Looking up, I saw the homemade cookie in Auntie's hand, moving from side to side. I watched its every movement, hoping it would fall. Inside minutes, I was prancing around the circle, showing off with my head up and in show ring step.

Auntie spotted another puppy school dropout and gave me the cookie. Head down, chewing under the Director's lead, he wrongly pulled up on the leash. I almost choked on the garlic liver cookie. He can be so annoying. Prancing around, I strained to hear Auntie's discussion with a Shepherd and Rottweiler.

"A pinch collar? In my class?" Auntie questioned.

"Cause it works, that's why," the Sheppard said. "I'll prove it. See! She does not pull with this on."

"A dog cannot reason cause, only effect. You are creating an anti-social dog. What a mess."

"No, you are wrong. It works and I'll prove it! I know my dog. You don't." The closing argument as the Shepherd droned on with a nasal whine was, "My husband said this..." and, "My husband said that..."

A new approach was required. "Yes, I agree. However, if your dog must wear a pinch, at least wear it correctly. The prongs go on the outside," she said, turning the collar inside out. "It works better that way," Auntie said, smiling wide. Auntie was changing the world, one Shepherd at a time.

The second class, which the Producer took me through, had no good citizens in it despite being called Canine Good Citizen.

The Director had prepared me earlier. He read: The goal of the class was to develop behaviour that is reliable, controllable, predictable and inspires confidence in the person the canine is interacting with. "'Inspires confidence," he repeated with a little more emphasis than I thought was necessary. Most of all, he noted the dog is outgoing, friendly and confident in new settings.

"Friendly, that's good," the Producer added.

Of course, like most ads, none of this was true. This class should have been called Intro to putz dogs. I never saw a bigger group of assholes in my life: barkers, biters and shitheads. I was confident that one of these so-called friendly dogs was going to bite me. We had to walk in a figure eight pattern that meant weaving in and out of each other. Not prancing, choosing instead to bob and weave, I watched for puckered lips. Luckily, the more vicious types had a cloth band around their noses. One pointer setter mix named Lucky was having nothing to with this class either. Jerking his leash free from the Shepherd's hand, mouthing it, he ran. All eyes were on him. I was jealous.

Jealousy is not a trait found in canines. Secondary emotions such as jealousy, pride, embarrassment and shame are the exclusive domain of Shepherds and perhaps chimpanzees (who have the cognitive capacities required to support the complex range of secondary emotions).

Anything that even resembles jealousy in a standard poodle is simply that I'm lacking attention at that moment. I was envious of all the attention Lucky was getting.

On one talk show, animal behaviourist, Dr. Paw-n-mouth said," Dogs are intensely jealous creatures that experience a range of complex human-like emotions." But, he was from Kansas. Enough said.

"Run away from him," Auntie called out. But Lucky's Shepherd was not responding, instead choosing to chase after Lucky. This of course only made Lucky run faster in the wrong direction. After running for an extended time, the Shepherd stopped. Depression lines filled his face.

We learned a new word which was halt. It means sit. 'So, why not say sit?' I thought. English is very confusing to me. For example, Lucky is a pointer-setter cross. (Does that make him popular at Christmas time?)

I was switched over to the Producer, who said, "Sit. Which is halt." She wasn't very convincing.

And then, she said, "Friday sit or halt-sit, whichever you like best?" That is the joy of training with the Producer. Nothing is that serious. We have an understanding on walks that it is more important to take in our surroundings. (We both have the wandering gene.)

I had no idea what Auntie was talking about with that halt thing. I guessed that meant when the Producer stopped, I needed to sit. As you know, puppies guess wrong most of the time. However, holy-moly-sister-sally, this time I was right.

Auntie said, "Good! Good, someone is getting it "The Producer and I looked at each and smiled knowingly. We are a fine team.

Shepherds all around us were complaining that their dog only worked well at home. But, nowhere else? This was easy for me to understand. I don't generally either. Dog park, home, and dog school are three different places to me that have no connection to each other. At dog school, I do not try to balance food on my nose. And, at home you don't answer the phone by saying, "Sorry, wrong department. Like at work? " Do you?

Plus, here's the other problem. Your expectations are not reasonable in the dog world. When we go for a walk, I am supposed to walk and or prance in the freezing cold? When you stop my ass goes in the cold snow, not yours. I think not. I checked with the only sane dog in the good citizen class, a boxer named Earl. He agreed with me. Our next exercise was one of my favourites. It is called, 'Ready? Give a treat.' The Producer says, 'ready' and gives me a treat. This I understand and appreciate. We did this ten times and every time I got a treat, for nothing. I was living the good life.

Then the words changed to 'Watch me! Give a treat.' In this exercise, I had to look up when the words were said or I did not get the treat. Although full, I continued snacking.

I think it is important that I point out a canine feature true of all canines, except the anorexic Lhasa Apso. Being full has nothing to do with eating a cookie. I always want a cookie. My understanding is that Shepherds have this attitude toward French fries. What puzzled me about this exercise is that when the Producer said, "Watch me," and I looked up and she was not doing anything. I got the treat for looking up? What am I watching?

I think whoever came up with dog training exercise should consider a change. I was thinking, "Watch me bake an apple pie," or "Watch me balance a pillow on my head," would be more fun. The Producer would agree.

Our next task was the recall. Auntie held one of us by the collar while our Shepherd walked across the bridge. Upon reaching the end, they called for their dog and clocked the time. The first Shepherd called out "come" and we all took off. Big mistake!

Unfortunately for the Shepherds' arms, all but one of us was not attached to an arm. Auntie reminded the Shepherds to call out the dog's name first. For example, "Rocket come," or "Dakota come". This was a solo task, not a group activity, with the exception of Lucky, who was still running, leash in mouth, up and down the bridge full speed at all times.

Auntie said, "Who's next?'

The boxer, yelled out "Earl" in perfect English. I was impressed! Earl is a speaking dog? Now, I will have to rethink my book tour. Earl will be my spokesdog. My thoughts combined with his words, lecturing across North America. Anxiously, I went over to him and asked a question that was still burning in my mind: ' Is kugel pronounced koo-gel or ki-gel?'

He thought about it, turned towards me he said, "Earl." I guess if you can only say one word then it might as well be Earl.

"Okay Earl, I guess it is your turn," Auntie said, laughing. Earl ran the whole length of the bridge, slowing at his Shepherd's feet. (Odd behaviour?) He had a reasonably fast time until he down shifted and coasted to a stop.

I remember from the radio that domestic dogs vary in size and shape so significantly that it's difficult to get a bead on just how fast they can run. However, it seemed to my watchful eye, the dogs that follow Earl on the bridge recall training exercise travelled at between 18 to 22 miles per hour (mph), with 19 or so being the average. A dog with a stolen tennis ball in most dog parks can reach speeds of 25 mph. This puts dogs at slightly over a three-minute mile on average. The human per-mile record is slightly under four minutes. However, on the Nature Channel, the African wild dog reaches speeds of 49 mph. (With a lion on his heels, 50 mph.)

Lion free, I was shooting for close to 30 mph, the same speed Lucky was running at. Auntie held me by the collar while the Producer walked to the end of bridge, waiting to clock my time. Or, so I thought.

I leaned forward to get a good start, with my weight on my back legs. The Producer said, "Friday, come!" and I was off. At the twenty foot mark, I was reaching mid speed of 20 mph. Lucky passed me so I knew I would have to dig deeper. Reaching the forty yard mark, I was neck and neck with him, clocking 30 mph. I pictured a lion and my fast twitch muscles kicked in. With one final push, I breezed by Lucky and the Producer at an outstanding 34 mph. (Two miles faster than my ice cream truck chasing time.) I hoped the Producer had everything documented on her blue square watch. Since I don't sweat, my excess body heat was dissipated through my mouth and feet. When I came to a screeching halt by the river, I was double panting hard.

Auntie came by. "Put some lukewarm water on Friday's belly to cool him down. Once cool, give him a drink. He will be fine. Next week, we will practice stopping."

Feeling better, we moved on to jumping up on things: benches, rock walls, floating docks and more. It was scary at first then a lot of fun. The Producer is fun to train with. Sometimes, she jumps up with me. We talk about shoe shopping and the colour brown between exercises.

Lastly, we did supervised isolation. I was tied up to a bike rail three feet from the next Canine Good Citizen, who thankfully, was also tied. The Shepherds left us all for five minutes while Auntie stood guard. I received two death threats and one marriage proposal. Dakota, a terrier, had such a bad case of separation anxiety that he barked nonstop the whole five minutes, preventing me from using my earlier class lesson, sleep/stay. Trying to refocus Dakota, I told him a joke. Two fleas are coming out of a bar when one asks the other 'Do we take a dog or do we walk home? He told me to piss off.

After class, I went home to nap. My sofa was occupied. SammyFarber had come by to visit. We chatted.

"How's life puppyhead?," SammyFarber asked.

"It sucks, too many secrets. I want to be very clear here. Telling secrets to another dog you trust is permitted. I told him about the Snowman incident, Frank, the Director, wanted by the cops and Anna, the Producer being very ill.

"So, besides that, how did you enjoy the play Mrs. Lincoln," he said

I had no idea what he was talking about.

He continued "Every year, in Assiniboine park of Winnipeg, Manitoba, a Delphinium flower garden blossoms. It is a hardy perennial that grows well in northern climates. The flowers grow tall and come in a variety of colors including purple, pink, white, red, orange and yellow. The spot is known as the English Gardens. No one knows who planted the garden, one bulb at a time. On March 12, 1852, a fire swept thru the entire park reducing it to ruin, destroying the structures, surrounding shady trees and gardens. If it were not for a Alaskan Malamute named Katauyak who cleared the path to safety, many more villagers and wildlife would have died."

"Katauyak," I asked.

"Yes, it an Inuit name meaning, rainbow. Alaskan Malamutes were bred for endurance. They were designed to be able to carry large and heavy loads for long distances, lots of stamina. They are the largest and oldest of the Arctic sled dogs, named after a native Inuit tribe, Mahlemuts"

"The next summer the Delphinium bulbs beneath the ground returned."

"How?" I said

"When a Delphinium loses its petals they float into the sky and band together to form arcs of colored light. In honour of Katauyak those arcs of light that forever bind us to our departed loved ones are called rainbows."

Delphinium petals connect our hearts to loved ones who have passed away?

"Do dogs pee on flowers as a sign of respect because they want their message to be carried to their loved ones?" I asked.

"Yes, on petals projecting outward like rays of light from the sun. Eventually, the flowers fade into the air to form the rainbows. When a loved one dies, Delphinium petals are visible in the air for a brief moment. If you see them, the everlasting connection is complete."

Chapter 14

Little Mountain Park

"Guard dogs wanted," blared the radio. Hmm, I thought? To my goals of licking the dog park fence without getting my tongue stuck and outrunning the African wild dog, I added becoming a guard dog. I started with what I thought would be a guard dog checklist.

4. Sit
7. Dig up treasures in neighbour's yard
14. Learn the secret of darkness
9. Sniff butts

It was 8:00am and I had already accomplished number 4. After my morning run at the park, I would work on numbers 7, 14 and 9. When the Producer and Director were dressed and coffeed, we took off in the car. We drove for two seasons, winter and spring, till we reached our destination, Little Mountain Dog Park.

"Wow, we made it in under thirty minutes," the Director said, looking at his watch. "It seemed so much longer to me."

'Me too. Much longer.' I made a mental note to remind him to get me my promised watch.

Walking around, I wondered what this new and exciting park had to offer. It was big, really big. I had to stay on leash till the Director and Producer got the lay of the land.

"Is it safe. See any dogs? Sure we are in the right place?" the Producer asked.

"Yep, it says, Little Mountain Off Leash Dog Park." the Director replied.

Finally, we were at a real dog park. I was jazzed. Legal and all. I have to tell Pageant Patti. The Producer unhooked me, leashless, free to explore. It was the largest park I had ever seen, much larger than the half city block I was used to. Even bigger than Cantope, which is gigantic! After half an hour of no dog sightings, I let my nose take over. Soon, I was in a wooded area, surrounded by dogs.

'Hi,' I said to the longhaired rough Collie rolling in the mud. 'I thought I was the only one here?'

Note to reader: Before I translate what he said into English for you, I thought I should explain that these dogs were uncanine -like in mind and action. I did my best. I hope it is clear.

'As ye kin see over on the right hand side thar, thays a slew of dogs who live here, good lord wiling and the creek don't rise. We wuz born in what yu city olk call a puppy mill. Us older ones go back n furth, a'fussin n a'fitin over the same patch of groun all dey till we wuz too riled up and starved to care anymore. Tiny wire cages at night for the youngins. Urine and crap was sopposed to fell thru the wire, cept, most time the crap stayed in cage en pups played with it. Sum pup areas were stacked three high and the lower ones getting a poop shower daily. Angry red sores on everyone of us.'

'What's your name?' I asked, holding back the puke and rage building up inside of me.

'Ain't got one. Nun of us do.'

'Where are you all from,' I asked, thinking it was odd to have no name.

'Up North, Manitoba.'

'An awful place?' I asked.

'Now I knew alkuhol makes ye sleepy, I atched my plan.'

'Your plan?' I asked.

'Twuz a beeyootiful fall evenin, jes warm a nuff. And, I up en bolted. The guy who was sopposed to watchin us he wuz a'sleepin. Whut I had figgerd on wuz how tired a bidy gits after drinkin till three am, thatz when the restrunt closed. So I mosey in Big Bob's BBQ restrant backdoor and avail myself to a case of vodka that I lug back to da mill.'

'Were you scared?'

No, I told em other dogs that they needed to accept the truth befor it twuz too late. We'd been wronged. Our keepers woke en drank the whole case. They passed out, we ran. When they wok, they chased us for miles and miles, drunk as skunks, not wantin to give it up. But finally we shook em off our tail. Her, the bloodhound over thar, lead the way here. She wuz born in Winnipeg,' he said.

I wondered how it was possible that the bloodhound had been here before. Why did she leave? How did she know the way back home? I had heard of dogs who had made incredible treks. But, till now, I did not believe it.

The pack had gathered in, watching my every move. They were suspicious of me, showing signs of extreme fearfulness. Uncanine signals coming at me from all directions, I kept a safe distance. The exception was the alpha leader to whom I was speaking. He was not scared. However, he was very protective of his pack.

The tension in a springer spaniel in the shadows was building into a rage. Glassy-eyed, he stared at me not really seeing my movements. He was having a mental lapse. I watched him closely, fearing he would attack soon. Next to him was a bull terrier chasing his tail. Not like Ivan the Stupid, this terrier was not having fun. I could tell by their distorted body structures that many of these dogs had been beaten. Some severely! Only because they had conditions that they could not control. (Tears rolled down my nose.) The longhaired collie continued.

'Never going back,' he said. 'Never-ever, nun of us. We ook after each odder. A stream runs thru ere and most times we got bounds of food like mice, rats, and squirrels, and more. It's a sooper seekret place. Plus, in really cold, the thunder gods deliver.'

"Thunder gods?' I asked.

'Three, sumtimes four of 'em. Never caught hair of them. Come real early. The youngin chocolate lab pup, he has seen em.'

I turned to the puppy and asked, 'Thunder Gods?'

Being a puppy like me, he opened up. 'I ain't seen 'em just their thunder wagon filled with chez, am, and urkey. Comes twice a week, early morn. Always dinner, 'cept one krismas night wiz got 32 fruit cakes.'

'Thunder wagon? A red radio flyer wagon, perhaps?' I asked.

'Yeah, a red wagon. How'd ya figue?'

'Lucky guess,' I said. 'Did they ever say anything?'

'No, not a word. Left dinner and go,' the puppy said. 'Cept, once we had overcooked noodles, raisins, and curds of ipe cheez.'

Kugel? I knew he was lying about not talking with them. But, I said nothing. Puppies lie to each all the time. We accept that. Then we looked at each other and mouthed, 'Oy, am I thirsty!'

I tried not to react. But, the puppy was sensing I was hiding something too. 'You know em? Ya gonna tell sum one bout this place?'

'No,' I said, 'I am a keeper of secrets. Can I do anything for you before I go?'

'Yes.' the puppy said. 'We ould all like a name. It gets so darn confusing ere sumtimes for me.'

I can do that. I lined them all up and I gave them names. Well actually, it was numbers. I called the longhaired collie 99, the bloodhound 16 cause that is more like a girl number, next was the Springer spaniel who I called 21, the bull terrier 31 and the cute lab puppy I called 7. I went thru the whole pack giving each of them a number. When I left they thanked me and asked my name. I told them my birth dog name, onety-one.

'Thank you onety-one. Ya made your mama proud tadey.'

"Friday, Friday where are you? Come! Come!"

'I'll find a way to deal with that mill,' I said, leaving my new friends. 'And, your sooper seekret is safe with me. With that I ran off before the Producer or Director stumbled on their hideout. Not because I feared they would act irresponsibly. But, because I made a promise to keep their secret and my mom taught me that everyone in life needs someone safe to tell their secrets to.

"Have fun?" the Producer asked, helping me into the back of the car.

'Yes,' I wagged.

On the way home, I thought about puppy mills. How the dogs are mistreated in puppy mills, not learning the basic skills of the canine world. It saddens me greatly that a puppy would miss puppyhood and not be allowed to be in contact with their mom and dad. It was fully apparent in their canine language skills, or lack thereof, that life in the normal canine and Shepherd world would be difficult for them. A dog who has lived with poop as his only toy can be very difficult to house train. Even rescued, they face an uncertain future. If you pass a few tape worm segments on the bed covers, you might as well pack your food bowl and move outdoors. Some Shepherds just cannot deal with such things. When I become full grown then I will do something about that puppy mill. That's a promise! For now, if you are considering getting a puppy, adopt from a shelter or rescue or purchase one like me from an ethical breeder that you can investigate, rather than buy from a newspaper ad or over the Internet or anyone named Olga. Urge Shepherds you know to do the same. When the demand stops, the puppy and breeding mills will be forced to shut down. And, do not tell anyone about Little Mountain Park. It is a sooper seekret.

When we got home, I did the doorway dance that I had worked out in the car. Running to the front door, I pretended to go into the house, pushing in front of everyone on the pathway. The next distraction is a very difficult move that takes skill, timing and more than a little luck. When the door opens, you move forward, stopping suddenly in the entranceway to scratch, which makes it necessary for them to step over you or trip. This is the point where you need luck and luck I found in the ringing phone. The Director had already tripped over me while the Producer scrambled by to get the ringing phone. The doorway dance had worked. I slowly backed out the door. I had been watching the neighbour for some time. I was ready for item 7 of my guard dog training program, dig up weapons in neighbour's yard.

From our kitchen window, I can clearly see into Mr. Neighbour's backyard. (The Director calls him that.) One day, the Director told me all the rules of city life when it comes to neighbours. I remember exactly what it smelt like when he told me, freshly watered roses. I remember his actions, how he pointed at things in Mr. Neighbour's yard while explaining rules 1 through 7, and fed me a cookie. The cookie had rolled oats, butter, cornmeal, sugar, chicken, cheddar cheese and egg. Every ingredient of that cookie is etched in my brain, but not the rules. Nope, not a one. I have a puppy brain, easily distracted by a good cookie.

I noticed that Mr. Neighbour spent a lot time mapping the garden, pacing off each section. Satisfied with his diagram, he dug up the ground. And then, he planted cookies. They bloom in northern climates. To camouflage his efforts, he laid in a vegetable garden overtop. Not your normal row types. There were circles, squares, hexagons and plants in raised beds. Seemed like a very clever disguise.

Some dogs, such as terriers, are relentless diggers. Digging for them, is an essential part of their hunting repertoire. Underground there are countless bugs, dead animals, old trash pits and live game with a side of kimchi. However, the most common type of digging is caused by the denning instinct. Evolution has provided dogs with an instinct to dwell in a protected area. If such shelter is not provided, the dog will dig to obtain it. (I have a den so I do not dig for that reason.)

Guard dogs put a high survival value associated with being intimately familiar with the local cookie stashes. Ready for action, I realized that I had forgotten my lesche knife, resorting to the paw method. Digging deep, I found the vegetable garden ground was softer than I had thought. Only inches from the prize, I heard the Director calling me.

Running to the front door, I entered with my tail wagging to hide my mission.

"I was looking everywhere for you. You want to go to the park? Or, if you like, we might do some training instead," he said. I suspect this was not the first time that he told the Producer we were going to the park and detoured to the basement while she attended Pilates class.

'Item 14. Learn the secret of darkness,' I suggested.

"Let's go down the basement and you will learn how the light switch works."

My heart skipped a beat. Finally, we were learning something useful to a guard dog.

Chapter 15

Lights Out

First, we did the touch command. The Director held a margarine tub lid in front of my nose. Every time I smelt it, a click sounded and I got a treat, dried lamb jerky. Mighty tasty! From there, we moved on. The Director put the yellow lid on the floor about a foot away and said, "Go touch." I stared at him, then sat down and waved in hope of another click. No dried lamb jerky appeared. The Director put a treat on the lid this time and said again, "Go touch."

Now I understood and went to the lid each time he put it somewhere. And got clicked. Thrilled with me, a good student, he continued clicking. My nose touched till the doorbell rang. Picking up the lid, I proffered it to the Director, reminding him that a Guard dog never ever breaks training. Not even for a split second! He paid no attention to me.

While he was gone, I gave some thought to my plan. A lot of which has been written of the Guard dog is plain wrong. I agree that some Guard dogs may have been ruthless killers, dressed in black collars, infiltrating enemy camps under a strict code of honour, fighting to the death. But not all of them. Some Guards, like myself, loathe violence and abhor death. Was I not remorseful over that whole snowman mix-up in front of SammyFarber's garage?

What is true is that every Guard, including me, is Sooper Sekrit. So, it is imperative that you eat this page after reading it. Respectfully, I have written the next two pages on rice paper. Eat quietly, the Director is coming. (I can smell him.)

When he came back the mood had soured. Inspecting my muddy paw, he was visibly upset with me.

"Friday, that was Mr. Neighbour. Remember, we spoke about him? He tolerates your barking at imaginary lions in the middle of the night. But, as discussed, not digging in his garden is rule number 4. However, punishing you for acting like a dog doesn't make much sense to me or to him. But, I can reduce your inappropriate conduct by training you in a concrete way."

I hated it when he sounded like a textbook. He continued, "It is not fair or logical for me to expect you can understand mimicry. The technical term for this is allelomimetic behaviour. From our kitchen window, you watched Mr. Neighbour dig in the yard and you wanted to imitate his behaviour. Correct?"

'Huh? Do I look like a cheetah to you? Did you know that the higher a monkey climbs the more you see his behind?' I could not tell him I was looking for buried treasure. Let's go with that mimicry theory of yours. 'Okay,' I said and leaned. 'Does this mean I am out of the running for employee of the month?'

"Okay. Let's continue," he said, ignoring me.

The Director put the lid down and said again, "Go touch." So, I did. Once I got that perfected, and could do it at any distance, things changed. The lid was taped to the wall without my knowledge. I smelt everywhere on the floor for it. Then I realized, if not A then B. If not on the floor, then it must be on the wall. We were clicking and dried lamb jerky was flowing freely every time I pawed at the lid top taped to the wall at nose height.

Most Shepherds would stop here. Not my Director! We were going to be here as long as it took, all night if necessary. This is not a good way to train a dog. But, I am not any dog. I am Guard Onety-one. We pressed on. He raised the lid to the height of the light switch making it necessary for me to run to the wall and jump to hit the yellow lid with my paw. I was certain what was coming next. I would paw the yellow lid taped over the light switch and darkness would be achieved. Wrong again. After a few successful smacks, 20 I think, he finally held the dented lid over the light switch and when I ran and jumped this time he moved the lid, causing me to strike the switch.

"Light off," he said, clicking me a treat. From then on, waving his hand over the light switch and saying "light off" or "light on" sent me springing into action. We practiced for the next hour all over the house, turning every light on and off. I was exhausted. Tomorrow I would try working the toaster.

The Producer came home from her Pilates class carrying a bag of wonderful smelling aromas.

"Did Friday enjoy the park?" she asked, dumping the contents on the kitchen counter.

"Yes, very much. He is resting."

On the counter she had wet, dry, moist, semi moist food laid out, ranging from chicken, fish, meat, lamb and even duck. Smells from heaven! She read the label of each can before putting the contents on separate blue china plates, making notes on each one.

'A counter buffet with a menu,' I thought, licking my lips.

The Producer went upstairs to change.

Now here's my problem. It looks bleeping high. The old chicken on the barstool dilemma.

'But wait,' I think to myself. Had I not learned anything from Canine Good Citizen class? Remembering the rock wall jumping exercise. Confidence built, I leapt. My light frame and strong legs guiding me, reward was mine.

Oddly enough, cat food and dog food appear similar at first sight, but it really is not. Dogs and cats have different nutritional needs and each food is formulated appropriately for the animal. Cat food often has much more protein and fat than dog food, so feeding me large quantities of cat food and especially cat treats can cause weight gain, nausea, and in my case, hyperactivity.

I ate everything, tender turkey in a Tuscany sauce, white meat chicken with cheddar and garden greens, wild salmon, yellow fin tuna and my favourite, tender beef tenderloin tips with long grain rice. Licking the last plate clean, a rush of energy engulfed me.

Hearing the Director approaching, I jumped down from the kitchen counter. The most important thing to remember if you have a hyper dog is that you must project calm energy toward him. Of course, that did not happen.

The Director caught up with me first. "Friday, the stairway is not a racetrack. Stop it, stop it right now!" he yelled. "You will break a leg. You idiot poodle!"

I paid no attention to him, running up and down the staircase, this time skipping every other step. Bored with stair climbing, I moved on to other venues.

When the Producer came down stairs, holding me by the collar, she yelled. "Put trampoline bed dog outside in the yard." Once outside, still energized, howling at the moon and stars, I knew I could beat the African wild dog easily in the 100 metre dash. I was pumped. Having no one to race, I started to bark and dig in the soft mud. I do not know why.

Not wanting to further upset the dachshund across the street while I answered my call of the wild, the Producer took me back inside. I decided that now was a good time to show her what I had learned. I ran from room to room, jumping at every light switch. Muddy paws tattooed the walls.

"What the hell?" the Producer said, lights flickering on and off everywhere. "What on earth is he doing?"

"Beats me," the cowardly Director said. "I do not know where he gets this stuff."

"Did he eat anything odd at the dog park?" she asked.

"No, I don't think so. Just played with a few dogs. Nothing unusual," he said.

I did not believe what I was hearing. 'Dog park? What dog park? What about Guard training? Okay buddy, pin this on me and there will be payback. You will not see it coming! But, b-b-but there will be payback,' I stammered. 'I promise you that. Yellow is not your color.'

My earlier statement that dogs love unconditionally is an exaggeration. While it is true that I seem predisposed to form long term relationships and develop strong bonds with Shepherds (what they call love), not all dogs love all Shepherds. The roughly 300,000 Shepherds that have to undergo medical treatment for dog bites every year would probably attest to that. What bothers me is that these unrealistic expectations of unconditional love can lead to frustration, unhappiness with the pet and sometimes, the dog is given up or euthanized. This unconditional love concept is not in the best interests of pets or Shepherds.

You want proof! At this exact moment, I would not say that I love the Director unconditionally. What I can tell you is that the Guard code has a section on payback. And, he's gonna get it!

The Producer spotted the empty dishes of cat food. "Perhaps, a reaction to the cat food. I never thought he could get up here. He will calm down soon."

Thirty minutes later, and a hundred laps around the yard, I did not calm down. I crashed! Sound asleep for five hours before waking up in the middle of the night. Ready for revenge!

So what can I say about my first Guard dog outing, without breaking the strict code of canine Guard silence? One thing I can say for sure is that I have never been hired out to the highest bidder for assassinations, espionage, or sabotage of any kind. (No, I am not counting Mr. Neighbour's yard as sabotage. There could have been treasures.) I take full responsibility for what I did next. It was time to rip the Band-Aid off.

Under the cover of darkness, I crept into the living room where I found my largest, hardest marrow bone. I could hardly lift it. Quietly, I crept along the floor till I was at the Director's bed side, bone secured between my teeth. Leaping on to the bed, I positioned myself directly over his head. He stirred but he did not wake. I dropped the bone.

"What the hell," he said, waking up.

"Isn't that nice? He wants to share his bone with you," the Producer said, wiping the sleep from her eyes.

The Director breathed in heavily through his nose. He was not sure if it was a gift or an attack. Mission accomplished, I exited before he made a final decision.

The late night knock on the door was different, more assertive. It was how I imagined a grizzly bear would knock. Then again, grizzly bears probably do not knock. I had a clear line of sight. The Director cracked the door open, stepping outside he said, "Morning, how may I help you?"

'Are you Frank Richards?" That was first time I heard our last name. Up to this point, I thought our last name was Poodle.

"Yes, yes I am."

"May we come in?" the voice on the outside of the door asked.

"Why?"

"We have a few questions. Will only take a minute or two."

"With all due respect, I do not consent to having you enter my home. You can ask me out here."

"We simply want to ask you a few questions about your whereabouts on the afternoon of January 5th. Specifically, our photo radar shows your car speeding on that day on highway 59."

"Yes, I am aware of that. I sent a cheque in for the ticket. Is that what this is all about? If you need me write a new check then I can do that or, if you want, I can show you the cancelled cheque. Or, I can pay again."

the Director rattled on.

I do not know the proper way to act when you are interviewed by the police. However, I do know you have to keep your excuses simple. 'Tell him you were driving with your head out the window and didn't notice the speed,' I suggested. 'Or bribe him with a free meal at the new Eduardo's Gourmet Burger Palace where they have a Kobe beef patty wrapped in gold leaf, foie gras, caviar, lobster, truffles, imported aged Gruyere cheese, melted with champagne steam, a kopi luwak barbeque sauce and Himalayan rock salt. They make a mean burger! Did you know they just opened up?' Of course I was ignored.

"In that case we will need you come downtown with us."

I always wondered why police stations were downtown and never uptown. Odd, don't you think?

The police officer read the Director his rights.

You have the right to remain silent and to refuse to answer questions.

Anything you do say may be used against you in a court of law.

You have the right to consult an attorney

"Do you understand these rights?"

"Yes, but it's only a speeding ticket? Isn't it?"

"Come with us Sir."

"Can I bring the dog?"

Holy moly sister Sally, let's not push this unconditional love thing. I am not serving 20 years to life.

"No Sir. No dogs!"

Phewf, I breathed easy. And then, I thought about the hours of training, the caregiving when I was sick, ball playing in the park. I really did love him. So, I tried to get out the door. I was coming. 'If you take him you gotta take me,' I said, squeezing out the crack in the doorway. 'We are a team. Let the prison term begin.' Looking in the Director's eyes, I added, 'I get the upper bunk, right?'

"It's okay Friday. You stay and guard the house. I will be back soon Buddy."

At this point, the producer wrapped in her pink robe, was at the door. "What is going on here? Where are you taking him?"

"It's all right honey. It's about a speeding ticket. You stay here with Friday. I will be back soon. It's all just a misunderstanding."

"Are you sure you do not want me to come?"

"Yes, I am sure. No need to worry. I will take a taxi home. Go back to bed now. It's nothing."

When they got to the Police Station the Director was escorted into grey walled room with metal table in it. He sat in a rather comfortable armchair which surprised him, expecting a steel folding chair. The conversation was being taped.

Police officer: I'm just going to ask you some questions, Mr. Richard. Do you want coffee or water?

Mr. Richards: No, thank you.

Police officer: Where were you on January 5th at approximately one in the afternoon?

Mr. Richards: I was driving home on highway 59.

Police officer: Who was in the car with you?

Mr. Richards: My wife, Anna.

Police officer: Anyone else?

Mr. Richards: No.

Mr. Richards: Yes, I mean, no. Does my dog count?

Police officer: What did you talk about in the car?

Mr. Richards: Honestly, I do not know. Frankly, I would guess holidays.

Police officer: Where do you like to go?

Mr. Richards: Honestly, South, anywhere warm.

Police officer: I hear you. My wife loves Florida.

Police officer: Did you see a car accident on the road?

Mr. Richards: No.

The thought of Anna being questioned bothered him. Was she next to be interrogated? Wiping his sweaty palms on his pants, he looked up.

Police officer: What time did you get home?

Mr. Richards: However long it took. I do not know. Why do you care?

Police officer: Answer the question.

Mr. Richards: At about two thirty.

A new person entered the room. A stocky build was evident thru his grey suit. He whispered something in the police officer's ear. The police officer gave Frank a short look and then excused himself. The man in the grey suit followed.

Frank sat reviewing all his answers, wondering if he answered correctly, wanting to change one. The man in the grey suit returned alone. He sat quiet for five minutes, arranging papers on the desk and scribbling a note in his pad. And then he said. "I am Detective Robertson."

Detective Robertson: I understand that you like to go south for holidays correct?

Mr. Richards: Yes, Frank said, nerves peaking.

Detective Robertson: And, you did not see an accident on highway 59?

Mr. Richards: That is correct. But, I did not see the accident but I saw the car and trailer in the ditch. He said, correcting his earlier answer.

Detective Robertson: So, you did not see the actual accident. However, you did see the after effect?

Mr. Richards: Yes, that is correct.

Detective Robertson: What colour was the car?

Mr. Richards: Green, I think. Maybe blue?

Detective Robertson: What was the license number?

Mr. Richards: I do not know.

Detective Robertson: Did you get out of your car?

Frank Richards was crossing his hands (defensive position), sitting on the edge of the chair, with very relaxed posture, tilting his head upwards to the right, as he thought of his next answer.

Mr. Richards: Yes, but only briefly. I looked in the car. The man was dead.

Detective Robertson: Mr. Richards, did you call 911?

Mr. Richards: No.

Detective Robertson: Why not?

Mr. Richards: Cause I heard the sirens of the oncoming police car so I left.

Detective Robertson: You mean you sped away. Why at such a fast speed? What was your hurry?

Frank paused: I did not want to be in the way of the rescue team.

Detective Robertson: I thought you said the driver was dead.

Mr. Richards: I do not know. I am not sure.

Detective Robertson: Do you own a fire extinguisher?

No response.

The Detective repeated: Do you own a fire extinguisher?

Mr. Richards: Yes.

Detective Robertson: Where is it?

Mr. Richards: I do not know. It may be in my garage. I have not seen it for a long time.

Detective Robertson: How long?

Mr. Richards: I do not know.

Detective Robertson: Okay Sir. Thank you for your time, Mr. Richards. You are free to go.

The Director took a taxi home, knowing he had messed up on more than a few questions.

Chapter 16

Ragdoll

Later that night, when the director came home I could hear him whispering to the Producer. I strained my big orange ears, no luck. It was serious. Wanting to help, but unable to, I counted myself to sleep.

In the morning, awakened from my nap by thundering wheels on the driveway, I knew it was here. I could hear it ticking. Having practiced weeklong for this moment, I was ready. Running over to the Producer, I sat at her feet and enunciated, 'Wooch.' unable to say Watch.

Unlike my mom, my muzzle is slightly longer than most standard poodles, which might explain why I cannot pronounce words clearly. It might also explain why I am soooooooo nosey.

The Director went into the bathroom for what seemed forever. From the sounds and the stink, I could tell his nerves and bowels were in a battle. Bowels winning!

For the longest time, I looked for a secret exit out of the bathroom. Over the years, hidden passages have been used to hide really good stuff, facilitate whelping, and conceal large bins of cheesy hound rounds. Many Shepherds do not know that the original secret bathroom exit sparked the idea for today's doggie door. Yesterday, I checked under the bath mat for a trapdoor. No luck!

Some secret entrances are invisible, such as a normal-looking wall that can be walked through, while others give a slight visual clue, such as a cave behind a waterfall. Although I have never seen the bathroom waterfall in action, I had heard it. I head-butted the shower wall thinking it was hiding an invisible exit. Not a good plan!

If by some miracle, the Director gets there before me, like this time, and shuts the door then I would claw, whine, bark or paw at the door incessantly till he let me in. This is not a standard poodle thing. In fact, most dogs have heard about this secret exit out of the bathroom. Unfortunately, no canine, to my knowledge, has ever found it. Protecting the secret, the Director always exits the same way he went in, reminding me that he has experience and my presence is not needed. This does not fool me. I will find that door.

'Wooch', I said returning to the Producer. 'Wooch, wooch, wooch,' I repeated, having practiced saying the word over and over to white bear.

"Outside?" she asked. Gee whiz, if I wanted to go out I would have sneezed.

Not making any progress, I ran into the vacated bathroom and retrieved the canine magazine from the woven basket. Flipping to the right page, I smacked the picture of the girl taking a bubble bath, above and to the right was a large white cat. The girl's wrist, dangling out of the white porcelain tub, had my wooch on it. Being specific, I pointed to the bottom of the page where the five different colour bands were, knowing the Producer would like that wooch feature. My oval shaped paws are rather small and arched which makes pointing difficult. Wrongly, I thought her wide smile signalled understanding.

'Puh-leeze give it to me,' I said over and over in my head. The opening front door disrupted my thoughts.

"It's here. It's finally here. Friday will be so happy," the Director said, signing a paper at the door. In his hand was a crate, not unlike the one I came in. I reasoned that everything good must come in a crate, I did.

The smell was strangely familiar and not in a particularly good way. When the crate door swung open, I peeked inside. Striking blue eyes stared back at me. The white patch of inverted 'V' on the face indicating a bicolour pattern confirmed my nose. He was a Persian, Burmese, and Siamese mix known on Ask the Vet as a Ragdoll cat.

At first, I thought this was a lot of effort to go to for a chew toy. (It does not take a border collie to know what had happened.) I raced back to the magazine and sure enough, the cat over the tub, although much larger, was the spitting image of the guy at the door. I was not overly concerned. There had to be a 14 day return policy with proof of purchase. At the front door, I investigated further.

One of the things I like about white bear is that he agrees with everything I say and do. The second really favourite thing is that if I bite his back, he squeaks. At first, this scared me. Then, I realized that he liked it too. The squeaking is a fun game that we play when we are bored. I squeeze, he squeaks. We laugh. Eager to see if my new toy squeaked, I bit him. Not so hard the stuffing would pop out like white bear, just enough to make him squeak.

This was the first and only time in my life that I was scruffed by the Director. Reba, my mom, used to scruff us kids when we were misbehaving so it was not that foreign to me. The Director lifted me up by the back of the neck, pulling me off the kitten, shaking me gently, but firmly, he said, No! The direct eye contact confirmed I was being scolded.

"Bad poodle! Bad! Bad! Bad!" the Producer barked.

I was so upset, I whimpered. Lowering my tail, I slinked into the other room.

To say I felt guilty or regretful would not be accurate. However, I did feel sadness. The sharp tone of both the Director and the Producer, coupled with their changed body positioning, threatened me. It was my first real blush with Shepherd dominance. I knew then and there when it came to the kitten, I was not the pack leader. Not knowing what to do next, I ran to get white bear. 'Pack your stuff, we are leaving for the woods at break of dawn! I screwed up,' I told him.

I was not the only victim here. The kitten, having been assaulted by me, hid in the basement for three days. The Director would check on him frequently but he was not coming out. He moved around a lot in the basement, one cubby hole to the next, always making sure he had a clear exit and cover from me.

With my keen sense of smell, I always knew where he was. The Director had to search. I thought I owed it to the kitten not to give up his hiding spots. It was the least that I could do.

Later that week, I could tell the kitten was calming. His movement was more deliberate, more confident. Before we were reunited, the Director took me to the dog park. After an hour of play, we walked for what seemed like forever and arrived at a really big hill.

"This is a landfill site," the Director informed when we reached the top. I double-checked because I am more qualified and have a bigger nose. I have 220 million scent receptors as opposed to the Director who has a mere 5 million. I am a scent machine.

The problem here for me was not finding the scent, it was sorting it all out. I quickly broke down the smells, starting at the lowest levels. It was rubbish, then scrap, then garbage, then more garbage, then gobbledygook. Yes, the small nosed Shepherd was correct. We were at the dump, no doubt about it.

He threw my tennis ball down the hill. I eagerly chased after it, wanting to please him so I would be back in his good books. I am a predator and as a predator I am wired to chase things that move. And a big, slobbery tennis ball fits nicely in my mouth. After the tenth time, I was getting pretty annoyed with him. This whole retriever thing is overrated. That is why I became a writer. By the time we got home, I was in a bad mood. And then, believe or not, I went on a seven mile run with the Producer. Something was not right?

Finally home and exhausted, I stumbled into the den. Dead tired, I could barely see the white fluff ball on the Producer's lap. Hmm, they had tired me out on purpose. But I knew, Cantope kennels sent me here to accomplish a certain number of things. And, right now I was far behind.

His beady blue eyes never left me. On a long sit-stay, I was instructed not to move forward which was more than fine with me. I did not want to get picked up by the scruff again. After a few treats for my prolonged sit-stay, I started to relax. The Director and Producer were unusually calm. I wanted to talk to the kitten to apologize. But, I knew that he did not speak dog and I certainly did not speak fluff ball. As you know, I am a pack animal and form friendships quickly. He was more cautious. More territorial. More solitary.

My current philosophy on life, spitting into the wind only gets you a wet nose, was surfacing. I had to try to make the best of things. (Wanting to avoid the woods, white bear agreed.)

At this point, my paternal instincts were kicking in. Thinking of adopting the little guy, I named him Skippy, like the peanut butter (not the rope). The Director took Skippy's towel out of the crate and offered me a sniff. What the heck? I sniffed. It stunk! Stale nicotine, tar and arsenic assaulted my sensitive nose. Nicotine is the most awful smell a canine can be exposed to. And this comes from someone who likes the smell of poop.

Both poop and urine are like your business cards. They carry info about age, sex and readiness. Between the roof of my mouth and the tip of my tongue I have what is known as a vomero nasal organ that I use for gathering dating information from urine. That is why I get so close to smell it. I checked again, hoping to be wrong. He smokes? Does my little boy Skippy smoke? I wondered as I became even more annoyed.

Skippy was securely on the Producer's lap while the Director moved me forward. My short leather leash was attached, enough rope to hang myself. Feeling his firm grip, I behaved. Next, in an affirming voice, the Director spoke to both of us.

"A pat on the back is only a few inches from a smack on the butt, understand?" he said. We did, sniffing at each other while the Producer and the Director gave us comforting strokes. After a while, the Producer set Skippy on the floor and although the Director still had a firm grip on my leash, we interacted freely.

Over the next three days, we crossed paths in the daytime, nodding hello. It was all new to me. At first, there were subtle changes in the home, more dishes on the floor than in the cupboards. My dinner was seasoned with cat hair. And, if you never had had a lint roller stuck to your butt then take it from me, it is not a fun experience. Desperate to learn, I listened to the meow mix theme song on the radio for clues. I could not break the code.

One morning, I stumbled on a solution. If the ears do not work then use the nose. I would communicate by smell via a language I call pheromone. Those produced by his face were friendly sayings like, 'let's you and me be friends'. His paw pads gave off alarm pheromones and messages sent by his rear meant, 'piss off dog'. Sometimes, he would approach me with his tail held high. He would then give me a head butt, swing around and say, 'wanna smell my butt'. This I understood. Although he was much smaller than me, he liked to take the lead in most social settings. If he retreated when I moved forward than I knew he wanted to be left alone. Not unlike my friend Earl, Skippy was capable of many sounds.

By that I mean, his high-pitched pheromone meow directed at me by his face meant that he was glad to see me. The same high-pitched meow directed at the Shepherds meant, feed me NOW! Sometimes, he would do what I call the silent meow. (I wondered what other feline secrets he was hiding.)

One morning he mouthed the word, meow, without saying anything causing the Producer to give him a treat.

Being a quick study, I mouthed, woof, to the coffeeing Director. Not the same result. The newspaper swinging, Director told me to close my mouth before a fly flew in.

"Ack-ack," alerted me. I turned quickly, remembering from my late night journey home that someone or something was going to die. In this case, it was a fly. As a puppy, I believed flies only had 24 hours to live. I do not know why I thought that. I later learned that if they did not fly by Skippy then they had two to four weeks to make buzzing noises over my poop.

Skippy was a much more skilled hunter than I ever imagined. He came programmed from birth with the chase hunting gene. Through play, he must have developed the coordination and timing needed to successfully capture the target. He would adjust his speed to the speed of a moving fly. Not unlike how Lefty figured out the safest way to cross car-filled streets. After gauging the distance, he would pounce. Once he had the fly trapped, he quickly removed the wings. I had two thoughts on this. Having chased a tennis ball more than ten times up and down a steep hill, I knew that it makes no sense to catch something and not secure it. And secondly, Skippy would be living in a relatively rodent-free environment, limiting the opportunity to catch real live prey. Therefore, when he caught a fly, he might want to prolong the "great" event as much as possible. Had our relationship gotten off on a better paw, so to speak, then I would have asked if he was a mouser. But, I did not think this was the time. What interested me most is, how did this apparently sleeping cat actually catch a fly.

Here's what I found out watching him take hold of more than his share of flies. He sleeps a lot, even more than me. When the room temperature is to his liking then he stretches his body out full. However, if chilled then he will curl up in a tight ball. As a lone hunter, he relies on his makeup. By this I mean, he needs a mechanism that allows this protein eating, big sleeper to get both the nourishment he needs frequently and the naps. Lucky for him, like me he has a third eyelid, the translucent nicotating membrane that appeared when I was ill. But, he uses his differently than me. He keeps his outer eyelid partially closed so that it does not look strange to the prey. When a shadow crosses the membrane, he springs up, adjusts his speed, gauges distance and pounces, thereby accomplishing the task of sleeping and hunting at the same time. Cats are the original multi-taskers, although they rarely get the credit.

I moved in closer. He hissed at me, a clear warning that it was his fly and I should back off. When he was done, he came over and head butted me, not a very canine thing to do if you want to exhibit fondness. By far, the most uncanine sound was as how he expressed happiness, a mix of purring and drooling. The first time I heard him do this I yelled, 'Swallow!' fearing he might choke. Also, he leg weaves, shows me his tummy and licks. It takes him about an hour to groom one of my paws. He will never make it as a dog groomer, because he is far too slow.

If this is not enough, he can chatter, chirp, murmur, hiss, growl, and spit. Most of the time he chirped, a friendly greeting. He was not a big talker. The first time I heard a caterwaul I ran to the window and looked out expecting to see Silent Bob. This high-pitched screech was most annoying. I considered Skippy was in heat and then realized that he was too young. Another call told me that the sound was coming from the telephone pole in the alley. Skippy listened. Understanding the message, he went back to chasing a rolled up piece of paper. I would ask him about this later.

I was planning on doing some further investigation at night. I have always wondered if a kitten was the result of a lion's sneeze. (Stop snickering. Oh, like I am the only one who ever thought that?)

Before entering the den where he was sleeping, I turned off the hall light. Slipping in and out of the darkness unnoticed, I would soon discover the truth about this creature. Or not? Much to my surprise, he not only was able to see me in total darkness, but when I approached, he was reading a cat survival magazine. His kitten paws moving along each sentence. The title was: No matter what you've done wrong, always try to make it look like the dog did it.

I must have startled him because I learned that his claws, which were not visible to me when I approached, can strike me in the nose fourteen times before I can even lift my paw. Retractable claws? I would have approached differently had I have known this fact. Nothing on me is retractable.

Making matters worse, his pupils can dilate to ninety percent of the eye. Cats can see in seven times less light than Shepherds and in almost total darkness. Better night vision than me? He had more cones than me evidenced by how easily he moved around in the darkened room looking for his next place to strike.

It occurred to me that he might have gotten those claws out of Mr. Neighbour's yard. Either way, I decided plan A would not work. I went to Plan B. Be friendly. I asked him, 'And how about those Shepherds?' It was friendly tone, the same way Shepherds ask about their favourite hockey team.

"Well? I am the new guy on the ice so I am still getting used to the net. The one that calls me, Mali Wali Bally Bu and always wants to wrap me in a blankee is fun. She grooms me a lot. She said the nicotine smell should go away soon."

'Oh, that is the Producer. She's nice, always baking.'

"The other one, the no claw, no scratch, no bite one is odd. At first, I thought my name was Stop-it! But he did take me to the vet and had the goo cleaned out of my eyes. I see better now."

'That's the Director. You'll get used to him.'

"And the third one is really cool. I like him the best."

'Third one?' I asked.

"Yes, when I first met him he said, 'Who let you out of the bag?' and then he fell back to sleep."

'Really, SammyFarber is here? We will have to go visit with him when he wakes up.'

The kitten continued, "I was born in a house similar to this one. I have five siblings, and then there's Mom and Dad. The seven of us Ragdolls lived there. It was a nice house with lots of cats. I miss my Mom and Dad but not the blue haze. My Shepherd smoked all the time. Very hard on my little lungs and my eyes were full of puss. My littermates and I played games, trying not to think about all the smoke. Do you like to play?' he asked.

I told him about my puppy games, *made you look* and *made you come*. But then, I proudly explained that I had learned a few new games. The first one (amusement time two minutes) was: I would stare at the back of someone's head until they turn around. And the second (amusement time 12 days) was: The rating game where I stare out the window and rate passersby, secretly awarding points as they go along, offering (unsaid) expert criticism over their clothing, hairstyle and footwear choices.

"Hmm," he said. "I will teach you some new games."

We talked. His is name was Malibu, not Skippy. He was born not far from here. Also, he is very sensitive to noise, especially the vacuum cleaner. 'Me too,' I said. We decided if they really cared about us they would get a good job and be able to afford a broom. I told him that I was the official keeper of secrets so he told me one.

"Shepherds think a cat, unlike a dog, will not eat any more than is necessary to regulate their body. Get real," he said. "This entrepreneurial cat named Morris made that up."

Another secret is that he gets stress headaches. Like today, when he jumped up on the dinner table and knocked over the wine glasses while stepping in and out of the stew pot. "All I was doing was apologizing for being late for dinner. And, my good intentions were misconstrued."

He continued. "Like just before you got here I was chatting with the African violet in the living room. He asked me which way to Africa. So, I freed him from the pot with my claws and pointed him south. 'Batten down the hatches and cast off,' I said, seeing clear sailing from the crow's nest. I am sure you will hear about that one in the morning."

'Crow's nest?' I asked

"A crow's nest is a structure in the upper part of the mainmast of a pirate ship, a lookout point."

'You mean the new carpeted tree in the living room?' I asked.

"Shiver me timbers, you landlubber dog. Ain't ya never seen a pirate ship before? Someone needs to be posted to keep watch on the horizon for other ships or signs of land. You got a lot to learn Captain Friday before you set sail. You got a crew, ain't ya?"

I ran to the crate and brought back white bear. 'First mate,' I said.

"He'll do fine." Malibu answered, putting white bear in the crow's nest.

'What did you mean when you said I will hear about the uprooted plant in morning?' I asked, more than a little concerned.

"I am a kitten. I can do no wrong. You are a puppy. You will always be blamed, enough said."

We played pirate for a while and then switched to hockey.

Much to my surprise, the little guy was an incredible hockey player. Moving a rolled up piece of paper between his paws, he approached. He positioned his body sideways to the net, which in this case was the fireplace. I readied myself in the net. I had my lesche knife digging pads on to protect my knees. Raising his right paw up and straight, he shifted his weight to the back paws. Raising his eyes, he picked his spot just over my left shoulder. Knowing where he was aiming did not stop the result. His paw came aggressively forward, transferring his weight to the front paw. He struck the puck on its bottom edge and followed thru with his hundred mile an hour slap shot.

"Goal!" he yelled, small white paper ball sailing over my shoulder into the fireplace. Nearing the end of the third period, he was ahead by 51 goals. Realizing the game was out of reach, the goalie was pulled. I took a nap. It had been long day.

Chapter 17

Caterwaul Warning

In the morning, I went straight in to the living room to visit with SammyFarber. Malibu was already there.

"Lumpy," Malibu said, walking on the sleeping SammyFarber "Does he ever do anything?"

'Yes. Once he ate a pickled egg from a big jar,' I said.'

Unexpectedly, SammyFarber woke up.

He looked at Malibu and said, "Did you know a cat usually eats its own vomit? Disgusting, but convenient."

Malibu head butted him affectionately.

SammyFarber had more to say. "'I stopped by to tell you and your new squeaky toy that I will be not be around for awhile. Me, and the boys, will be out every night this week looking for garage sale donations. Got anything? He was in a playful mood, stroking Malibu who was resting on his belly.

I thought you should know where I am, Friday, just in case the lottery commission is looking to give me the big prize."

Lifting Malibu's tail, he said with a laugh, "What kind of poodle is your friend?"

Before I could answer, a screech filled the room.

'What the heck is that?' I said to Malibu, covering my ears from the screaming.

"It's a caterwaul warning. A new message is coming," he replied. "Messages are sent over the wires from cat to cat, mostly weather info. It was started by Siamese cats wanting to chat with relatives in the sacred temple of Siam in Southeast Asia. Because of the time difference, caterwaul messages are usually transmitted at 3am."

'Is it accurate?' I asked.

"Nope, never,"' he said, as if everyone knew this fact. "Dumb birds screw it up, always sitting on the wires and interfering. That's why we chase them."

'More than chase them,' I thought.

He continued, "Like last week's caterwaul posting was mice are coming. So naturally, I sharpened my claws all night," he paused, looking down proudly at his handiwork. "At 6 a.m., I realized that it was ice coming, not mice. Once I asked the caterwaul wire why snow is white?"

'I always wondered about that too,' I agreed, falling into his trap. 'How is snow white?'

Malibu looked at me and said, "Pretty good, according to the seven dwarfs."

That was the first time I realized cats were tricky. Not wanting to be outdone, I told him that it's very lucky to spit into high winds.

He smiled. "I'll go see what it is." Malibu ran over and jumped up on the windowsill and listened. I buried my head under a pillow.

'What message did you get?' I asked when he returned

"Actually, it was for both of us. It says, "May you take comfort in knowing a rainbow will connect you to your loved one someday. Our hearts are with you in this time of sorrow and loss. Remember: do what is asked of you when the time comes."

'Who are we losing?' I asked.

'I dunno. Damn bird got in the middle of the message.'

'What kind of bird,' I asked for no real reason

'Raven,' Malibu said,

'What's a raven,' I asked.

Malibu did not answer. He can hear a package of cat treats opening half a block away, but he cannot hear me in the same room. I could tell he was deep in thought about the message. What he was not telling me was that Ravens are said to predict death and pestilence (disease). Folklore has it that the raven's sense of smell is so acute that it can smell death before it comes. No one wanted to see a raven fly over a house! And, unbeknownst to me, this Raven was on the telephone wire in my backyard.

"Friday," the Director said, breaking the eerie chill in the room. "You have competition obedience tonight, class one. You can earn these by practicing before class." He opened his hand to reveal three cheesy hound round dog biscuits.

I agreed. Then again, I would agree to jump off a bridge for a cheesy hound round. When we got into the yard, the first command was wave. I have been doing this since I was a puppy. I can wave with my right or left hand, high five and clap. I did my whole paw routine insuring I got the cookie. It was delicious. I did not know that cheesy hound rounds also came in peanut butter flavour. I ate it too quickly.

'Next,' I said, eagerly looking up, guessing the command to be 'watch me'. It was not. It was, strut. Yuk! This one requires a lot of patience on my part and it is easy to screw up. You have go from a sit to prancing in a figure eight with the Director, lag behind or forge ahead and it's no cookie. To make matters worse, I cannot heel wide or crowd him on the sharp turns. I must stay focused!

On the ready command, we take off. I am tuned in to every knee movement. At the end, I know I have done well. I look up for my treat but there's nothing coming. I have missed something. Standing, I wrack my poodle brain. And then, it hits me.

He stopped at the end and I should have done the silent sit or halt as Auntie calls it. Realizing my mistake, I put my butt on the ground. He looks down, shrugged shoulders, thinking eyes are on me. I lean. He gives in. The second peanut butter round is mine. I savour it for nearly ten whole seconds. That's a new record for me.

The third and last task is a five minute down stay. During my down stay, he gets my training bag and fills it with assorted collars, leashes and this yellow plastic thing. After what seems like two hours, he returns and gives me a pat. "Good job, Friday. Exercise over," he says, walking away to load the car.

I am pissed. A great injustice has been done to me. He had showed me three cookies and I only got two. Nothing for the 5 minute down stay. The Director thinks I cannot count so it would seem reasonable to him that I would not know one cookie is missing. And, that is why he ate it. You, having some insight into the fact that I can count, although not in any logical order as far as you're concerned, might agree with his conclusion that I cannot go from 1 to 2 and then to 3.

Here is what you are missing. It is correct that I do not have the concept of three that you have. However, I am a sophisticated creature, especially when something interests me like cheesy rounds. You incorrectly assume that I would have to understand the counting concept. Simply put, I would have had to count the wave-cookie as one, the strut-cookie as two and down-stay cookie that I did not get, as three. What happened in my mind was not counting. It was a picture of the three cookies promised to me. I simply broke the picture down in my mind each time I received a treat, which left me with a picture of one cheesy hound round still missing. Not subtraction or addition. It's sensory picture formulation and adjustment, if you do not get it then that's okay. You are not a canine.

If you want proof, show your dog three cookies and then drop them in your yard. You will notice that after you dog has found the third cookie, he will stop looking or smelling. Go figure! (This will work with twelve cookies too. Get the peanut butter flavoured cheesy hound rounds.)

There are many things in your world that I do not get. The other morning the Producer stopped to admire a rainbow that was clearly visible in the western sky. We sat together. Well, to be perfectly honest, I was bored to tears. I have no concept as to why Shepherds stare at those things. One day I would learn of their great power, not today. Instead, I was looking at two piles of dog poop, one slightly higher than the other. I was wondering if the bigger pile came from a bigger dog. I can stare at poop all day. I find it far more fascinating than a rainbow. You may not. Later in life, I learned the secret of rainbows. The information filled my heart with sadness and joy. I really want to tell you about rainbows because happiness adds and multiplies, as we divide it with others. We act as though love, good treats and a warm doggy bed were the chief requirements of a happy life, when all that we need to make us really happy is something to believe in. But, you will have to wait. I got to go pee now.

Later that evening, I attended competition obedience. When we got to Auntie's place, I had fond memories of the driveway. It was where we played pass the puppy and run like a crazy dog. Maybe, just maybe, this class was going to be as much fun. At the end of the driveway, we entered the white training hall. I had made it. This was to be my finest hour.

At first glance, I was very intimidated, the only poodle in a sea of border collies and shelties. Then my confidence built. Out of the corner of my eye, I could see Ivan the stupid was in the class. And yes, he was chasing his tail.

The first exercise was sit, which is harder than you might think. I was eight feet from the Director on leash in a stand-stay position. He called and I moved forward, but not too fast. Backing up from me, he coiled the leash as I approached until he had a firm grasp of my collar. He put pressure on the collar and pulled it up slightly.

We practiced this a few times until I could approach with my head up. Next, the movement was the same except while backing up he changed direction and stopped. I sat and I felt his knee gently nudging my left side until I was sitting perfectly straight.

After a few of these, we did the same exercise, but this time it is from a recall with no leash. I looked over and the border collies were fronting perfectly. Jasper, the sheltie, was almost square to his Shepherd but he was leaning slightly to the left on the sit. His Shepherd corrected him with a tap from this long white plastic stick. I would have been in last place if not for Ivan, who was chewing on his leash, not allowing it to be coiled.

I tried again and each time I forgot to look up so I was never perfectly square to the Director. Auntie whispered something to the Director and we tried again. This time when I got to him, I smelled something above hanging out of his mouth. I could've swallowed a fly, it was the missing third peanut flavoured cheesy hound round. Head up, I sat perfectly square and the cookie was dropped into my waiting mouth. I was fronting!

The next exercise was the drop on recall, which I believe should be re-named, brain fart. In this exercise, I am supposed to come running from one end of the training hall and suddenly put on the brakes and hit the ground. I do not get it. This is what I thought. He called me and I came. While I was running, he said, "Down!" which to me meant that I am to come and when I get there, I lay down.

How in the world am I supposed to know that the second command, 'down', cancels the first command 'come'? We might as well have been playing rock/paper/scissors.

The rules of your Shepherd games do not make any sense to us. Equally so, I have found some of our canine games do not make sense to you. Let's take the canine game, got your nose. In this game, the canine jumps up and touches the Shepherd's nose with his nose. Each time the noses collide, the puppy gets a point. Five points or any other number that pops into our puppy brain, and we win. Having spoken to many canines, I have never met a single dog whose Shepherd understood this fun game. In fact, one Siberian husky told me his Shepherd was so canine confused that he kneed the husky in the chest for playing this game. Oddly enough, the Shepherd was a nice, intelligent person. Go figure? (If you do not want rowdiness and exuberant jumping, especially when young, then get a basset hound, not a husky.) Furthermore, if you do not want to play the game, then simply back away and turn when it starts. Dogs are not stupid. We understand sometimes you don't want to play. Yes, sometimes we check back later to see if you changed your mind. If you have not, back up when he jumps and turn away again. No kneeing, puh-leeze!

We try again. Same result. Then again. This time I come real slow and he does not say down. At this point, I think I have him trained. If I keep coming really, really slow on the recall it causes him not to yell, down, and I can get to him without error. Things were going well under my direction when Auntie butted in. I am at one end of the training hall and she called me. I was excited to get to her and forgot about the slow walk.

While I was running toward her the weirdest thing happened. A set of car keys came flying at me. The airborne keys landed with a loud clang a foot in front of my right paw, startling me.

"Down," she yelled and I did what any sane dog that was suddenly attracting flying keys would do, I downed.

"Good dog!" she said loudly. I had no idea what was going on. We did this a few more times. When I saw her key throwing hand go up, I hit the ground and covered my head.

Finally, the Director took over and I went back to my slow approach. At this moment, I was seriously considering turning off the lights and exiting. Equally confusing, the Director put a plastic rectangular box in my path. Like that's going to help? I was called and I jumped over it, half expecting him to yell 'wave' or 'sit' in the middle of this new technique. I do not have a lot of box jumping experience, so I slowed down before the jump to measure my distance.

I have a wider field of vision than Shepherds because my eyes are set further toward the sides of my heads. The tradeoff is that I am not adept at focusing on objects at close range or at judging distances accurately. On the next round, the Director picked up on this and told me to, "Down," when I slowed in front of the plastic box. At this point, having nothing to lose, I laid down. I had had enough of the flying keys. And, you guessed it, he yelled, "Good dog!"

I got it! The box was removed, the keys pocketed and Friday the Poodle (that's me) could drop on recall.

Now, if you are anything like me then you are wondering why anyone would want to have this skill. Here is how it was explained to me. If you call your dog from far away and then you suddenly notice that a train is coming in between you and the dog, then it is crucial that the Shepherd can stop the recall and get the dog to lay down until the train passes. My thought is this. If there is a train track between you and your dog then not calling him might be another solution.

Lastly, we did dumbbell retrieving. I am faster than most border collies. And, oddly enough, so is Ivan. My yellow dumbbell made its first appearance out of the Director's bag. It came from the supermarket style pet store and cost two dollars. Most of the other dumbbells in class were custom fitted to the dogs bite and cost upwards of two hundred dollars. We were on a wait-stay. The Shepherds threw the dumbbells and before anyone gave the go command, Ivan and I were off. We each had three dumbbells in our mouths when our Shepherds caught up with us. To make matters worse, I was not letting go of any of mine. For a moment, a very brief moment, I thought I had done well. Ivan and I were tied for first in dumbbell collection and awaited our prize. The stares from the outraged Shepherds let me know that I had not won anything. Finally, dumbbell free, we walked back to the car. (The Director was practicing his avoidance technique during the long walk.)

Over the next few weeks and more gruelling lessons, I knew I was not measuring up. I had to ferret out the secret.

Here is what I learned. On the long sit-stays some of the Shepherds, out of Auntie's earshot, were whispering the word, sit-sit-sit, to their dogs. On another exercise, I noticed one lady had a piece of chicken sticking out of her semi closed hand at the dog's eye level. No wonder he followed her perfectly thru the figure eight. What annoyed me most was that one dog who I spoke to told me that he had not eaten for two days. Sometimes, before a competition, he would be starved for almost three days. I knew this was wrong. When no one was looking, I gave him a cheesy hound round.

At this point, I thought about my great gift that was yet to be unlocked. I can tell you after having endured eight torturous weeks, plus two private lessons on dumbbell retrieving which almost ended in me getting my ear pinched, I can say, without doubt, my great gift is not competition obedience.

Chapter 18

Strike Three

The powers that be had decided that we were moving to new, smaller house. If asked, I would have suggested a yard twice as large as our postage stamp one. I was not asked. For a week, our house was invaded by cardboard boxes, small, medium and extra heavy. The Producer would take a glass, wrap it in newspaper, and put it in the medium box. And then, she would take another glass, wrap it in paper and put it in the same box. After all the glasses were wrapped, she closed the box, taped and labelled it glasses. Two hours later, she opened the box took out a glass and had a drink of water. It seemed odd to me, hiding glasses and then finding them later. I bury things that I do not want at that moment. For example, I keep a marrow bone under the couch cushion in case I have an unexpected dinner guest.

During the pre-move period, the Director tried to keep my schedule as normal as possible. I went to the dog park in the morning and light training sessions in the early afternoons.

The day of SammyFarber's yard sale had arrived. I was pleased to learn that the Director was on staff. And, even better, he hired me as his

Yard Sale Assistant, YSA. We walked down the block to SammyFarber's house. Oddly enough, I was fired on that same day. (Go figure.) The going daily rate for the YSA is three cheesy hound rounds. Meet and greet was my job description. I brought white bear to work with me. (Oh, like you do not have a stuffed bear assistant?) The Director was empty handed except for my leash. Once we were set up, the Director laid out a very simple philosophy and that was anything that could not possibly be given away, had to be sold or burned. The only exception was a pail of motor oil. Setting it on a step stool, out of my reach and white bear's, he reminded us to stay away from it. No worries. I did not like the smell of it, old and fermenting.

Waiting for our first customer, the Director taught me to weave. He showed me a really lame, little, tiny, miniscule lamb treat. Then, he took a big step with his right leg and dropped his right hand straight down. I had to go through the outstretched leg to get the treat. (Did I mention that the treat was really, really small?) He repeated the same exercise from the left side. Within minutes, I could weave in and out as he walked. I was a quick study. Realizing this, the Director made me weave ten times before he would let go of another itsy-bitsy treat. Which supports what SammyFarber had told me: Never make things look too easy to a Shepherd. Having no choice, and being who I am, I changed the game. By stopping in the middle after three or four crosses, I found that he tripped over me. Now, we were having fun! A customer interrupted us.

"Yes, that is two dollars," the Director said to a very nice older lady who gave me a tasty red lifesaver during the meet and greet. "Yes, I agree with you that it would be convenient for you if I held this broken lamp in our lay-away plan till Christmas. But, it is not our corporate policy."

I recognized the tiny lamp from my outing with Meeko and the boys. More than a little nervous, I said nothing.

The older lady was persistent so she changed tactics by offering her Visa card, claiming she wanted the points. The Director countered. "Perhaps, I could pay you cash to take it now," he said, tiring of the negotiation. He took a dollar out of the shoebox we were using as a cash register and handed it to her.

And, she actually had to think about his offer before she said. "Okay, I'll take it." First customer and we were already in the red. Our business plan was flawed. No one consulted me, even if I was catching onto this business stuff quite quickly.

Desperate, I expanded my job description to include marketing before he sunk the family business. The price tag was $2 for the electric can opener. I suggested that we call it a deluxe cat caller and charge five bucks. Like most employees' suggestions, mine was ignored. Did you ever notice that no one is listening until you fart? But, I did not give up. One nice older gentleman picked up an old throw pillow, quickly setting it down. Springing into action, being a super salesman, I picked it up and pushed it at him. Putting it back for the fourth time, he looked at me and said, "Okay, Mr. Pushy, I'll take it."

Another dollar added to the shoebox. Sales were booming! From then on, I always had a feature item in my mouth that I would showcase to potential buyers. One gentleman had a Springer spaniel with him. I zeroed in on the dog.

'Yes, this is a great bone,' I said, dropping a used, tasteless rubber bone at his feet. 'Lasts forever and tastes like peanut butter.' (I felt bad about what I was doing. But, SammyFarber's family needed the cash. This rubber bone has little rubber nubs on it that can come off. Rubber nubs are not digestible.) 'It's delicious. Real peanuts!' I was eager to seal the deal.

The spaniel picked it up and just like that it was in a box his Shepherd was carrying. I am new to garage sales, but my poodle senses were in high gear with this guy. He put a few expensive items in the bottom of the box and covered them with cheap stuff like the rubber chew bone. "Is ten bucks okay for this?" he asked, showing it to the Director.

"Make it fifteen," the Director said, without looking in the box.

"Done," he said, paying fifteen dollars and exiting with fifty dollars worth of stuff.

Business was what you would expect given our poor location. A bigger yard and better signage would have generated more sales. I continued with my 'meet and greet' when I noticed out of the corner of my eye a young male child.

"Mommy, mommy I want this," he said, holding up my stuffed white bear assistant.

I panicked. 'What the bleep do you think you are bleeping doing?' I said rushing over to him. Having learned a thing or two after the snowman adventure, I decided not to go for the jugular. Instead, I weaved between his legs and stopped, causing him to topple over and release white bear.

"Waa, waa," he cried. His mother lifted him up. Oddly enough, I felt slightly airborne myself. The next thing I remember was that I was face to face with the fuming Director.

"What are you doing?" he asked. And then he turned to the child's mother and said, "I am very sorry. I am sure it was an accident."

Turning back to me, he said, "Wasn't it, Friday?"

I said, 'Don't you know it is bad management style to micromanage your employees?' He did not answer. Wanting to be put back on the ground, I remained quiet. The nice lady said her boy was fine. When she was gone, free cat collar in hand, the Director set me down. But, not before he told me that it was strike two for me and I better smarten up. I gave him my 'you will be hearing from my union rep' look, which caused him to turn back and say, "And, yes I know about the red candy. No food from strangers." For Shepherd eyes, he certainly saw a lot. I was determined not to have more strikes called.

After three hours, and earning less than five hundred dollars, he was done bartering. Any offer was accepted. He even let one old guy take a toaster home for a test drive. But, when it came to me he was very protective. Every third person asked how much for the doggie. I was flattered.

The Director had an answer ready each time. "I would sell him but we are using him as a down payment on our new house?" or "I would, but then who would mow the lawn?" Sometimes, he would say that he could not put a price on such a perfect beagle. When they told him I'm a standard poodle then he would act all surprised. He'd tell them that he should have known better than to buy a dog from the trunk of a car. "I bet he can't really make chili either," he would say in a serious tone.

I amused myself by guessing people's occupation by the way they were dressed. Most of the older people, who winter in Florida, were pot and pan salespeople except one who was obviously a crocodile wrangler. We had three fortune cookie writers, a juggler, and, of course, more UPS drivers than I cared to count.

Bouncing, as if on springs, a dark reddish-apricot female poodle entered our showroom. Her untrained Shepherd was twenty feet back, attached to a flexi lead.

"I had to see your poodle. Standard poodles are the best dogs ever made," the Shepherd said without taking a breath. "Poodles are God's creature of choice. You know? I do not know why anyone would want to spoil a perfect animal and turn them into a labradoodle. It should be illegal. Lexi, my standard poodle, is the most beautiful standard poodle ever. Yours is okay, sort of!"

At this point, I want to share with you my Shepherd family history. The Director, having researched a number of breed choices, decided on a jet black German Shepherd dog. Generally speaking, there are only two kinds of human Shepherds. 'Questers', who want a particular breed and 'Doggers', those who want a dog. Of course, it goes without saying that both types want to have a happy, healthy dog to share their lives with.

Breed specific Questers, like the Director, want a specific size, temperament, and work ethic in their purebred. He was on a quest to find a dog's centre point from which a dog's view on life emanates. In this quest, he wants his dog to reach its fullest potential. The Director will tell you that every dog is purebred. By this he means, you can look at any dog and determine what the majority breed is, thereby understanding the dog's role in life. By identifying that 35% or more of the dog is a Rottweiler then he would say you have a guard dog. 35% Terrier and you have a vermin hunter, 35% Bichon frise and you have a companion dog and on and on it goes. He becomes visibly upset with Shepherds who say they have a mutt, or even worse a Heinz 57 dog. Because, he believes, they are not taking the time to understand their dog's innateness. At the dog park, one gentleman bragged repeatedly that his dog was a rescue. The Director said there is no such thing as a rescue breed. What you have there is 35% Belgian Tervuren. You have a herder-guard dog. Stop forcing him to retrieve.

Questers like the Director are more than a little strange. They would never look at another Shepherd and comment on personality traits according to ethnic origin. To them, this would be absurd. However, in the dog world, they believe their point of view is correct. You can find them reading dog food labels or at dog shows. Questers are attracted to shiny things like dog trophies, obedience medals and cans of gluten free dog food.

On the other side of the dog bone is the Producer or Doggers as I call them. To her, it does not really matter what I am. She loves dogs. The Producer will tell you about the time I bit the head off a snowman or when I calmed a crying child. You will never hear a Dogger talk about bloodlines or breeding traits. If you want to find a Dogger, they too can be found in the dog food store. However, unlike the Questers reading labels, the Doggers are picking out fancy coloured collars. When I go to the dog store with the Producer, we bounce every ball to see which ones bounce higher. Did you know orange and blue ones bounce the highest? It is so much more fun than going with the Director.

Here's a little quiz I prepared for you. (What? You thought you would read a whole book and there would be no test?). Read the statement and then using your I Love Poodles pen, mark down who was talking to whom at the time.

21 - Enough label reading already. Real Dogs don't eat anything that makes its own gravy. Get the cheesy hound rounds and let's go. My radio show is on soon.

7- Yes, it is lovely, but could he try the dark blue one on again, please.

5 - Don't get your panties in a knot. I need seventeen hours of sleep. Deal with it.

If you answered, Me talking to the Director, Producer talking to sales clerk and SammyFarber talking to everyone then you win. Go and help yourself to a cheesy hound round.

Now you are probably wondering how we went from jet black German Shepherd to a standard poodle. The answer is simple. The Director has a twin sister who I call, Twin. She lives in Colorado with her firefighter husband who I call, Captain Fire. They have two standard poodles, Mikeleah and Finnegan, my cousins. One year, Twin and Captain Fire come to our house and fix everything the Director has broke. Twin makes everything look beautiful while Captain Fire makes everything work. I have so much fun playing with them. Anyway, Twin told the Director and the Producer how much they loved their standard poodles and that is how I came to live in Winnipeg. I love Twin and Captain Fire.

Sorry, sometimes I ramble, back to the yard sale. As you know, SammyFarber's Shepherd mom was very old and not very good with money, which in this case turned out to be a good thing, a very good thing.

How much for these?" an elderly well-dressed man asked. Before the Director could answer, the fidgety man said. "I will give you four hundred dollars. Not a penny over."

The Director turned to face the windfall. In the man's hands were the vintage metal dome 1968 Snoopy Lunch box and Elvis' Christmas Album LP. The Director was stunned. He quickly realized that SammyFarber's mom, having no idea of the value, had meant to label the items three dollars and fifty cents for the album and one dollar and fifty cents for the vintage lunch box. However, she had left out the decimals, which made the two items five hundred dollars instead of five.

'Sold,' I said hearing the offer price of four hundred dollars. Yes, even with YSA status, I was ignored. 'Worth Every Penny!' I added.

The hesitation of the Director was wrongly assumed by the potential buyer to be a negotiation tactic. The buyer responded with "four hundred and fifty dollars and you throw in the that fire extinguisher. I need it for my cabin way up north. Deal or no deal?"

If the Director was light grey before, he was now zombie white. I recognized that dreaded red fire extinguisher as if it was yesterday. It had been the focus of many a sleepless night for me. The other two items looked vaguely familiar as well. There were only three possibilities. The Director had brought over all three items with the twofold goal of helping out SammyFarber's Shepherd's yard sale and disposing of the dreaded murder weapon. Or secondly, Meeko and his gang had been in our garage again. Possibly, during my visit to SammyFarber's house where I terrorized the snowman, I had brought the three items in the gym bag with me for the sale. If not A, then B or C. Rather than cast the shadow of blame on others, I decided that I had done it. How else could they have logically gotten there? Yup, it was me. I could live with that decision. Having no evidence, the Police would free the Director of all charges. He did not tamper with anything. I did. Case solved. I nudged the Director's leg, trying to get him out of his trance.

Putting the items down on the table the buyer looked up one last time. I knew the deal was going south. 'Let me talk to my Director about what we can do! I offered to deaf ears.' All my efforts were to be in vain, if that fire extinguisher did not disappear. 'What can I do to put that fire extinguisher in your cabin today,' I asked? 'Wait, there's more. It is the one kitchen appliance you'll wonder how you ever did without! It slices, it dices, and so much more!' I rambled on. Nothing was working?

The Director needed to step up to the plate. I was running out of sales lines I had learned on the radio. Shopping with the Producer, I had a lot of experience with buyer remorse. She would pick out a green collar for me. Take it to the cash register, then backtrack to get a red one. This process would happen three or four times, switching from green to red then back to green over to yellow and more. Finally, I would leave the store with nothing at all. I knew if the Director did not act fast the sale would slip away.'

Finally, the Director opened his mouth. But, no words came out. He tried again. "Does this purchase bring you joy?" The man hesitated then broke out into a big smile.

Nothing sucks more than the moment during a sales presentation when I realize my approach was wide of the mark. However, the Director's sale pitch impressed me. In fact, it made mine look a little cheesy.

"Sold," the buyer said, forking over four hundred and fifty dollars. Our running total had skyrocketed to the one thousand dollar mark. Things were looking up. I loved the Director so much for the choice he made. The case of the red fire extinguisher was over. You probably recall that puppies make a lot of wrong decisions. This was one of them. As I was to find out later, the case was far from over.

Back to work. I was listening to this lady go on and on about how wonderful her apricot standard poodle was when she said something that peeked my large, floppy orange ears. The word was, Cantope. I moved closer. She and Director exchanged information, Watson, Reba, Diane and Peter were all mentioned and then it clicked.

The apricot poodle who was looking over at a broken bicycle that the Director claimed got very good gas mileage on the highway, smelt familiar to me. Wanting to test my theory, before acting inappropriately, I called out. 'Hey, number 3?'

Turning to face me, she said that no one had called her number 3 for a very long time. Her perfectly groomed body, beaming in the afternoon sunlight, was perpendicular to me. I charged. Ramming my head into her exposed chest, T-boned, she fell over on her side. Still not done, I bumped the step stool, causing the grease pail to fall on her perfectly coiffed hairdo.

'Paybacks a bitch, ain't it number 3,' I said. 'It's me, onety-one, the one you would not let have any of mom's milk. You selfish bitch!' Not having enough of mom's puppy milk almost killed me. You shithead."

And, you guessed it! Strike three. I was fired without pay.

I spent the rest of the afternoon with the Producer packing and unpacking stuff. This Obsessive-compulsive disorder (OCD) is an anxiety disorder characterized by intrusive thoughts that produce uneasiness, apprehension or worry; by repetitive behaviours aimed at reducing the associated anxiety; or by a combination of such obsessions and compulsions. According to talk radio, this is very common in people who have CJD. Symptoms of the disorder, for the Producer, included excessive hand washing; shoes on then shoes off, repeated and opening and closing a door a certain number of times before entering or leaving a room and more. Now, she was taking the glasses out of the packing box for the fourth time. It was very hard to watch. I so scared for her. I loved her deeply.

Most evenings, I passed the time listening to the radio or playing pirate with Malibu.

In the morning, the tension in the air was thick. From my viewpoint, the only time I moved, it was Cantope to Winnipeg and that was spooky enough for me to want to stay put forever. My canine senses told me that we were relocating but I didn't know where? When the moving men came, Malibu and I were locked in the basement. The men working above smelled of nicotine, coffee and glazed donuts in the morning and baloney sandwiches with mayo on white bread in the afternoon. I did not trust them with my stuff. Malibu was concerned they would sail off on his pirate ship.

When they left, the only smell that remained was SammyFarber's sofa. Everything else was gone. Malibu suggested that they were probably waiting till SammyFarber was home before the sofa was moved with him on it. I agreed. Finally, the moving men came back and took it. Now, Malibu and I were alone in the house basement with only our two crates. I looked in mine and luckily white bear was safe. I told him what was happening and not to worry. I think he read the discomfort on my face.

At that moment, it occurred to me that the three of us had been left behind. Forever!! I was so scared. Quickly, I made a plan. Somehow, I would travel to all the dog parks till I found Meeko, Silent Bob and Lefty. From them, I would get the directions I needed to make our way to Little Mountain Park where we could hide.

You may be thinking that having been to Little Mountain Park before, I could find the way or at least hire a bloodhound to lead me. Here's the problem. In tracking, I follow the tracks that I made on a previous journey. Nose to the ground, moving from one paw print to the next. Not a good plan when you consider I went there by car.

In trailing, which is more common amongst my breed and other non-tracking breeds, I follow nose high scents left behind by the skin of the animal or person I am trailing. Trailing, although efficient, can be very difficult if too much time has passed or the winds are too strong (like today). The only options left to me were either air scenting (land marking) which, is what I use primarily to find my way home from SammyFarber's garage or the obvious, get a good travel agent. Hence, I decided to find Lefty and ask him the best route.

The trip would be hardest on Malibu. He was not familiar with the ways of outside world. I asked him to get a weather report from the Caterwaul wire before we journeyed out. He agreed. While we waited, I pelted him with questions.

Why does a cat always sit on whatever you're trying to read? Do you add roughage to human's food by shedding cat hair on it? Is everything not nailed down a cat toy? Have you ever been mistaken for a meat loaf?' Of course, he ignored me. Cats do that.

Without telling him why, I asked him if he could jump up to the high window ledge that was allowing the cool breeze to waft in. He said with a good, white, bouncy springboard he could do it.

'Springboard?' I asked.

He did not reply. He just stared at me with those piercing blue eyes.

Why am I always the last one to figure anything out? Of course, the springboard was going to be me.

Within fifteen minutes we had our Caterwaul report: Hot tamale winds and chili tomorrow. I figured we better leave soon before it got too spicy outside. Malibu was tough for a kitten. If necessary, he could ride on my back while I teeth carried white bear to our new home in the park, certain 99 would welcome us.

Had I have gotten the Director's memo then I would have stayed put. It said: "Once he and the Producer had everything settled in the home, we were to travel by dog crate and cat carrier." The Director's idea was that the crates would serve as a familiar "home base" or "safe zone" that would help us cope with our arrival in a new home, with its unfamiliar sights, sounds and smells. With the move in complete, the carrier and dog crate would be placed in a quiet room. He would then open the door to the crate and carrier allowing us to explore the safe room at our own pace. Our meals would be served in this room, by the Producer until Malibu, white bear and I had adjusted to the move. Once comfortable, we would be allowed to gradually start to explore the rest of the home. For me, this process was expected to take a matter of hours, whereas for Malibu and white bear it would probably take a few days before they started feeling comfortable.

Of course, I knew nothing of this plan so I put mine into action.

I positioned myself a few feet from the window, balancing my weight. Running at full speed, Malibu jumped on my back and sprung toward the window. At the point of contact, I pushed up hard as I could. His sharp nails dug in for a second and then released with my arching back. Looking up, I saw him sitting comfortably in the open window. Standing on his back paws, he used his front paws and head to push the open window up a little higher. I hoped it was high enough. I nosed his crate toward the window. It was smaller and lighter than mine. Job done, I nosed my crate halfway between his crate and the window ledge creating steps. Now, all I had to do was run as fast as I could, leap onto his crate, then mine, springboarding out the open window. At least, that is what I thought would happen. Sometimes, I think too much.

Let's consider the cinnamon bun on the table. This is a true to life thinking example. There were three cinnamon buns on the kitchen table. The Director ate one and the Producer another. As you know, I reason if not A then B. Hence, it was logical for me to think that if the Director saw a bun was missing and he, being A, did not eat it, then the Producer, being B, must have eaten it. I reasoned this to be the same thought process the Producer would have. Specifically, if she didn't eat it herself then it had to be him.

Now, do not get ahead of me here. Of course, I ate the third bun. Wouldn't you have, given the premise? But my point, which I was not able to explain to either of them, was not who ate the third cinnamon bun but that I was able to think. To this day, had I not had any cinnamon glaze stuck to my ear, I think I would have gotten away with it.

Lastly, consider the concept of my tail. You may know that a straight up and down tail wag is a warning as opposed to side-to-side tail wag, which is a friendly greeting or approval. We wag hello. For this to happen, our minds must be more than a jelly donut. Dogs think!

It was go time. I ran faster than I have ever run before and I leaped for the stars. My back legs landing on Malibu's crate propelled me forward where my front paws hit my crate and added to my upward journey. My calculations were off, as discussed earlier I am not good with depth perception, so my head banged into the top of the window.

Luckily, my fat ass went through the opening first. Dazed, I was on firm ground outside the house. Releasing the squeaking white bear from my mouth, I took a deep breath of fresh air. When my head cleared, I looked around for Malibu. He was missing. Then, I looked up to see his smiling face nestled in the Producer's arms. The Director looked at me and said, "I do not want to know." I waited while he got the crates in the car and then all of us proceeded with his plan. My head was pounding.

Later that evening, Malibu and I explored. Tired, white bear remained in the crate.

Malibu was very happy to see his pirate ship anchored in the living room. With the exception of being half as large as our previous home, it was very similar with two notable exceptions. We had two pools. The outside one, rather large, was covered with a black tarp. And, the much smaller one inside had rocks, plants and two goldfish swimming in it. I was very excited. Pressing my ear to the tank, I waited and listened. Finally, the age-old question that great minds want to know would be answered? But alas, it was not to be. The Director, like clockwork, pulled me away from the tank.

"Friday, please don't do that. Okay?" he said, tired from unpacking.

When the Director left, Malibu was pressed up against the fish tank glass, scratching at anything that moved. Unable to contain my excitement, I asked him. Do you hear anything? Can they bark?'

Squinting his Siamese eyes, he said, "Yes". And then he added, "'I did hear something, now that you ask."

'What, what? Was it a bark?' I asked.

"No," he said. "Two of the fish were swimming when suddenly they crashed into that big rock. And then, one turned to the other and said, 'Dam!'"

'Not funny,' I said. 'Not funny at all.' Before lying down to nap, I told him that his pirate ship was sinking, which sent him racing into the living room.

Chapter 19

Mira

At one end of the spectrum are the wolves that mate for life. At the other end, sponges who do not mate I am exactly halfway between a wolf and sponge in my mating habits. My current heartthrob is a tan and black German Shepherd mix. I passed her on a walk one day. A dog knows he's in love when he loses interest in peeing on trees. I think that is also true of old people. The Shepherds took me to the Assiniboine Forest, which they referred to as The Woods. With the exception of the missing poodle layer, the smells mirrored Cantope. Signage at the entrance, noted that dogs must remain on leash at all times. Ten seconds into the woods, the Producer unleashed me. Perhaps, I had read the sign wrong.

After walking through carved paths for about an hour, we came upon of all things, more signage, this one a reflective yellow sign with a black deer prancing in the middle. The words CAREFUL DEER CROSSING were underneath. Believe it or not, there was not one, but four deer waiting to cross, supporting my theory that deer can read. (I am not implying they are reading classic novels, that would be foolish, just the magazines in the Safeway checkout line.)

The huge buck lead the way, loping out of the overgrown clear cut field into the flooded glade, exploding the icy water into sheets of spray as it pounded through the ice layer. (Just so you know, I heard that description on the Nature Channel. There was no overgrown field, flooded glade or icy water. I do not even know what a glade is but it sounded cool. We authors like to take liberties sometimes.)

Anyway, there was a small dirt hill. From the top, I watched nervously as the whitetail buck bounded straight for a densely treed area, its huge rack swaying from side to side. Following behind him, were a doe and two small fawns. And then, Miss tan and black was barking vigorously. The massive antlers of the lead buck disappeared into the woods.

I noticed, even when chased, deer rarely run at top speed for long. This grouping maintained a good lead in front of the object of my affection, by simply loping through the woods, stopping frequently to listen and scan for alarming scents. Miss 'tan and black' finally gave up the chase, returning to where I was, love at first sight (for me not her).

Having been at the groomer's the day before, I was concerned about my own aroma. Winnipeg winters are cold and dry. I had been bathed in Comfy Cosy Doggie shampoo that contains colloidal oatmeal and botanical extracts of peppermint, burdock and comfrey. Although lovely smelling to the Producer, I feared it might not have the same effect on my canine love interest. At this juncture in my life, my legs were shaved, leaving bracelets on the hind legs and puffs on the forelegs. The entire shaven foot and a portion of the shaven foreleg above the puff are visible. The rest of my body was left in full coat, shaped to insure overall balance. A pompom on the end of the tail bobbed when I walked. I was a neon sign shouting, GQ not alpha male dog.

Not having any options, I approached. She smelled and looked great!

'What's your secret,' I asked, sniffing her entire body.

'Before I hunt, I roll around in decaying feces from herbivores, and other nasty smelling things that are natural in the wild. (Wolves came up with this plan.) This masks my own scent so I hunt prey with much more ease. If, let's say a deer, is standing there munching on some vegetation, it's going to be smelling the air with its powerful nose to alert it if anything that wants to eat it is around. Now, if I smell like a rotting carcass, or like deer poop then I am able to sneak up on the deer much better. This ensures a higher chance of making the hunt a success. Unlike you who smell more like a fresh baked oatmeal raisin cookie. Just sayin.'

Sigh. I like them smart, don't I?

'You kill them?' I asked.

'No, I am a city dog. But when I come to the woods, I like to revert back to my canine instincts.'

'Where do you train?' Trying to find common ground, I listed my schooling, Competition Obedience, Adult Obedience, or Canine Good Citizen?

'McDonalds and Wendy's drive thru,' she said, scratching her chubby gut. 'Do you really think being able to do a five minute sit-stay would help me catch a deer?'

She was right. Given her career path, Competition Obedience may not be the best choice. 'Ever catch one?'

'Most days, I don't. They stay well ahead of me, allowing an opportunity to plan their escape. Wise bucks are well known for jumping over fences, running through thick brush, swimming sloughs and doubling back in order to lose me or throw me onto another track. I have to stay alert. Some days, a badly wounded deer can be caught and I invariably bay it, rather than attack. I get enough protein in my diet from burgers.'

We had so much in common. Given the choice of killing a meal in the wild or going to Costco, a poodle will always pick Costco samples.

She continued. 'My Shepherd takes the wounded deer to a wild life preserve not far from here. They fix it up and return it to the woods. Then we go to the Drive Thru on the way home. I have the quarter pounder with fries. Most window people know me by first name.'

'And that is?' I asked.

'Mirzam. Or, Mira as I am called. I was named after the "greater dog" constellation that follows the hunter Orion in Greek myth. The constellation is depicted as a dog standing on its hind legs, pursuing a deer. One of the stars that make up the greater dog is Mirzam. Hence, I am Mira. And you?'

'Friday Poodle is my name. Poodles are very rare and expensive in Japan. So, people were shaving sheep to look like poodles and selling them as poodles. To stop this practice the Japanese government insisted that all real poodles, the ones that barked instead of baaing, were called "Fridays". And, that is how I got my name.

'Really? Is that so? I notice that you never let facts interrupt the flow of your conversation.' she said.

Of all the brainless things I have made up in my life that was by far the dumbest. Love can do that to a guy.

From my point of view, things were going along nicely. She would chase me and then I would chase her. The first thing I look for in a dog is not good looks, although that is certainly a bonus. I look for matched energy. Mira and I were a perfect match, similar in size and age. I do not know why some dogs like other dogs. But, I can tell a large part of my attraction to Mira came from watching her compete with the deer.

A dog's prey drive isn't something they can turn on and off. It's hardwired into them and it's one reason why canines are good at doing specific jobs. German Shepherds require daily physical activity to burn off excess energy and maintain a stable and healthy mind. A bored dog with high energy like Mira can dismantle a living room in just a few hours when left alone with nothing to do. Her behaviour isn't her fault if she doesn't get proper exercise. If you don't enjoy going for long walks or finding a dog sport your dog can participate in, a canine with a high prey drive or herding gene will not be a good choice.

Off leash and free from the Shepherds' watchful eyes I had a chance to unburden my soul with Mira. After listening to my story of the Director and fire extinguisher she asked.

'Was the death harmful or helpful to the guy in the car?'

'Helpful, I think,'

'That is good,' she said. 'My advice to you Friday Poodle, is to let sleeping dogs lie if you know what I mean. Is there something else bothering you?'

'Like what?' I asked. Not sure if I should say too much.

'Well, your female Sheppard is dying. Does that concern you?'

'Huh? What?' I said trying to act surprised at the news.

'When I smell her, I am not just registering a smell. I get an entire story because I can smell pheromone, which is not only found in the urine and feces, but on the skin. From this I can tell a lot about your Shepherd, including she is female, what she ate, where she has been and more. Did you know she had a cupcake for breakfast? And, this disease is a type of cancer. But, it may not be fatal.'

'Wow! You know a lot about this?'

"Yup, been there, done that. Lost my Shepherd to breast cancer last year?

'Is there anything I can do?' I asked.

You have to consider if your actions will be regrettable or admirable before you do anything. It is not like the canine world where we end the suffering of other canines without remorse. This is not their way. You will know what is the right decision when the time comes. Their world is different from ours.

'Mira, you are the girl of dreams. Thank you.'

She smiled.

A rustle in the bush revealed Uncle Tom. He was a very old deer. No single factor can be used to conclusively judge the age of a deer in The Woods. However, as you can clearly see by looking at the detailed drawing at bottom of the next page, he was old. (Right there! Bottom of the next page in the right corner!)

Made you look! Ha-ha! Made you look! Of course, I cannot draw an old deer. At best, I can draw a two-legged stick dog facing east next to a square house with spiral smoke coming out of the roof chimney.

Uncle Tom's teeth were worn, his antler and body had deteriorated. The loss of muscle tone was an indicator of his old age. His head had loose skin, and his eyes were squinty, like the other mature bucks on the Nature Channel. His rump did not appear rounded anymore. I've noticed also that just like old Shepherds tend to get grey hair, an old buck tends to look lighter in color than the deer who passed by earlier. His left leg had a heart shaped scar on it and the hoof was abnormally large.

'Pardon me, mind if I play thru,' Uncle Tom said to no one in particular.

'Who's that?' I asked Mira.

'An old deer, been to reserve three times for his leg. The lights are on but someone's been playing with the dimmer switch,' Mira said.

I was scared. I knew how tiring it could be to turn the lights on and off.

Sensing my discomfort, the Director said, "Not to worry it is a friendly deer".

"Like Bambi," the Producer added.

I had no idea who Bambi was.

Oddly enough, Mira stood in front of me, blocking Uncle Tom's path to me, should he decide to charge. Hmm, Mira liked me?

A standard poodle never pretends what they perceive to be a dangerous situation as safe. Having said that, I might act like I am not scared. This is not the same thing. Acting like you are not scared is what SammyFarber taught me about avoidance. From a safe distance back, I avoided Uncle Tom. Speaking two languages caused a problem for me. Although the Shepherds said he was friendly, my brain was still picking up a picture of this very large animal with sharp antlers. My canine language of pictures will always overshadow your English language of words when safety is an issue. Mira knew I was anxious.

Uncle Tom looked at me and said, 'Based on your haircut, am I to assume it is tourist season in the woods?'

This was the first time I looked at the world from an old deer's point of view.

He continued. 'Given the shape of your poodle mouth, even if you could speak, you could not sing Sly Sam Slurps Sally's Soup.'

``Time to go," the Director said. I would like to have learned more from Uncle Tom.

Over the next few days, I considered what had happened in The Woods.

Poodles suffer from confirmation bias. Our brains are wired to see correlations as causes. Not unlike when a Shepherd picks up a leash, then I can expect, with reasonable certainty that I am going for a walk.

The downside of having a built in confirmation bias is that it I am what you might call superstitious. Once, when we were in the car, I looked out the widow closest to me. Unrelated to my window glance, a car cut us off which caused the Director to shout and use hand signals at the other driver. Incorrectly, I assumed that looking out the closest window of the car caused other cars to cut us off. So, being superstitious, I only look out the window furthest away.

I am not an intact male hence I cannot have puppies. Which is a good thing, because if immune-mediated thrombocytopenia was hereditary, then I would not want to pass it on. And, there are lots of puppies to adopt in the world already.

Yes, I ramble. Get over it. Sometimes, I ramble when I do not want to face life facts. Mira had told me that someday I would have to make a major decision. This fact, which would come to fruition, worried me more than I can express.

Chapter 20

Ping

On most engines, the spark occurs a few degrees before the piston reaches top dead centre. If the spark occurs too soon (over advanced timing), cylinder pressures rise too quickly and peak too early in the cycle resulting in a loss of power. This can cause engine damaging "detonation" (spark knock or ping) to occur.

The truck entering our driveway was pinging. I have absolutely no idea how to fix that. But, 1-800-cartalk did a whole show on pinging. Having listened with white bear, I consider myself an expert on pinging sounds. There will be more about this pinging truck so keep it in mind.

Normally, I bark at registered letters delivered to the mailbox by pinging trucks. Why? Cause I'm a dog and that is what I do. However, I was very stressed out. Too frazzled to bark. I tried to calm myself.

The Director had noticed two of my calming clues, belly down and tail wag. You would probably think at this time that I would be overjoyed, although he missed eighteen clues, he was finally starting to speak canine. However, I was more nervous than overjoyed. The Director is not capable of small changes; think of him as a boing-a, boing-a

Springer spaniel not as a Saint Bernard. By the way, the Monks of the St. Bernard Hospice deny that any St. Bernard has ever carried casks or small barrels around their necks; they believe that the origin of the image is an early painting. I didn't know St Bernard dogs could paint.

A big change was coming to our household. I am a perceptive creature and therefore highly sensitive to the emotionally charged atmosphere around me, and the subliminal clues being sent out. Here's the problem. The Director wants to take the lead in calming me. He goes into training mode. Oh, yuck! Not now.

Do you see his problem? He does not want me stressed. There is enough stress in his life already. Here's the solution the Director proposed to me.

"I have been committing a fundamental error in our relationship. I now believe having watched you try and calm yourself, that the ranking of animals is not only unnecessary, it is limiting. Naturalists call the dominant leader of a pack of dogs the alpha male. This causes most Shepherds and some dog trainers who encourage them, to always act the role of the alpha male. I believed my role to be alpha at all times until now. The theory is that for the dog to live in harmony with their Shepherd there has to be a clearly defined pecking order whereby the lower ranking, that's you, submits to the will of the higher order member. That's me. For our relationship to grow, we need to redefine our roles, when appropriate, as a partnership and leave the pecking to chickens. Do you see value in testing my idea?"

'Yes,' I lied. From my canine perceptive, I do not see the value of ideas. I only see the value of things I can smell and touch. 'In support of your partnership theory, I am willing to put it to the test. Get a box of cheesy hound rounds out of the cupboard and divide it into equal portions. You eat half and I will eat half while we work out the details. Okay partner?'

Ignoring me, he continued. "Some dogs are less pack orientated than others. Although they stay with the crowd, I do not think that is necessarily pack mentality. For example, a golden retriever will leave the security of his pack to chase a tennis ball. And, you are not fooling anyone. You will go with anyone, anytime, anywhere provided they have an abundant cheesy hound round supply. I am not suggesting that the simplistic view of let the dog be a dog will work either. I have never met anyone who claims to follow this belief actually letting it happen. If you roll around in poop and think you are going to enter the house then you are sadly mistaken. Do not even consider car chasing, thunder anxiety, social anxiety, shedding or any other so called being a dog activity. People, especially those with the let the dog be a dog mentality, always put their lifestyle interests first. And, that is okay. I would not put you in charge of the cheesy hound rounds. I am in no way suggesting that you are the new pack Alpha. However, in this situation, I need to partner with you."

And with that, he redefined our partnership. I decided that I would wait and see how things developed under this new relationship before commenting further.

Many dog owners fervently believe that their pooch has this capacity for guilt. This is based on experiences where they have come home, found their dog with its head down, ears pulled back, tailed tucked between its legs. The dog then runs and hides under the bed. The owner finds the garbage strewn throughout the kitchen or new red pumps chewed beyond repair. The implication is clear, the dog did the dastardly deed and he is feeling guilty about his actions. The truth is that 999,999 out of 1 million dogs do not feel guilt. (The exception is SammyFarber.)

Here is what is really going on. The right side of the Shepherd face more clearly expresses emotion. The left side of the Shepherd face is more devoid of emotion. All canines focus on the emotional side of the Shepherd's face when the Shepherd enters the room. This emotional side gaze bias is significant because dogs exhibit this tendency only when looking at Shepherd's faces. We are examining the more emotionally rich side of the face for clues that are suggestive of the Shepherd's mood or emotion. We have an enormous capacity for detail. Once we have a clear read, then we react. If you were not emotionally charged by seeing the destruction then we would not react in the manner that you refer to as guilt.

It was training time again. The Director reminded me of our partnership deal before we went outside.

For the next hour, the Director threw the ball and I retrieved. Each time I would return the ball to the Director's feet. No release command required. I love playing ball especially when I can jump high and catch it before it lands. It is my most favourite activity in the whole world. The single most important thing to learn about our world perspective, is to understand that we see details. I love the way the ball bounces and spins. I do not expect you to understand. Simply throw the ball often. Happiness, from playing catch, is not something you experience, it is something you remember all your life.

I have a raised metal dish that sits in a metal stand at nose height. The Director believes that a raised food dish can prevent dog bloat (or volvulus), and mega-esophagus, which is a condition when the food accumulates in the esophagus instead of descending to the stomach. This is more common in large dogs that bolt down their food. The Producer agrees to this bowl for a different reason: keeping Malibu's cat hair out.

I am a quick eater, sometimes too quick. Canines think that when a floor changes color then the dark spots are deeper than the lighter spots. This happens because in the outside world depth changes are often associated with color changes. Our eye structure adds to the problem. Every time the shiny metal dish that holds my food jiggles then the outside light streaming in would osculate and dance on the sides. A reflecting bright surface is scary to canines. I mean I still eat. Gimme a break here, I like food. With my snack finished, The Woods were our next destination. I was anxious to see Mira.

A little while later, and no Mira, we came across a Dalmatian mix that was less than friendly. Dalmatians are very protective dogs and can be aggressive towards other dogs if not properly trained. I could see in the dog's lips, he was readying for the attack.

The Dalmatian inched forward, lowering his back and flattening his ears.

At this point, I had no choice but to offer canine wisdom. I looked the Dalmatian in the eye and explained as calmly as I could. 'Why don't you go to the other side of the woods and play, hide and go f**k yourself?'

He growled.

'Don't piss me off today,' I replied, threatening tone in my voice. 'If you come at me, I will not consider that deep down you are a good dog. Dalmatians when properly exercised and trained are loving, sensitive animals. I will have only one thought on my mind and that is I'm running out of places to hide the bodies. Am I making myself clear?' I showed him my pearly white teeth.

'Yes,' he said, deciding that flee was a better option. At that moment, I was glad that SammyFarber had taught me to trash talk. We would have been in big trouble if he did not buy my act. I do not know how to fight.

At first, I did not recognize the Putz the Wheaton in The Woods. He seemed larger than I remembered. True to form, he wanted to fight. Stressed out, I had more than enough aggression in me to pound the snot out of him. Enough is enough, I thought. Good fighter or not, it was time to drop the leashes. I circled, watching for his exposed jugular. Body lowered, hackles raised, pupils dilated, I pulled my lips back ready to attack. Yes, I was scared. But battle lines were drawn in the dirt. I was pumped. Before you start to worry about me, I think you should know that many dogs bite stronger than others not because they have greater physical power, but because they do so with more will and determination. I was single-minded in my goal to see his head mounted on my den wall!

Suddenly, I was airborne. Argggh, not now! Tagging in, the Director had lifted me by the collar. Of all the times I wanted him to be able to read my body language, this was not one of them. I would have been happier if he had joined me at the taxidermist, picking out the right plaque for the Putz's head. I would have whupped that Putz's dumb ass.

This partnership thing was not working out.

You might jump to the conclusion that there is a lesson to learn by letting a dog fight. Regardless of what your dog is afraid of, or why he is afraid, resist any advice or temptation to force your dog to 'face' its fears (this is called flooding). Your dog will sink. If your dog has anxiety take him for a run not a brawl.

Another day in The Woods had ended. At our next partnership meeting, I would have to talk to the Director about merits of watching the wrestling channel.

Chapter 21

Table for One Please

The problem with smart dogs, really smart dogs, is that they very quickly figure out what behaviour brings them the reward they want. Having seen my performance at most classes, you already know that I am, at best, in the middle of the curve, certainly not at the top. I am happy there, because there is too much pressure in being a Big Head. However, I do have my moments.

For social dogs like standard poodles, any form of Shepherd attention is rewarding. For example, some Shepherds believe that the best way to stop a dog from excessive door barking is to show the dog a treat. This forces the dog to smell the treat and since the dog cannot smell and bark at the same time, it quiets them. The dog is given the command 'enough' and then the treat or pat or both are offered to the barker.

Being a big fan of treats, I figured this out in seconds. I also figured out what started the process. I got up from my mat every ten minutes and barked at the door. Like clockwork, the Director came with a cheesy hound round and a pat.

The only one objecting was the cat. 'Puh-leeze, enough already, enough with the barking, let me sleep.'

In the afternoon, the Director took me to dog class. I was so excited, running like a crazy dog is my favourite exercise of all time. When we got to Auntie's, the puppies lined the driveway. The Producer stayed to visit with the puppies. However, the Director took me into the training hall where my stomach is a' rocking. Scientists have many different theories about why anxiety causes an upset stomach. One of the key beliefs is that anxiety causes changes in neurotransmitter function, particularly serotonin. There are serotonin and other neurotransmitter receptors in my gut, and so when my body is experiencing anxiety, it's likely receiving chemicals that tell it to respond with that upset feeling. Another theory, and the one I subscribe to, is the lack of cheesy hound rounds causes constant worry. Very stressful and I am just saying, please pass the glazed donuts this way. I need sugar.

Unfortunately, I cannot tell the Director how to train me, what hand to use, and in what order to do things. A book, even this super-duper one, will not teach you to read a dog's body language. Our partnership was to be tested. The Director decided at our most recent staff meeting, which I was not invited to, that he would use 'ach' instead of 'NO'. The difference is that the word No can be said in anger. With 'ach', there is little chance of it sounding angry. Unless of course you are a senior and the cashier has forgotten that it is double coupon Tuesday. Agility is an anger free zone. I can tell you that if I do not get something in agility then there are four distinct possibilities: I am either confused, distracted, afraid, or feel I have a better plan.

The warm up exercises were easy. I noticed that the Director was using a high pitch for "sit" and a low pitch for a "down". I found this new tone changing easy to work with. Auntie went thru the hand signals with the Director and me. I was doing excellent. The Director on the other hand, was failing miserably and received correction after correction from Auntie.

"Try doing the stay signal with your other left hand," she would say.

"He should only see the palm of your right hand on the drop. Try again. Concentrate! Your about turns are very sloppy. Remember the T."

I figured with a few more private lessons, he would get it. Before she left to join the puppies, she explained one of the many jumps in the room, the broad jump. This is a series of three low level jumps that I had to leap when I heard the word 'over'. Thinking I had to land in the middle of each one, I picked confused from my list of four options. The Director helped me by moving the blocks a little closer together. By the end of the hour, I could sit, wait and broad jump like the best of them. I was only 'ach'ed once for overeager jumping before the hand signal. Looking up, I saw Auntie and the Producer returning.

"Anything good?" she asked.

'Yes, I showed Auntie my broad jump. Hand signalled by the Director to a spot and then a sit stay, I waited. When signalled, with the wrong hand, I approached aggressively and smoothly. I am a tuck and kick jumper. Up and over the broad jump with no effort. Auntie was pleased.

When it came to the tunnel, the Director threw a cheesy hound round in and I raced through. The Producer clapped.

On the ride home, the Producer questioned the Director. "Do you think he wants to be a show dog?"

"By birth, the answer is yes," he said. "But, it's not for him. You need a whole team readying him for a show. He wouldn't like that. His long hair cut is a real challenge. Each week, eight weeks prior to the show, he is bathed, specially conditioned, brushed, dried and clipped, a four-hour process. Once at a show, an hour is spent styling and hair spraying him for the show ring."

"Spraying is adding the beauty on top, correct," the Producer asked.

"'The beauty is in the headpiece," she added.

"Special care is taken to prevent hair from breaking. During show season he is crated at night, reducing the risk of the coat breaking. No ball playing, whatsoever. When it's hot, he is not allowed to scratch, rub or destroy his hair in any way."

"Is the hair spray left in all season?"' she asked.

"No, because it puts pressure on the hair. We would have to manage the long hair with the least amount of damage."

Fearing a life as a show dog, I decided to be the perfect companion.

When we got home, I did not bark at the front door. Instead, I amused myself by tapping at the back door. The Producer let me out into the yard, praising me for alerting her that I needed to go to the bathroom. She threw my ball for me, which I love, but I resisted. Then she offered me a treat, which I refused. I thought I was playing the role of the perfect dog, sitting quietly at my Shepherd's feet on the deck. However, I overacted. The Producer was catching on that something was not right. She called Auntie. I could barely hear her.

"What's his problem?"

"He is not his usual goofy self and he does not want to play or eat. He just slumps at my feet. No barking. No energy. Something is up with him?

"What do you mean, congratulations you have a balanced dog?"

Auntie went on to explain what a balanced dog is. She told the Producer that my native instincts and drive coupled with my physical, mental, and emotional development made me a balanced dog. She said I was born that way, explaining that trainers put in endless hours trying to have a balanced dog.

"Friday, for whatever reason, is balanced. I knew it the moment I met him," she said. "And, he's smart! Too friggin smart. He's playing you. He needs a job. Bring him to Canine Good Citizenship."

"This balanced dog thing is overrated,' I thought.

When the Producer and the Director went to bed I called it a night as well. With only ten minutes of shuteye on my dog bed, I felt Malibu walking on my head, meowing in my ear.

I knew I had to take the leadership role if I was to get any sleep. Malibu followed me into the den. I turned the lights on and off and then on and off again to signal class was starting. Malibu sat on the sofa. There is a spotlight over the den door. I switched it on and stood center stage. Basking in the light I said, 'Pekingeses, Bull Mastiffs, Maine Coon and everything in between please put your paws together and give a solid Winnipeg welcome to Malibu the ragdoll cat, having just completed a two month sold out performance in Kitten Cirque du Soleil in Las Vegas.'

Intro complete, I started class. 'This is Friday's rambunctious and obnoxious puppy class for 'cats who do not sleep'. Please check your syllabus to insure you are in the right classroom, 'climb the curtains' is next door.' I introduced my teaching assistant, white bear.

Malibu, focused on a blue throw pillow with white tassels, was not paying attention. I could hear him thinking. 'Hmmm, what's this? (chomping on the pillow) Is it something to eat? No? (tossing it around) Can I play with it? Maybe. Can I shred it?' I watch as his teeth pierce the pillow, stuffing peeking out. Obviously, not knowing how sharp his teeth are; he is very busy learning how to be a cat.

Wanting the class to be fun, I bowed. Playfighting with me will develop his reflexes, coordination and physical skill. After a few minutes, he bit me hard enough to hurt, so I squealed in shocked indignation. Malibu was surprised by my reaction. (I am a great actor when I need to be.)

He hesitated a moment, unsure of himself, then tried to bite me again. This time, I yelped even louder, spinning around above him, growling, showing him teeth and scowling at him fiercely. Turning my back to him, I stormed away, completely ignoring him and any further attempts to entice me to play.

Malibu quickly picks up the message, if you can't play nice, I won't play with you at all! - quickly. Understanding dog language, Malibu played calmly.

Moving on, I went to the doorway and stopped. Malibu went through. Big mistake. With a menacing growl and using my teeth, I grabbed him by the scruff of his neck and gave him a shake, pulling him back. He hissed at me. I gave another little shake, tougher this time. I waited. He acknowledged my instructor status by relaxing his body, retracting his claws and keeping still for a moment.

During the next hour, I showed him what I know. He was a quick study. At one point, he had had enough of my training and raised his lip, showing his sharp teeth. I did what any good, caring doggie dad would do. I knocked him over with my right paw and pinned him to the ground, growling angrily while pinching him with my teeth. Malibu went limp. He got up, shook his fur back in place and sat on the couch.

I know what predatory aggression is because I have it. Oddly enough, it shows up every time a bushy tailed squirrel passes my line of sight. I feel good about killing a squirrel in the dog park, serving him to my friends for a snack. It is not an act of rage. I simply bite down hard and shake him to death. It is not a loud screaming territorial fight that you see when two dogs go at it, rage circuits firing everywhere. It is a quiet ritual that I enjoy. Squirrels, nature's speed bumps.

However, I do not have emotional aggression. A few cheesy hound rounds and a good radio program and then I am set for the afternoon. It occurs to me that Malibu does not have aggression issues either, unless you consider de-winging a moth as aggression. His breed of cat may not be genetically predisposed to violent behaviour.

I came up with a plan, tug-of-war. I am bigger and stronger than Malibu and would have no trouble winning every time.

The Director does play tug-of-war with me, believing that it does not cause aggression if played properly.

Now I know what you're thinking. Almost every book I've ever read about training dogs tells me that I should not, that it produces aggressive behaviour, that it will make them think they're the alpha, that it'll make them bite the mailman. Well, I'm here to tell you that I am the alpha, get over it. Those people are doing an enormous disservice to their canine friends by limiting playtime to "shake a paw" and "beg". Please keep an open mind and keep reading.

It's not that you want your dog to get so riled up he bites your pinkie off. What you should want is for your dog to associate being around you with the highest levels of satisfaction possible. Now, how satisfying do you think it is for me to be flipped over on my back and shown who is the boss? Furthermore, how satisfying do you think those little treats are after you have given me a few hundred of them? It's not like you are offering me a vanilla cupcake with sweet yellow cake and a thick layer of creamy white frosting. Most dog treats taste the same. Clearly you need to up the ante with me, so that interacting with you leaves me feeling like I just had the best day of my life, again and again. One of the best ways is playing tug-of-war or ball.

You see, I need to bite stuff. It's a stress release especially after dealing with you all day. Only kidding, but I do have stress. Unfortunately, many Shepherds discourage their dogs from biting anything. Like any other repressed but innate activity, the biting will find an outlet for itself like peeing on the hallway carpet or chewing a table leg. If you play it right, your dog will be able to bite hard enough to release quite a bit of the tension that they are carrying around. The result is a happy dog. Did I mention it is okay for me to win sometimes?

After I learned tug-of-war, I was taught 'pull hard'. It is like tug-of-war except you pull an object. Like a towel attached to a dryer door, opening it. Think about it? Perhaps you hurt yourself and cannot bend over then I can take your socks off for you. At training, we do 'pull hard' at the end of every session. I learned to plant my feet and balance my weight for maximum pull power. Of everything I will ever learn as a poodle, pull hard will change my life forever. Even now, when I hear those words my ears flatten, tail tucks between my legs, cowering and lip licking begin as the hair raises on my back. Sorry, I digress.

I gripped the pillow in my teeth and showed it to Malibu. Immediately, he snatched the free end and yanked. I won a few rounds and I let him win a few rounds. I noticed if he won too often that his aggression built. I considered winning them all. But I do not think that would have solved anything. Instead, when he got too aggressive from wins, I stood rock-still till he calmed. It was my idea of a kitty time-out and it was working. Wanting to continue play, he quieted.

In the cat world timing is everything. Malibu was learning that tempered aggression got results while emotional aggression got your ass kicked. We were having loads of fun! During one hearty round, both of us pulling as hard as we could, the Producer walked in. The pillow split down the middle and there we were flat on our back, five feet apart. The evidence was clearly in our mouths.

Sometimes a dog's got to do what a dog's got to do. 'Exercise over,' I said, not knowing what else to say. I ran over to the Producer and leaned on her right leg. Much to my delight, Malibu leaned on her left and purred. With shrugged shoulders, she vacuumed.

Normally, I do not go out at night, except for training. But, thinking the pillow fight was a sign of pent up anxiety, the Shepherds took me to The Woods. The reduced activity at night was a benefit to me. I ran along calmly enjoying the cool night air and reduced sounds. My biggest sight advantage at night is due to the tapetum. This mirror-like structure in the back of my eye reflects light, giving the retina a second chance to register light that has entered the eye. The problem with the tapetum is that it scatters some light, reducing my vision to 20:80.

Walking off leash for about a half an hour, I zigged instead of zagged. The Director and Producer called my name repeatedly. I tried, without success, to smell them out. The problem with tracking is that Shepherds frantically looking for their lost dog run up and down the same path one hundred times, causing the weaker scents to blend with the stronger ones. At one point, I thought they might have climbed a tree. Tracking is not my forte.

It was a long time, two minutes, before I reappeared, head high, raised tail, carrying what I thought was a large tasty stick. Getting closer, I realized that it was an animal leg with a heart shaped scar on it. The hoof, still attached, was abnormally large. In the case of small prey, the dominant dog, me, would eat first. But, with such an abundance of deer meat, sharing with my Shepherds was acceptable to me. It was very scrumptious, only a few hours old. Eventually, the Director separated me from my snack. I guess he was hungry too. For those of you who are wondering if I knew the leg belonged to Uncle Tom who passed away at 92, here is my two word response, 'Piss off! Do I ask you if your steak dinner is Buttercup, Elsie or Clarabell?'

Before we got into the car, The Producer stopped to read a lost dog poster.

"Lots of these lately, and this one has a five hundred dollar reward for a dog named Huckleberry. It is so sad, especially in this climate, when a dog gets lost," she said.

We drove home, turning into the driveway, the Director narrowly missing a collie-lab cross.

"Don't scare him," the Producer said, getting out of the car. "Do you think he's vicious?"

I could tell them that he's a she and she doesn't bite. But I didn't.

"No, he looks calm enough," the Director said, getting out to help. "Bring him in the house. I'll park the car and bring Friday in."

Once we were all safely in the house the entertainment began.

"I'll take his picture and make 'dog found' signs. I can post them within a ten mile radius of our house. Friday will help," he said excitedly.

'Do I look like a minimum wage employee to you,' I asked. 'Dr. Laura will be on soon and what about the homemade doggie beef dinner you promised?'

"Is he the one in the park poster," she asked.

"No, Huckleberry was a Labrador retriever. Nothing like him," the Director said, aiming the camera phone at our new guest.

Before I could intervene Malibu walked by, which was odd since he normally went to the basement for three days whenever we have company.

They exchanged greetings. 'Hi Malibu,' she said.

"'Hi Carmela," he responded.

'Is it working?' Malibu asked.

'Wait for it,' the visitor said. 'It's coming, any second now. '

"Maybe we should feed him first. He probably hasn't eaten in days," the Producer said, reaching into the fridge. "Do you like homemade doggie beef dinner," she asked, showing her the bowl.

'Yup,' Carmela said, licking the bowl clean.

'You know her' I asked Malibu.

'Yes, she lives across the street. Sometimes, I visit with her.'

Hmm, I thought. That's why it is so hard to find you. You found the secret passage out of the bathroom, didn't you?

'Meow,' Malibu said

'Huh?' I responded, knowing he was not about to give up the secret.

'What part of meow did you not understand?' he said walking away.

'And you Missy, what's your story?' I asked Carmela.

'Yes, I do live across the street. Sometimes, I like to dine out so I go to a nearby driveway and I wait. Works every time.' 'Carmela said.

I was impressed. 'How do you get home?' I asked.

'My chauffeur picks me up after dessert.'

"Maybe after she has eaten you should take her to the Tuxedo Animal Hospital and see if she has a chip or registered tattoo," the Producer said, realizing it was a girl dog.

After Carmela ate (my dinner) we all piled into the car and drove to the animal hospital. When we arrived the staff greeted her.

"Hi Carmela, we will call your owner," white coat number one said.

"Take one cookie for dessert and go in the back and wait," white coat number two said.

Then white coat one told the Director not to worry. She explained that Carmela comes here once a week and that her owner would be here within the hour. Munching on her dessert, Carmela walked into the back room to wait for her chauffer.

Back home. I had dry kibble with a small can of salmon tossed in. I was pissed off.

Later that night, Malibu and I were in the backyard playing tag when a white, rusted pickup truck pulled up. Ping-ping went the engine. It was the same ping I had heard before. You remember, right? I could smell one small dog in a wire crate in the truck box, a mix of fear and ground rosemary seeds assaulted my nose. Although I could not see her, I knew it was Pageant Patti.

A fat man, beer gut hanging over his black belt, unshaven and gritty, stood up in the back of the truck near the crate taking pictures of us with a telescopic lens. At first, I thought he had a really big nose. The other one, rake thin, reeking of onions, threw pieces of hotdog at us. I have never had a hotdog before, not counting the stuffed one the Producer gave me. It was delicious. Malibu ate a few pieces between poses as well.

When they left Malibu asked me who they were.

'Movie talent scouts,' I guessed incorrectly.

I do not think so. I think something really, really bad is going to happen to us. My cat friends talk about this sort of thing on the wire. I am not sure what these two are up to. But I am really scared.

Trying not to show my fear, I said, "not to worry little buddy, I will protect you.' I had no idea what it was that I was promising.

Chapter 22

SammyFarbers Secret

Two days later, I went to Canine Good Citizen class. I could hardly wait to get out of the house. Malibu was keeping me up all night with his nocturnal quest to make our home moth free.

On the way we stopped at large red brick building. The Director got out of the car and walked up to a green machine. After a few minutes, money started spewing out.

'We won! We won!' Off the hook and pumped over the moon, I howled out the window. 'Wahoo! We won the lotto! Yippee, we are going to get a real house now.' I could not contain myself, hanging halfway out the window, barking incessantly.

"It's an ATM machine you over enthusiastic poodle. Please stop barking," the Director said getting back in the car.

When we got to outdoor arena class, I thought I was doing excellent, interacting with my classmates in a positive way. That is until a bichon frise, not in our class of eight, walked by during a prolonged down-stay. I broke from the pack and went after him, chasing him into the parking lot. My emotional aggression had kicked in and I was pumped. The little scared dog hid under a parked beige van, allowing the Director to catch up with me.

Auntie explained that I was protecting the pack. The thought of eight of us needing to be protected from a bichon was puzzling to the Producer. Auntie asked if there was some unusual stress in my life lately. And then gave me a gift from her bag.

The Producer and the Director lied, claiming all was good at home.

Yeah right, I thought. He was facing manslaughter charges, 20 to life, and she was soon to be pushing up daisies. You bet your sweet ass there was stress in my poodle life.

The gift was similar to a harness, the neck strap wraps around my head and sits high up behind the ears on the back of my head; underneath it was just above the Adam's apple. This piece fitted snugly; Auntie squeezed one finger underneath the strap as a test. The second piece looped around my nose, sitting at the corners of the mouth and just below the eyes. It was loose enough so that I could open my mouth but not so much that it could slip off the end of my poodle nose.

Auntie showed the Director how to use the two-leash system. "One, on his normal buckle collar, and the other one attached to the nose ring," she instructed.

The product worked by leading the dog by his muzzle, just like the alpha dog would direct me in our natural environment. I did not object to the new addition to my wardrobe. I think I secretly wanted the help before I ripped some little dog to shreds.

We finished the class without further incident. I wore my gentle leader for the next seven days. The Producer and Director took me everywhere, working at gentle corrections and praise. And, believe or not, after seven, four hour days of practice, I was cured. By that, I do not mean by any stretch, that I was a balanced dog again. The stress in my life was crushing.

Looking back, I think all I needed was confidence, a safety net. A combination of my changed attitude toward what I had to face, coupled with the Shepherds' awareness, and most of all, their desire to deal with the problems, guiding the pack through this rough patch. When I went for a walk, I always positioned myself between Producer and Director. At the park, I paid more attention to their needs. I wanted to help

Right before dinner, I remembered that a few days prior, I had invited my friend, Dusty, to join us for the evening meal. She is a husky cross, one year older than me. As a puppy, she lived behind 7-11, surviving on Slurpees. For anyone who does not know, a Slurpee is a frozen carbonated beverage (although not carbonated in Canada) sold by 7-11. Dusty's two favourites are Mello Yellow and Bubble Yum. I prefer the watermelon flavour. On a road trip, her Shepherds found her living outside 7-11 and brought her home to Winnipeg.

The temperature this evening had dropped to well below zero and I was getting concerned. Dusty has a thick-furred double coat, sickle tail, erect triangular ears and distinctive white and brown markings. But even a dog with two coats can freeze to death if the wind picks up. Huskies are very stubborn and independent dogs, traveling miles away before realizing that their Shepherd is not in sight. Dusty does not remember her dad so it is hard to say what the cross was. Judging by her lightweight, smaller frame and fondness for rice, it may have been a visiting Akita.

After dinner, I considered that she might have decided to reschedule due to the harsh winds building outside. Two hours later, I heard footsteps on the driveway. At first, I thought it was Carmela. But then, I smelled Dusty. She climbed up our steps and sat on the small porch, curled close to the door where the heat escapes. I barked to announce my dinner guest had arrived. Finally, after more than a few barks, the Director looked outside the front door and saw nothing. Shepherds tend to look at their sight level, which is not good if you are a frozen dog curled up on the step. Seeing nothing, he went back to watching TV. After a minute or two, I barked again, this time much louder and higher pitched.

"Enough Friday," he said. "Enough with barking. The sound is snow falling off the trees. Not lions attacking."

Ignoring him, I barked some more. There is nothing more annoying than to have two Shepherds go right on talking while you are barking. When I added howling, the Producer had no choice but to open the door and check. Luckily, she looked down. There, curled up on the step, was my frozen dinner companion.

'Sorry I am late,' she said, entering our house.

Since dinner was over, I ran to the couch and pulled out my emergency marrow bone that I keep hidden under it. Dusty chewed eagerly while telling me her story.

'After studying the map of the two legged dog facing east walking toward the box house with the curly smoke coming out of the roof that you drew for me; I went east. The increased wind chilled me to the bone. After a few blocks, I picked up your scent trail and travelled north. Not far from here, I saw three dogs pulling a red wagon so I crossed over a few streets. They did not appear too friendly. A little while later, I picked up the trail again which had me winding back away from your house. Eventually, I found myself on a snowman's driveway. He does not like you. Anyway, lost and really cold, I considered going home. But, I did not know which way that was. I am a sled dog, not a tracker. Finally, I ran into a dog named Carmela who was sitting on a long driveway of an English Tudor home. She said she had dinner reservations. Anyway, Carmela pointed me in the right direction and here I am.'

At that moment, Dusty's Shepherd rang the doorbell. Dusty was overjoyed to see her. I said goodbye to Dusty and told her we should have lunch next week.

That night I slept on my back, knowing the solution to my pack's problems would be found.

When the Shepherds crank up the heat, I sleep on my back, trying to cool down. Cooling down is hard for me because I only sweat through the pads in my paws. During the day, I pant to adjust my body temperature. But panting while sleeping is almost impossible. On my back, my paws breathe and my belly is less covered with fur hence when it is exposed to the air I get cool. Sleeping on my back is really comfortable.

At 3 a.m., needing a drink of water, I went to the kitchen. And, there was SammyFarber enjoying a rum and coke. We drank and chatted. I had water with three ice cubes. He had a double shot of rum. I shared my love and my concern for the Producer with him. What he told me surprised me.

'Little poodle, I do not normally speak of my past. However, I feel your pain. And perhaps, when you hear my secret you will see the path.'

'But, but, but, I already know your secret. How you got the inventory for your garage sale. Right?'

"Canines and Shepherds alike, can have more than one secret, little puppy. But there is a major problem with evaluating information labeled "secret", Shepherds tend to inflate the value of "secret" information simply because it is secret whereas canines know really important hush-hush data when they hear it. And this is mine.

'More than one secret?' I asked. 'That is very confusing?' I said. 'Tell me more.'

'I will if you shut up for a second,' SammyFarber said, sipping his rum. 'We are predators and therefore are hardwired to kill. Contrary to popular belief, we do not kill for food. Killing is fun for animals, but not them all. You cannot train a horse to be an attack horse. Simply, they are not wired for it. We canines are, however. A dog that believes he is the alpha in the house or pack is dangerous. Oddly enough, obedience training established your Shepherd as your alpha. That is why you are at the crossroads. You feel the need to take charge. However he is the recognized alpha. Correct?'

I agreed. For the first time, I was starting to understand my mixed emotions.

'Do Shepherds see death differently?' I asked.

'Yes. First, it is very likely that the dying Shepherd will be surrounded by their friends. They mean well but, in the end, each Shepherd must die their own death. Shepherds consider dying as a journey one takes alone with a crowd around them.

Years ago, my Shepherd sat in the sunroom, no longer able to make it to the master bedroom. By trade, he was a pharmacist at the local drugstore. He was sitting in a spartan room in their two bedroom bungalow, where he was about to take his own life. How odd is that?

At the age of just sixty-two, his multiple sclerosis has worsened to the point where he had to "fall" off the couch in the morning and could only creep around his house. Crawling on his knees to where he filled my food and water dish. He edged snail-like over to the door, to let me out to pee. He crawled through the day. How sad it was to watch. And there was the pain. Oy, the pain he endured year after year. Yet not wanting to give up. He had suffered with the disease for five years, and in the past two years had gone from walking stick to wheelchair. He twice tried to kill himself with a drug overdose. "His life," he said, "was like walking down a cold, dark passageway that was getting narrower, with no doggie door".

Enough is enough, he told me that fateful morning, wanting permission to die. As he prepares for his death, he says, poignantly, that he has "fallen in love" with his wife all over again. He looks to me for acceptance. Instead, I suggest that there are many people he needs to say goodbye to first. For me, he has so much life left in him. He shook his head apologetically and replied, "The die is cast. Help me steady my trembling hand."

Soon afterwards, as the summer sun heated the room, he calmly filled his wineglass with the poison that ended his life.

Yes, I could have knocked the glass out of his trembling hands instead of nudging it toward his lips. I could have betrayed his trust in me. Defied his last request. I did not.

His cold body was aglow. Thru the window, I saw hundreds of delphinium petals of all colors banded together by beads of sunlight, forming a connection to my heart. I watched as his soul left his body. I imagined him running free in the park. Turning, he looked back and smiled. Joy filled my heart. More than anything, I wanted to follow. But just as quickly as it had appeared, the fragrant smell of the Delphinium flowers was gone, leaving arcs of coloured light that will forever bind us. In time, I accepted his decision, realising that I was being selfish for wanting him to linger longer. He knew his tolerance for his condition had ended. My Shepherd was of sound mind, lucid.

It took me a long time to accept his view that his quality of life was so diminished that he no longer wanted to go on living. No last walk in the park. As his dog, I did not want to see him suffer any more. I knew if the roles were reversed he would treat me with the same kindness and respect.'

Hearing SammyFarber's secret, I shed tears.

Chapter 23

Creamy Vanilla Yogurt

The Producer, my resident nurse, includes the traditional combs and brushes, toothbrush, liver toothpaste and ear solution with cotton balls and vitamin C pills in her doggie repair kit. I have my vitamin C wrapped in vanilla yogurt. Last week, I wrote to Ben and Jerry, suggesting squirrel swirl yogurt. To date, I have received no response. Perhaps because it is very hard to say squirrel swirl five times fast.

I am not a good patient, big surprise. I can smell vitamin C two blocks away. So what? Am I supposed to eat the yogurt and ignore the orange after taste? Not me. I lick the yogurt till I get down to the vitamin C pill then run for high ground. Once caught, they try to get me to swallow the yucky pill with more yogurt. This time, I separate the pill from the yogurt in my mouth and spit the pill out. After four or five attempts, approximately a cup of really good vanilla yogurt, I give in. Feeling a little pudgy, I swallowed the pill. Plus I wanted to go for a walk before it got too dark out.

Walking, I love to meet new people. Yes, I can be a tiny, little, itzy-bit judgmental. See that lady up there with the green shamrock and pompom knit hat, she is a Shephound, part Shepherd and part hound. She will totally ignore the Director and focus all of her attention on me. Before she became a Shephound, she wore designer blue jeans, colourful tops with matching accessories. Now, she wears a black t-shirt that says, 'in dog beers I have only had one'. She knows the name of each dog on the crescent and which ones have ear infections. And thinks, Puh-pee is a dog breed.'

"Hi Friday. Are you going to the park to play Frisbee? "Shake a paw," she said, extending her hand. The Director will not allow me to shake a paw, thinking it is the second most stupid trick a dog can do.

I did not respond. "Beg," she said, holding a treat out for me.

'Are you expecting me to sing badly in front of an open guitar case?' I asked.

Now that she had requested what the Director believes is the number one stupid trick, begging. He was obviously aggravated. She continued, lip licking and cocking her head, "Are you going to the park to play Frisbee," she repeats?

"No, he licks his genitals for entertainment," the annoyed Director responds.

After patting and feeding me, she moved on.

I spotted a fluttering leaf and pulled east. At the exact same moment, a westbound squirrel went by. I zigged and then I zagged, pulling the leash taut, which really pisses the Director off. Adding to the chaos, I spotted an open box of Cap'n Crunch, with Crunchberries, which I gotta have, in a lidless garbage can. A dogs got to do what a dogs got to do sometimes.

"Stop it. Stop pulling me all over the street right now. Friday," the Director with the newly lengthened arms, cries out. Coming to my senses, not wanting to be taken home, I walk nicely to the dog park. Did you know, I am somewhat of an expert on dog park poop? Yup, big surprise. By now you probably have figured out I am a self-appointed expert on just about everything. But would somebody please explain to me those signs that say, "No animals allowed except for Seeing Eye Dogs?" Who is that sign for? Is it for the dog, or the blind person? More on poop, Shepherds have a variety of options. Some use the bend and pretend method. This saves on bags. Others have the off path / on path solution. In this group, only poop on the path exists. The third group are the stargazers. The moment their dog poops, they immediately start examining the constellations, pretending to have no knowledge of what their dog is doing. The fourth group, of which the Director is a member believe that Shepherds not picking up poop should be fined for the first offence with the second offence being a mandatory five years in prison.

Continuing with my Shepherd education, I think you should know, 'Every dog park has a crazy dog lady. She will tell you everything that is wrong with her dog in the greatest of detail. Banjo has ear mites, eats his poop, drinks from the toilet whenever he sees luggage and has thunder anxiety attacks on non-rain days. She also believes that dogs that eat grass are self- medicating themselves to vomit. Personally, I enjoy the taste. The grassy taste is reminiscent of the cattle or lamb product I had for dinner. I like freshly laid lawn sod the best. The crazy dog lady usually has the crazy cat person with her. Crazies attract crazies.'

'And then there are the stick throwers. They always have non-retriever dogs like malamutes, samoyeds, huskies, and elkhounds. If you want someone to fetch an entire tree then these breeds are your guys, otherwise their position is if I chase it then it better be edible. These stick throwing Shepherds can be very dangerous around water. They are oblivious to the idea that the lab Shepherds may not want their dogs in the muddy water. Face the fact that, most water dogs will take any opportunity to swim in the water regardless who threw the wood. Stick throwers should be smacked in the back of the head with a rolled up newspaper.'

I think that all dog parks should have one of those amusement park signs that say if you are not this tall then you cannot enter. I looked over and see a boxer puppy with a small boy's arm in his mouth. I do mean the entire arm. A dog, unlike a Shepherd is always ready. (Left in the car,

209

I always sit in the driver's seat just in case I am needed to steer, should it roll forward.) Springing into action, I grabbed an old tennis ball that was lying on the ground, dropping it at the boxer's feet, inviting him to play. Given the choice of the boy's arm or the tennis ball, he picked slobbery tennis ball. Laughing, the boy pulled his arm out of the boxer's mouth.

'What was that salty thing,' the boxer puppy asked me.

'They are called children. Shepherds who cannot have dogs have them instead,' I said.

Bored, I challenged the Boxer puppy to a game of super-stick. In this game, we pick one medium size twig and promote it to super-stick by peeing on it. We take turns trying to steal it from each other. Shepherds do not understand super-stick. To them, every stick is the same. But, we know there is only one super-stick on any given day.

The Director and the Shepherd, unaware of what was going on, continued their debate over the merits of registering the labradoodle and goldendoodle. The only poodle mix that I am truly in favour of registration for is the cheese doodle. Mmm, delicious.

When we got home I took a nap. Hey, I am good at it.

After dinner, wanting my input on five doggie games, the Director called a meeting. The first was Flyball. It is a four-dog relay race between competing teams. The Flyball course covers 51 feet in length and consists of four hurdles leading to the Flyball box. Each dog must jump the four hurdles, retrieve a ball from the box, and return over the hurdles and cross the finish line. I did not need to hear any of the others. My mind was made up. Flyball was my choice. However, being courteous, I half listened to the others.

Next was Canine Disc for dogs that think catching hard plastic is fantastic. The dogs get ninety seconds to score as many points as possible by catching long throws into the Bonus Zone. Knowing we could play Frisbee in the park anytime, I quickly crossed this one off the list.

Dock jumping was next. Canine athletes run and jump off the end of a dock into the indoor pool, the longest jump wins. This one really did not appeal to me, reminding the Director that I do not know how to swim, was essential.

Agility training was next. This is truly a Shepherd's idea of a team sport. Courses are complicated enough that a dog could not complete them correctly without Shepherd direction. In competition, the Shepherd must assess the course, decide on handling strategies, and direct the dog through the course, with precision and speed equally important. I shook my head. It's way too much work. As well, weave poles make me nauseous.

Last was Rally-O. It seems unlike regular obedience, instead of waiting for Auntie's orders, the competitors proceed around a course of designated stations with the dog in heel position. The course consists of twenty signs that instruct the team what to do. Unlike traditional obedience, Shepherds are allowed to encourage their dogs during the course. I laughed. I could not think of anything more boring. Voting Flyball, the meeting was adjourned.

Suffering from lack of sleep, I went to bed early. I dreamt about a dog, named Scout who starred in a Disney movie as Buddy, the basketball playing Golden Retriever. In my dream, I taught him the 3 point shot.

Our house has an alarm that is dog, cat and bird friendly. On setting number one, the motion detectors pick up the slightest internal movement. This setting does not work for us. Setting two, the one we use, protects the doors and windows, allowing internal movement up to 75 pounds on the main floor. Hence I have to watch my cheesy hound round intake. In addition, the windows can be open to two inches without triggering the alarm, allowing small birds to draft in on fresh air currents.

On this particular night, the open window allowed the smell of onions to drift in, waking me up. Thinking nothing of it, I went back to sleep.

A few hours later, the alarm sounded. Lights flashing on the exterior of the home, alarm horn blasting and the police alerted. Both the

Director and Producer were awakened by the racket. So was Morris the old hound across the street.

Rushing to the staircase, the Director called out, "Friday! Malibu!"

Leaving his pirate ship with white bear in charge, Malibu raced up the stairs into the Producer's waiting arms. Once again, the Director called, "Friday, come!" This time louder than the first, having to yell to be heard above the blaring alarm.

No response. The Director had choices. He could wait for the police to arrive thereby avoiding any potential conflict with the intruders. Or he could take his chances with a confrontation and save me from harm.

Had I responded, I am sure he would have waited for the police. His only loss would have been the stolen items and they were insured. Given that I did not respond, he assumed that I was dead and the murderers were waiting downstairs armed with knives to finish off the rest of the pack. Or else, somehow I had managed to escape and was running wild on the streets. Unable to accept either, he told the Producer to take Malibu and lock herself in the bathroom while he investigated.

Creeping down the stairs, he peeked into the living room. He stopped when he noticed the open window near my dog bed which had triggered the alarm. A noise behind him caused his heart to jump out of his chest.

It was the Producer carrying Malibu. "Find anything?" she asked. The next thing that happened taught me a very important Shepherd lesson. Not all Shepherds, in the exact same situation, react the same way.

Sleepy-eyed, I looked up from my doggie bed and saw them both staring down at me. As mentioned before, I immediately looked at the right side of their faces to anticipate what was going to happen. The Producer had a big, warm smile on her face, right side relaxed. The Director's right side was contorted; he was going to kill me.

"You can hear the lid come off the vanilla ice cream container from the other room, but you cannot hear an alarm sounding," he said, raising his eyebrows. "You freak out if a leaf moves on the driveway at 6 a.m. But, you cannot hear an alarm blaring," he repeated. "A single speaker connected to our deluxe Vibrex B141 alarm has recorded "loudness" measurements of 110 decibels. We have two speakers. The neighbours four blocks away can friggin' hear it," he screamed. "I knew I should have gotten a Doberman." Looking back, I think he was more scared than angry. I know he would be devastated if anything happened to me. In my defense, I have to point out that those ice creams lids can pop quite loudly.

When the police came they checked the entire house and grounds. Finding no one, they filled out their report. Before leaving, they assured the Shepherds that it was very unlikely that the thieves would return. They were wrong, so, very wrong. They were going to come back and get me, selling me to the highest bidder.

Chapter 24

How Much is that Doggie in the Window ?

Jumping eagerly into the car, excitement oozing from every paw, I was off to play Flyball. My dream team would be me, Malibu, Lefty and Meeko. Lefty would lead off, jumping the hurdles as if they did not exist. Then me, followed by Meeko. Malibu would anchor the team in case we needed that extra burst of speed at the end. Although I hate to admit it, Malibu is faster than I am. And, with a little growl from Meeko, he would really haul ass. I could see the headlines in tomorrow's paper, Friday the Poodle captains winning Flyball championship team.

When we arrived, I was in a large training hall that looked strangely familiar. Auntie stepped out and greeted the crowd, "Welcome to Rally-O!"

'What the heck?' I said. Looking into the Director's eyes, I quickly narrowed it down to either a 50% off coupon or a set of free steak knives, either way I was pissed. The Producer took me through the obedience course, spotted with signs. The first instructional sign was 'sit' followed by 'down' and 'wait'. I thought I was going to puke. This was soooooooo boring.

Sensing my mood, the Producer changed the game. This one says phone a friend and she did. The next one, scratch your ear. Give it a try. On each of the next fifteen signs, the Producer made up her own message instead of the obedience commands. Eat a treat and name my shoe colour were my favourites. We had so much fun.

After everyone had completed the course, Auntie asked who would like to do it again. The stupid border collies all started barking, 'pick me, pick me'. Reluctantly, I faked my way through another round. It only got worse. We had six more weeks of this to look forward to. I wondered what the Director was thinking.

When we got home, Malibu and I played the window game, rating everyone who walked by. Malibu likes clothes that sparkle, giving anything with glitter high marks, who would have guessed? After a hard day at Rally-o school, for dinner, I had dry kibble. Malibu, who played in the house all day, had a can of Spicy Crusted Sea Scallops, snow peas, mint toasted almonds, shaved fennel on freshly made cheese fettuccini. Go figure! After dinner, I took a short nap. Maybe five hours.
Exiting for our late night, do it now pee dance, Malibu and I exchanged probing glances. Something was off putting. I peed and went back inside.

Restless, wide awake, heart thumping wildly, I lay in my bed, tossing and turning, listening keenly to the sounds behind the rain. The resonance, I knew, came from somewhere down the back lane behind the house. It had been intermittent for the last two nights.

Tonight, when I listened hard enough, behind the rain pounding on the house's grey shingled roof I could hear a reverberating empty metal sound, like two hollow pipes being struck against each other, at regular intervals. It was as if someone were trying to send me a message through the chill wet darkness. Occasionally, straining to listen, my nerves exploding with tension, I was certain that I could detect voices, sometimes a male dog but most often a familiar female dog's whimper. Once last night, Saturday, I had even heard her shriek. Now, Sunday night, the hollow metal thuds came about every thirty seconds, and as I listened I tried to rationally construct a picture of the noise's source. If the noises had come during the day, I would have pictured construction workers with hard hats and metal shovels. The back lane was always being patched and mended. But at night, no one would be working on the lane, especially during a furious rainstorm. I thought it was an animal, but an animal couldn't maintain the steady, rhythmic beat. I was wrong. It was a canine trying very hard with her last breath to warn me of the danger that awaited me. I recalled that some old locals at the dog park had been talking about animals being abducted and held for ransom. In another story, equally, if not more disturbing, I learned that animals like me were abducted and forced to live in narrow cages and breed. I could not sit still while the animal in the truck begged for my help. I barked and then I barked again. The sleepy-eyed Director let me out. Malibu followed. I distinctly smelled onions. I wondered what delicious treat they had in store for us tonight, perhaps medium rare roast beef? Food always clouds my thought process. Quietly, the rusted dark white truck pulled up out of the shadows. The engine was pinging. (I wondered where I had heard that sound before.) It had been waiting for us. Attached to the top of the half-ton truck, were two large black poles with yellow nylon loops at the end. The loop was slightly larger than my head. This meant nothing to me. Many things are slightly larger than my head. (Refrigerators for one.) I did not connect the dots.

Dogs hate the truth. The truth hurts too much for us to enjoy it. We may even say we accept it, but we can't. Our character is made kindly so we need bad news delivered more softly. We feel uncomfortable when we stand next to someone who is mean to us for no reason, pushing us away and referring to us as dirty animals. We develop interesting little mind games to help us accept what we do not want to see or hear. We push the depth of our acceptance for the truth off to the side whenever possible, not always jumping right into the middle of the truth when it comes knocking at our emotional door. If the truth thumping at the door is there to reveal something we did wrong, ripping the garbage bag to shreds for a piece of discarded chicken, we work hard on avoiding to open that door. I am guilty of all of these things. So are you. That is the truth.

Their voices were low and garbled due to the red bandanas they wore over their mouths

"When I say go. Pop da fence and grab da shitheads," one Onion mumbled.

Before you translate the above sentence from mumble into English, I think it is important that I translate it into canine English for you to understand how I heard it. Canine English is what is spoken at training school, nowhere else on the planet. The rules are weird. The first rule is that if the canine does not understand the word then the Shepherd repeats it. In our canine world, this is meaningless. Repetition of words to a dog does not increase learning. And, in some cases, it can decrease learning. If you say sit-sit-sit and I sit on the second sit, then I assume that the third sit must have a different meaning. So, I lay down, which drives you nuts. But, in our world it makes perfect sense. If I am already sitting and you say sit again then it has to mean something else. If not choice A, then B. Do I have to keep going over this? Repetition is not learning. It is only repetition.

The second rule is that if the dog does not sit on the first command then obviously the dog has an elephant stuck in his ear. I have no idea how Shepherds came up with this conclusion. But at every training class there is a Shepherd who says the command louder and louder each time the dog does not do it correctly.

The third rule of canine English is that the last word is the key word, or trigger word, as I like to call it. Pay attention, this is important. It took me a long time to understand. But, I finally figured it out. If you say, "Let's take the car to the Park," then the last or trigger word is "Park" and that is where we are going. However, if you say, "Park the car," then the trigger word or last word is "car" and we are not going anywhere. Right?

Now that you understand trigger words as we hear it you will understand why training us by using the words "no" or "good" before the command is not the most effective way for us to learn.

Let's look at "No Bark"! The trigger word for me is "Bark" and that is what I do when you say, "No Bark" and, if you repeat it, while raising your voice then we are really going to have a fun time barking. (At least, I will!)

Now, let's look at "good sit" or "good stand". If I am already doing the command and you say, "good sit" then those of you paying attention, and not fretting over the long poles with loops that were about to be around my neck, will know that I will most likely lay down. (Keep in mind that the word, good, by itself reinforces my action. Simply leave out any more words.) Having said all this, let's look at what I heard next.

Sorry for rambling. I warned you that I avoid the truth when it is unbearable. Get over it. I was about to be snatched into a horrible life. The Onions inserted a metal rod in the gate opening and forced the protective bar off the hinges. Entering our yard, they said. "Come here, nice little shitheads. I have hotdogs for you shitheads."

The trigger word in both sentences was, of course, shithead. Lucky for me it was not hotdog.

Hearing the trigger word Shithead, I barked my warning bark to Malibu and he responded by meowing. A warning bark is a low, quiet bark, but the noticeable growl increases in intensity and ultimately turns into a howling growl. I use this to signify a potential danger, and therefore it is normally not associated with territorial intrusion. When I bared my teeth while continuing to sound the alarm, the message was clear to Malibu. This has nothing to do with territory, get ready for combat was the message. Understanding my alert, he hissed.

I am a predatory animal built to hunt and kill. I am less fearful than prey animals. That makes me potentially dangerous to bad Shepherds for two reasons. The Onions by their actions had triggered my killing bite instincts and secondly, I am not afraid to express angry aggression. I will fight to the death! Win or lose, me and Malibu were not leaving this yard.

Rage is about survival at the most basic level. It is the emotion I draw on when my life is at stake. When cornered, I can be extremely aggressive. (Do not let the fancy hairdo fool you!) With razor sharp claws extended, Malibu stood his ground beside me. Swinging yellow nylon loops circled our heads. Realising what they were, Malibu ducked his. I, on the other hand, having learned 'pull hard' decided to sink my teeth into the loop, feet planted, weight balanced, I pulled back as hard as I could. The Onion on the other end was caught off guard and fell, knees hitting the concrete patio floor.

There I stood, mildly crouched with the weight on my back legs, hackles up from the neck to my tail. My muzzle was tense, wrinkling and snarling with teeth exposed. My tail tucked under my belly. Ears back and flat against my head. He was eye to eye with me. I bent my legs in preparation for a quick attack. I planned to use my speed, strength, and aggressiveness, along with the pain from biting to overwhelm and panic him. Judging the distance, I leapt at him, aiming for his jugular vein. Once my kill bite was in, I planned to shake him to death like I would a squirrel. I launched. He blocked with his elbow. The forearm hit my jaw, knocking me down on to his left leg. I was more energized when he struggled because, once I attack, I am intently focused. He was trying to stand up. For me, it's all about keeping my prey off balance.

I bit hard into his leg, blood coloured my teeth. Four premolars line each side of my upper and lower jaws in back of the canines. These are the shearing teeth I used to rip the jeans from my attacker's leg. Tilting my head to the side, wolf style, I grabbed his meaty leg again with my premolars and ripped flesh off the bone. My top jaw has two molars on each side, and the bottom jaw has three. These are my crushing teeth, used to crack bones. I bit deep and hard. The son-of-a-bitch screamed in pain. I was winning and darn proud of it.

Looking up, I saw Malibu. His technique was different from mine. He was crouched directly on top of his paws, with visible shaking seen in some parts of the body. His tail was close to the body, standing up, together with hair at the back. His legs were very stiff or even bent to increase their size. Typically, Malibu avoids contact when he feels threatened, although he can resort to varying degrees of aggression when he feels cornered, or when escape is impossible. Hissing and snapping his teeth at the other dognapper's ankles, he fought hard. Malibu can claw at a rate of five times a second. I think he broke that record. Front paws, with sharpened claws, were striking lightning fast. Ankles bleeding more with each cat claw attack, the intruder left the yard. Mine would have left too, had my tooth not been lodged in his right leg. Finally, he yanked me off by the collar and stood up.

The Director and Producer arrived. Holding the only weapons available in the yard, the Director waved the BBQ spatula as menacingly as he could. The Producer, armed with the big fork, was at his side.

As odd as it may seem, in this life and death moment, all I could think was, are we having hamburgers? The intruder, hopping on his left leg, bounced out the gate, then speeding tires raced down the back lane.

What I want you to understand is that my life and that of my buddy, Malibu, were at stake. I am not a mean dog. If I did not fight, I would have been used for puppy mill breeding. Malibu would have been sold or held for a reward.

Many Shepherds think that their dog will fight back if someone tries to steal them. I can tell them that with the right introduction and medium rare sirloin, any dog, including me, can be snatched. Be careful out there. Lock your gates! The dogs most likely to be stolen are the pit bull terrier, labrador retriever, and chihuahua. The least likely animal to be stolen from an urban yard is the water buffalo. It's too hard to get it into the back seat.

When the police arrived, we went out into the backyard. The female detective smelled of Labrador retriever. Two dogs, I think, one young male and one older female. Both labs. While the Shepherds talked, I drew a picture of the thief in the dirt.

The version told to the police was accurate except the part about me biting the dognapper was omitted. Maybe the Director thought Animal Services may want to talk to me if they knew I had bit someone.

Handing the Director his card, Detective D. Barker commented, "Use a stiff, bristled brush and chorine on that," he said, pointing to the fresh blood splatter on the concrete.

We still have some unfinished business. At that moment, I knew this was the same police officer that had visited our house to ask the Director questions about the fire extinguisher mercy killing.

That night Malibu and I slept in the Shepherds' bedroom. We have been there ever since.

Chapter 25

Qannik

The next morning, I paid the price. I was neutered.

"Are you feeling okay?" the Producer asked.

'Thanks for asking, let's have pudding, Oreos and marshmallows. When I wake up from the sugar coma, I'll be a brand new dog.'

She did not respond. However, I could detect a giggle now and then. Try as I may to acclimate to being a wide-load, I was not happy bumping in to walls. Yes, you guessed it. I had a cone on my head. Deciding to make the best of it, I waddled over to my dog bed, catching a glimpse of myself in the hallway mirror. Trying different poses, I bust a gut laughing. I wanted to show Malibu my impression of a desk lamp.

A soft meow was resonating from the upstairs linen closet. My investigation revealed that either we had talking towels or Malibu was trapped inside. Assuming, still traumatised by the night before, he hid in there sometime during the evening. I ran to the Producer for help. Over and over I told her, 'Malibu is trapped in the closet. Hurry! Hurry!'

"Woof, woof to you too, Friday," she said. This Timmy in the well thing was not working. Not wanting to give up, I raced over to the

Director. Pronouncing each syllable, I said, 'The Cat Is In The Closet.'

"Enough, enough with the barking, Friday," he said. "Nice to see you too!"

With no one left, I tapped the fish tank glass. No response. Given the fact that Malibu paws their tank in a less than friendly way, I understood their reluctance to help.

Since English was not working, I switched to canine. When I picture Malibu in my mind, I see him in his pirate ship, precariously dangling off one of the higher yardarms. I needed to convey the canine image to the Shepherds. I barked at the pirate ship, also known as a cat tree, in a low threatening growl. Well, sufferin' cats. It worked! The Shepherds came running.

"Have you seen Malibu," the Producer asked? "No, the Director said."

'I have, follow me,' I said.

"I'll check the basement. You concentrate on the main floor," he said.

There is nothing more annoying than to have two Shepherds go right on talking while you are barking. The Director rummaged around the basement nooks and crannies while the Producer scoured the main floor.

'Help is coming,' I told Malibu thru the upstairs linen closet door. 'They should be up here in about a week to ten days,' I estimated. While we waited for our rescue team, we talked. I told Malibu that as long as I was alive, he could rest easy, no one would ever hurt our pack.

'Friday, I have two things to tell you,' he said. 'First, I never doubted that you would protect me. I love you Friday! You are my hero and always will be. Secondly, when I get out, if I find that your big apricot snout was in my food dish again then I will scratch your eyes out.'

Finally I gave up on the rescue team. I jumped up and grasped the doorknob in my teeth, pulling very hard I had it open in a few minutes. Malibu was free.

With the only casualty being the doorknob and my cone, Malibu showed his smiling face.

Time passed. I healed and life went on.

This morning, the Producer was putting on her running shoes when Blondie rang the bell. Blondie is a good friend of the Producer. She runs with us two to three times a week. Last run, she talked about Frye boots. Even bought a pair with the paige clovertab cuff, wore them only in the house and then returned them. Including me in the girl talk, the Producer said I was going shoe shopping soon. I wanted Frye cowboy boots for winter. I always wanted to be a Cowboy dog named Tumbleweed or Bandit. There are three kinds of cowboy dogs. Some learn by campfire stories. A few learn by observing the cattle movements. It don't take a genius to spot a mountain lion in a flock of sheep. The rest of them have to pee on the electric fence.

Blondie calls me Fri-fri, which I find trendy. Most times we run five miles. For me, it is barely a warm-up. However, on this day, I thought I might want to stay home and rest. But no, I was going, like it or not. Go figure? On today's extra-long trek, they never mentioned what happened the week before. I was glad.

Oh, Oh, I almost forgot something very important. Before we left, the Director called me over.

"Give this note to Blondie," he said, tucking a piece of paper in my collar.

'What does it say,' I asked politely.

He did not answer.

She read the note: "Friday insists on ten miles today." Before we left, I hid the car keys under the couch.

Around the end of mile one, a dog joined us. He was a Canadian Eskimo Dog, powerfully built, athletic, and imposing in appearance. I could tell he was loyal, tough, brave, intelligent, and lost.

'Can I join your pack,' he asked, running alongside of me. This was the first time I considered the idea of a pack of dogs. Later, I would learn a lot more about it.

'Sure,' I said. 'But, I dropped a bone on the Director's head the other night. So now, we are going ten miles in the freezing cold with no food stops.' Having not seen him at the dog park before, I asked if he was new in town.

'Yes, I am visiting. A light ten miler is good. My name is Qannik, meaning snowflake. Not to worry about snacks, I forage and hunt for my own food. I take pure delight in cold weather, often I sleep outside,' he said. He stayed close to me. But, not close enough that he could be grabbed.

Like most spitz breeds he was very vocal.

He explained he was in town for the annual Skijoring tournament just north of us. It is a sport in which a dog (or dogs), assist a cross-country skier. One to three dogs are commonly used. Qannik preferred to run alone. The cross-country skier provides power with skis and poles, and the dog adds additional oomph by running and pulling. The skier wears a skijoring harness, the dog wears a sled dog harness, and a length of rope connects the two. There are no reins or other signalling devices to control the dog. He told me that he is motivated by his own love of running, responding to the Shepherd's voice for direction. His speciality was the 15km race. Most of his friends are sled dogs. But his quest was to be a Skijoring champion.

I told him to picture a lion was nipping at his heels. 'It works for me when I need extra speed,' I said. He agreed to try it. 'On the run, I am not allowed to read the mail (sniff poop and urine). This is my quest in life,' he said. I yearned for mine.

Without notice, our house appeared. Something was not right. It was too soon to be home already.

At the end of the second mile, the Producer was too stressed to continue.

When we got home, Qannik was not breathing hard. The frazzled Producer put us all in the backyard. It took the Director about an hour to get a traditional buckle collar on Qannik. I do not think he ever had one on before. When it came time to load the car, the Shepherds faced another problem. Qannik had always used a portable ramp to get in a vehicle. Not speaking Eskimo, they tried "Up", "Hup", "In" and everything they could think of. Finally, with great arm effort, this one hundred pound plus dog was loaded in the back. Arriving at the no kill shelter, the Producer said, "If they don't locate his Shepherds in a week. I am taking him home with me. He needs to run."

I was so excited. We were getting a roommate. He could fill in for me on the long runs. Daytime TV, here I come.

The no kill shelter called a few hours later to say that Qannik had a microchip implanted between his shoulder blades. They notified his owners who picked him up. They said Qannik was very happy to go home, pointing out American Eskimos dogs are very loyal.

That afternoon, after locating the car keys, I went for a car ride. The Director called me aside and told me that he and the Producer were going on a holiday. She is tired and always misplacing things like his keys, was the excuse I was given. I knew it was more serious.

'Really,' I said. 'Where are we holidaying?'

Quickly I grasped where he was going and where I was going were not the same place. I was going to a doggie dungeon. He asked me to rate the doggie penitentiaries we visited on a scale from one to ten. The first four all offered long wire cells, doggie doors leading into an attached pee area. I would be caged, side by side with other dogs for two weeks. I gave them all minus five. I think the Director scored them even lower. The next few seemed more reasonable, they offered outdoor play areas, a pond and lots of walks and free time. At the best one, the Director counted forty dogs and three staff members. I would get eleven seconds of exercise per day, he calculated. Back in the car we went. I am sure some of the places were very nice. Safety is the big issue. I would rather be in a safe environment, although somewhat confined, than to be in an unsafe atmosphere. The Producer called Auntie and Lickety Split I was going to be a country dog chasing rabbits at Auntie's farm.

'What about Malibu,' I asked, watching my doggie bed and toys load into the car. "The Painter will look after him and white bear," the Producer said. The Painter is a family friend who visits often, making a big fuss over all of us. He likes visiting with us more than the Shepherds. He is always painting his condo a different colour and that is why I call him the Painter. He has the lovely smell of eggshell latex. This month it is sea green. Next month, possibly sky blue.

Of course, I knew more. I have been on a few vacations. Every time the Director says he knows a shortcut home we go on vacation from the right road. What I gleamed from eavesdropping on phone calls was that they were going on a plane ride. Having travelled in cargo before, I feel the same way about airplane rides as I do about diet dog food. It is better for some other canine. I was glad they were going to relax and I offered my travel advice. Do not insult the alligator till you have crossed the river.

When we arrived, I was feeling a little dazed. After the run with Qannik, I had spent the next half hour licking the candy coating off all the Advils.

The Director dropped off my dry dog food and my doggie bed. My toys were not brought in because Auntie said they might cause problems. Auntie has five dogs, Essa, Kirin, Mucara and Lara who are border collies. Draco is a Belgian turvener and SillyTilly is the cat. There were four dogs boarding, Banjo, Sky, Rudy and Rue totalling ten dogs including me. Later that evening, Banjo, Rudy and Sky were picked up by their Shepherds.

At eleven-thirty p.m., well past my normal bedtime, dinner was served. Not wanting to share, I ate my usual dry dog food quickly. The Director changes dog food bags every three weeks. This month the feature was chicken with eggs, including eight vital nutrients that nourish the heart while essential minerals promote strong teeth and bones, and antioxidants help maintain a strong immune system. It was a high-quality protein with no fillers or artificial preservatives, and gentle on the digestive system. Auntie referred to it as crap.

That night I slept in whatever floor space was available. My cozy doggie bed was taken over by Kirin. I did not mind. Auntie keeps the house very cold which was refreshing. Most Shepherds' homes are far too warm for us. I have different phases of sleep, same as Shepherds. However, my sleep cycles are shorter. I go through SWE, slow wave sleep, and REM, rapid eye movement sleep cycles. Dreaming occurs in the rapid cycle. I wondered if I was going to dream about another yard sale adventure. To enter the deepest REM sleep a dog has to be completely relaxed. I was about to enter REM when, I was awakened by Drako, leaning up against me, bonding. At least, that is what he called it. At first I thought everyone else was asleep, but then, I realized that Rue could not be completely relaxed when all his muscles tensed to keep him curled up in the corner. He had four metal tags around his collar that clanged when he tossed and turned. He was a walking tension headache. I wish I had saved an Advil for him. I have only one tag, the Producer's phone number embossed on a red metal dog bone, and the Director put black tape on the ring to keep it silent. Rue was more awake than I thought, planning his takeover.

The other dogs were sleeping comfortably with their feet pointed at the ceiling. Our day at Auntie's begins at sunrise. We go out to pee in groups of four, taken off the property to a nearby field. At first, having never peed on a flexi lead, I did not know what to do. But, when I saw Essa and Draco pee, I did the same.

When everyone was finished with the morning ritual, Auntie loaded us all in car crates and we went to the city pet store, oddly named, It's Raining Cats and Dogs. I was a regular there. When we arrived I was allowed to go in the store.

"Hi Friday," the store owner, Brenda, greeted me. I ignored her. I was on a mission. After a few minutes, I found my dog food and pawed the bag.

"Yuk," Auntie said. "That's crap."

Knowing the Director read all the labels I was somewhat surprised. I pawed again thinking she had missed the part about chicken being the #1 ingredient.

"Yuk," she said again, walking toward me.

Was it possible the Director and I had been bamboozled?

Auntie explained the trick to me and another curious buyer in the store. "The dog food company breaks up the rice into its components by listing three types of rice until Chicken rises to the #1 spot. 1st- chicken meal, 2nd- ground rice, 3rd- rice bran, 4th- rice gluten and on it goes. Of course, if you added up all the different types of rice then rice would be number one on the label. This is sneaky and deceptive but legal. And, take it from me, it is crap," Auntie said.

Auntie purchased raw food patties for me. Each patty is six ounces of chicken, rabbit, bison or other game animals. Arriving home, we were allowed to play in the yard.

I had been at Canine Good citizen with Draco and at agility with Essa. They were the alpha couple. But not a romantic couple. The other three had been at competition obedience with me and we were all friends. The unknown was Kirin, Essa's son, trying to move up the pack order. I remembered him as a trouble maker from puppy class. Even then, he was bent on herding the other puppies. During run like a crazy dog, my favourite activity at puppy class, you may recall that the larger dogs, ten pounds and more, ran together while the lightweights waited their turn. I did not know it at the time, but I suppose this was an attempt to stop pack mentality from setting in. It is hard for me to understand that a pack of puppies could be threatening. A dog like Kirin that seeks to dominate, even as a puppy, may use aggression as a means to elevate its perceived power and authority, or to make others respect its wishes and not challenge it.

On the last day of puppy class, I witnessed a dogfight with Kirin and a bull terrier, open-mouthed snarling, barking and really frightening attacks on one another. But in fact, they're just doing what comes naturally (in Nature, anyway, if not in your local dog park). There is something petrifying about watching dogs fight, the lunging, the frightening faces, the low growls. It's all designed by nature to help us decide who the CEO will be, thus furthering the advancement of the pack. Fighting is not fun for dogs. I was glad to see the bull terrier submit thus ending the fight. I live in a hierarchical society, governed by rules and understandings that to Shepherds would seem extremely unjust. Keep in mind, in our world, some dogs really are "superior" to others, having first rights to mating and reproduction as well as having responsibilities in pack leadership such as providing food and protection for the others. There are "alpha" animals, male or female (or the alpha couple in this case), who lead our pack and to whom others, including me, in the pack defer. The alpha male or female makes decisions about where and when the pack will hunt, sleep and who gets ice cream. As you know, I gave up my cozy bed to Kirin without question. It also determines who stays in the pack, and may oust or kill outright other dogs that for reasons of aggression, character, illness or age that do not fit into the structure of the pack. Rue, the visiting lab cross, was not fitting in, challenging for the leadership role. As a guest as well, I suggested to Rue that he chase squirrels. He ignored me. Unfortunately, he picked the exact moment that Kirin decided to move up the doggie pack ladder. The alpha animals regularly back up and reinforces their authority by fighting those who may challenge it. Rue challenged for a leadership position and Kirin objected. Being Essa's oldest son, he felt he was rightfully next in line. The pack, having strong ties to Kirin, agreed. It was 5 against 1. I had a choice. My first option was to make it 5 against 2 and be the appetizer. The alternate option was 6 against 1. I picked 6 against 1. I do not want you to think that every encounter by a pack of dogs is about killing a member. Most of times that our pack would fight it was over a better sleeping spot or a toy lying around. It is the same way that two-year-old Shepherds squabble over the red crayon in the box without bared fangs and loud, snarling barks.

Rue had a choice. When a pack of dogs asserts its dominance over a member, the dog can either run away or roll over on its back like the bull terrier puppy did, exposing its belly to the dominant animals. This is basically saying, 'Of course I like eating last and sleeping on the cold, wet spot. You are in charge!' The point in rolling over is acknowledging that the dominant animals could, if they wanted, kill the submissive one by tearing open its stomach. Rolling over may also serve to protect the submissive animal by recalling to the dominant pack leader the way helpless puppies roll and tumble about. The submissive Rue, by looking vulnerable, would cause the more aggressive Kirin and friends, to see him as puppy-like; needing protection rather than viewed as a threat. Keep in mind, dogs are social animals and given the choice, prefer to live in peaceful groups. But, Rue was not backing down. He was moving up the ranks at any cost. I joined Kirin's pack and chanted 'kill him' right along with our alpha. By the time Rue figured out what was happening, it was too late. He began a panic run. Our pack started a full-speed chase, running as fast as thirty kilometres an hour. Rue did not run in a straight line; he attempted to circle back toward Auntie's main gate. However, pack members use direction changes to their advantage in cooperating to capture prey. Draco, Lara and Mucara had fanned out, blocking the way to the gate while Essa, Kirin and I forced him toward the side fence. Border collies, having the herding gene, are in tune with each other's movements. Our plan was to move in and bring him to the ground by biting at him, tearing chunks off his abdomen. By the time Auntie showed up, the six of us had formed a tight circle around Rue. We had him trapped, kill was our next item on the agenda. Yes, I am a canine and that is what we do. I am sorry if you are disappointed in me.

Waving a shovel at us, Auntie threatened each and every one of us. The pack looked to Kirin for direction. He was undecided. There was no doubt in my mind, the six of us could have taken her and Rue down should that have been Kirin's decision. It has nothing to do with our love for Auntie, which was real. It is about who, and what we are. We separate the two things.

For the moment, Auntie controlled the space around her and Rue. Then she did something very strange. She relaxed the muscles in her face, smiling with her eyes, slowed down her breath, then turned away from the alphas rather than moving toward them and building the tension.

"Go home, all of you go home," she said in firm, quiet voice, lowering the shovel. Many of these border collies were competition obedience champions. (Essa has more ribbons then walls to put them on.) They knew what was being asked. With the tension dispersed, they agreed. Under the leadership of Kirin, the pack disbanded, walking back toward the house. Rue stayed close to Auntie. Reaching the house, she put him in a crate in the garage and called his Shepherd for immediate pick-up.

That night for dinner, we had rabbit patties. They were delicious. Over the next few days, my entire system cleaned out of the garbage dry food. I had a bad case of poopy-pants, (Yes, that is the medical term, I think?) Auntie took me out more frequently. By the fourth day of my raw food diet, I had more energy and clearer thoughts. And, my poop was half the size, far less impurities mixed in.

Over the next eight days, we played together like a family. Draco and I renewed our friendship. Kirin and Lara, always keeping me in their sights, accepted me in their pack. At night, Auntie played records for us, mostly opera. She sang along. I did not know that Shepherds could howl.

Chapter 26

The Plea Bargain

In the morning, the Producer and Director picked me up. As the car was loaded, Auntie explained the new food routine. Then we were off. No mention of the Rue incident was made. I was happy to be going home. When we got there Painter was leaving the house, stopping in the doorway to hug me.

Once inside, I visited with Malibu.

'How was your visit with Painter,' I asked.

'Great! We played cat-mouse-cheese. In this game, Painter pretends that a ball of paper attached to a string is a frightened little critter. It runs away from the fierce kitty, that's me. It hides around the corner, it ducks under the rug, then it freezes. I pounce. We have fun. There were paper bags set up to hide in. I utilize all my hunting skills like stealth, speed, agility and cunning to find it. More fun than de-winging moths! We also played cat checkers. This game is like Shepherd checkers except the rules are slightly different. In cat checkers, if you do not like your opponent's move you can bat their checker across the room. And, kinging is different. In cat checkers, kinging is flipping a checker over your shoulder and pouncing on it. The game ends when someone jumps into the middle of the board and sends the checkers flying in all directions, usually me. But, not always. And you, how was your vacation?'

'Good, just the normal dog stuff: play, eat, sleep, almost said nighty-night to Rue. You know, the usual canine pack stuff, kill or be killed,' I said.

After putting everything away, the Shepherds coffeed, listening to the radio. Everyone in our house has their own favourite radio section. The Producer likes the Dow Jones report, which was up 275 points. She was elated. Maybe we can afford the big bag of cheesy round hounds?

My favourite part of morning radio hour has always been the stalled car report. Today, early birds who used the Donald Street bridge to escape this morning's traffic were blocked by a stalled car in the left hand curb lane, according to a report received from the bridge, but we're getting reports of mostly open roads elsewhere in the downtown area.' I said to no one in particular. I considered stalled car reporter for my life's work. Of course, if cheesy hound round tester was available I would choose that job.

'Main Street was recommended as an alternate route,' Malibu reminded me.

The Director likes the sports scores, hoping that the Blue Bombers, our football team will make the playoffs. I think if every team in the league loses their next twelve games, we have a chance. There were lots of local junior sports announcements followed by one of particular interest to me. The announcer said, "At the annual Skijoring tournament in The Pas, Manitoba, a Canadian Eskimo Dog named Qannik set a new record time in the fifteen kilometre race, running as if he had a lion on his heels." He continued, "And now over to Caroline for our top story of the day," the radio announcer said, snapping me back to the present concerns.

'Cathy Northem and Arthur Smith, of Winnipeg, Manitoba, were away for a week in December when their two-year-old Pug 'Mia' disappeared from a friend's front yard after being let out to pee," Caroline reported. "That same month, Mary White's one-year-old Siberian Husky 'Timba' disappeared from a dog park in Charleswood in the middle of the day."

"Last month, Beth Bisery left Winnipeg for one week, putting 'Huckleberry,' her two-year-old Labrador Retriever, in the care of a dog walker who tied Huckleberry up outside Kohler bakery while she ran inside to buy a donut. When she came back, Huckleberry was gone. A handful of seemingly unrelated incidents, all taking place in one city within a few months' time. Statistical small potatoes, you could call them. Or they would be if anybody were actually keeping statistics on stolen companion animals, because the police, humane societies and insurance companies don't," she said angrily, handing the microphone over.

"You could put yourself in the grave with the worrying," Cathy Northem said. "It is a cold winter, is she lost outside, has she eaten today? I never cried so much in my life for anything."

"It has been absolutely devastating," adds Beth Bisery. "It's horrible not to know what's happened to Huckleberry. Is he even alive? It's like losing your child."

"Motives, you ask?" The announcer said. "A dog may be stolen for a variety of reasons. It could be by somebody who's simply taken a fancy to the animal and wants a well-trained pet of their own, or perhaps by an estranged partner. More ominous are thefts-to-order from puppy mill operators seeking fresh breeding stock. Pictures are taken of the dogs and once the pre-order deposit is confirmed, the dog is nabbed and shipped away. Even worse, underground dogfighters are on the lookout for likely breeds as well as live animals to be used in training."

"In Winnipeg, dogs are stolen all the time," according to Jennifer Verniski, a spokesperson for the Humane Society, though she can't give an approximation of how widespread the problem is. Unspayed females and unneutered males, especially purebreds, often comprise thefts destined for puppy mill purgatory. With prices for purebred poodle puppies running

$1200 and up, dog farming can prove to be a lucrative, filthy business.

"My heart aches for the family dog snatched from their yards," says Verniski. "They will never sleep on a clean surface again, will never run off leash in The Woods. Their eight-to-ten year dog mill sentence is grim. Only the very strong will survive the cold barns in the winter and the hot humid days of summer."

Caroline continued, "Such a fate appeared to be at the bottom of a recent case involving a purebred apricot standard poodle and a ragdoll cat in River Heights, a middle class community of Winnipeg, Manitoba. Detective D. Barker says the thieves were scared off before they could make off with their prizes. The suspect was arrested in the emergency ward of the St Boniface hospital where he was being treated for severe gashes on the left leg. Doctors say that they do not know at this time if it has to be amputated. Detective Barker, a dog owner, citing an ongoing investigation, refused to comment on what clues led him to the hospital to look for the alleged dognapper."

"Const. Leslie McDiarmid, media relations officer with the Winnipeg Police Force, says that in the jurisdiction of Charleswood, these reports are taken seriously and investigated as actively as possible. It might not be up there with burglary or other types of property theft, but dognapping is on the rise, says McDiarmid. Police reports don't make a distinction between pet theft and other property theft. There's no way to pinpoint the exact number of stolen pets each year, but anecdotally, officers say that Winnipeg's pet theft is increasing. A couple of these thefts that we tracked happened around Valentine's Day earlier this year, so perhaps some people stole a puppy to give as a gift," McDiarmid adds. Toy breeds, puppies, and purebred dogs that look expensive or unusual are most vulnerable, says McDiarmid. Among the stolen breeds tracked by the AKC and CKC in 2012 are Yorkshire terriers, standard poodles, pomeranians, shih tzus, bulldogs, corgis, a Norwich terrier and a mastiff."

"And now this new breaking story just in; a plea bargain agreement has been reached with the alleged standard poodle thief in exchange for the location of a puppy mill in Up North, Manitoba. The local authorities are closing down the mill at this moment. Multiple arrests are anticipated later this week."

"And now, here's Cynthia with the weather."

I did not listen to the weather report. All I could think of was that 99 and his pack were safe. The puppy mill closed forever, many more to go. Malibu smiled.

Blondie showed up and we went for our run. Life was normal again.

When I got home, tired and hungry, SammyFarber was waiting for me.

'How was camp,' he asked.

'Good sleeping temperature, feel refreshed. Ready to take on the world,' I said.

'Keep the dream alive. Hit the snooze button often,' SammyFarber replied. 'You look thinner, more alert. Eating different?'

I smiled.

In the morning, I woke up an adult dog. I do not know how it happened, it just did. I was no longer a puppy. Sensing the change in my behaviour, the Shepherds took me to a meeting with the Manitoba Rural Search and Rescue Team. At the meeting, I met Maxx, the Canine Search and Rescue alpha, and Captain, the Shepherd leader.

The Captain explained that many dogs are cross-trained and are able to do several tasks well. He went into limited detail on each type. I could tell the Director was fascinated.

The Trailing dog (this includes the bloodhound) is trained for scent discrimination. The dog is usually worked in a harness and on leash. The dog is given an uncontaminated article belonging to the missing person. The dog is trained to follow that scent and no other.

Next, the Air scenting dog is given an area or sector to work with his handler. This dog and handler team will clear an area of any and all humans within their given sector. The dog, working off leash, is perpendicular to the wind to locate airborne scent.

And lastly, the Tracking dog is trained to follow a path of a certain person. The dog is usually worked in a harness and leash. It is a footstep to footstep approach."

The Director looked down at Maxx.

"Maxx is cross-trained. But he specializes in the two tasks. The Disaster dog, (which includes FEMA)," the Captain said. "His goal is to find human scent in a very unnatural environment. This would include collapsed buildings and areas affected by tornadoes and earthquakes. Maxx is non-scent discriminating and he is specifically trained on unstable footing, small confined spaces and other settings not usually found in the wilderness."

"I should mention he does Cadaver dog work, trained to alert on dead human scent. But, I prefer he sticks with survivors. He is a first-rate worker."

Upon hearing the options, the Director said something that to this day still makes milk come out my nose.

"I think either Disaster or Cadaver dog training would work for Friday," he said.

'Does he have rabies? Now that hallucinations had set in, I checked his lower jaw for signs of foaming. Oddly, there were none? Me, jumping through window, some of which I assume are not even open, trying to locate a dead body in a condemned building? I wondered if Lefty would be teaching the course. Not sure what to do I looked at Maxx, the Roti. 'Is this for real,' I asked? He was favouring the right side of his body.

'Yep! I just got back from Katrina. I worked five days, ten hour shifts. On the last day, in one burned out building, which I thought had been checked for safety, I jumped in the window, ran upstairs and found a body on the second floor. Sadly, a small boy had suffocated. Answering my bark, the Captain came up the stairs to investigate. Unfortunately, his weight and mine were too much for the floor joist and we fell through. When the emergency response team found us, I would not let them near the stunned Captain. I didn't know who they were, friend or foe. One look at my teeth and they backed off. Luckily, the Captain woke up and called me off. We were on the next flight home. My right side is still killing me. I think I broke a rib.'

'Too much information,' I said, Way too much. I had to find a way out of this career path. And then it came.

After looking over at my manicured nails and show dog clip, the Captain said, "You know, we are starting a new division called the Elite K-9 Therapy Division and your dog might do well at that. This is the first year it is being offered in Manitoba. The pilot program is a six month training plan of action that when completed allows him to work as a therapy dog."

"I don't know. I'm not sure if a nursing home is his calling," the Director said.

"Maybe it is more," the Producer said.

"She's right! The Elite K-9 is much more," the Captain said. "We plan to train fifteen dogs the first year who will be on call for any national emergency. Once called, they will be flown or trucked to a school or other safe house where we will transport the disaster survivors. Stationed at food table, their job description will be 'loitering with intent'. Their goal would be to entertain the children, refocus frightened survivors and offer a caring paw to those who have lost a pet. It is not a job to be taken lightly. And, when not called, they would work at the major hospitals and other rehabilitation centres in Winnipeg. This is not one of those watch a video and attend one day of training program that those so called other therapy dog programs offer. This is an extensive training course for Elite K-9's who want to perform at a high level of canine therapy and wear the Manitoba Search and Rescue emblem.

'They had me at food station,' I said.

"You know, it may be the right thing. What do we do now," the Producer asked?

"Watch the papers and you will see an announcement for an open call. Be sure to come early, we are expecting a big turnout," the Captain said.

And with that, we left. I was both excited and nervous. I am only slightly more than one year old. And, even though I have a big head, I still have a puppy body. I did not know if this was right for me. I wondered how this new vocation might affect my afternoon radio show listening. Then again, could this be my calling, my purpose in life?

Chapter 27

The Letter

Some Shepherds believe that dog training is a cooperative effort between the Shepherd and the canine. My assignment, Zaide, was a strong supporter of this concept. Saturday mornings, we met halfway between my house and his condo in an agreed upon field where the Director or Producer would hand over my leash. Zaide is a friendly, caring senior who always has a warm smile and friendly hello for everyone he meets in life. His philosophy was that life is not about waiting for the storm to pass, it is about dancing in the rain.

Hi Zaide, I said, wagging my tale on the approach. How's it going?

"Kicking butt and chewing bubble gum," he replied. I loved how he spoke to me. "Time to skedaddle, Friday. No sense putting the elephant on the table." He grabbed my collar and held it tightly, and I thought, 'he likes me!' And then I thought, 'wow this sidewalk is icy!'

At first, under Zaide's control, I was confused because the only command was, Friday follow. I soon realized that on our walk it was his job to alert us of any cars at the intersections. He did this by stopping and saying, car. Given the fact, we were never struck by a car, he got top marks for his part of the trek. However, my part was to alert the near deaf Zaide of any bicycles coming at us along the narrow bicycle path. Zaide explained to me that bicycle riders thought they hung the moon. "Let me know if you see one, I do not want to be ass over teakettle," he reminded me.

I relied on the principles of classical conditioning that were worked out early in this century by Pavlov, called Pavlovian conditioning. In the original experiments, a bell was rung, and the subject (as it happens, a hungry beagle walking by) was given a cheesy hound round; eventually, the beagle began to salivate on hearing the bell, apparently anticipating the arrival of the cheesy hound round. I had heard all this from Ivan P. Beagle, great-great grandson to the beagle in the test. 'This is pure stimulant-response stuff, since the signal (the bell) always comes before the reinforcement, and my beagle great-great grandfather did not do anything to make the bell ring,' he said. So was the case with the bicycles, the bell would ring and I would pull over. However, on Zaide's walks there were no treats or salivating, only praise rewards, once he told me I was keen as mustard. I have no idea what that meant?

Testing me, Zaide would pretend not to hear the bell, only moving over when I put pressure on the leash. We were doing well until the exercise became more difficult. In the second half of the trail, the bicycle would approach from behind with no bell sounding. Now, instead of listening for the bell, I had to find a new solution or risk Zaide being run over. This is the secret. Bikes make noise!

Rattles are caused by play in the headset bearings allowing the fork to rattle over bumps. Poor shifting by young riders can cause this too. Squeakers have a poorly lubricated chain. Squealers need new brakes or to lose weight. Clunkers and tickers do not pedal properly. Skipping, cracking, and banging means you walk with the bike. And lastly, sloshers, who have a full water bottle attached to the frame in case they come across a forest fire.

Zaide believed that before passing us, every rider should speak loudly and clearly into a bull horn, while initiating the ambulance siren attached to their bike frame. Flashing lights, although not mandatory, would get the rider bonus points in Zaide's book. The other option would be for 85 year old Zaide to wear his hearing aid. He preferred the first option, which made me feel valuable on our Saturday walk. At the end of our stroll, usually five miles, we would call Baba, his mate, to meet us. After 4 or 5 tries, Zaide completed the call. Baba would walk a few blocks with us before turning back to go home to watch golf.

Zaide told me, "Baba is not comfortable walking very far. Nervous as a very small nun at a penguin shoot," he said.

Before she left, Baba always invited us over for babka, made from a doubled and twisted length of yeast dough. Instead of a fruit filling the dough, Baba used cinnamon and topped the babka with streusel. Delicious.

When we got home, the Producer read the announcement in the paper we were both anxiously waiting for, that Frye cowboy boots were ten percent off. Also, she read the following:

Therapy Dogs needed. Manitoba Search and Rescue are looking for qualified dogs to team up with Search and Rescue dogs at disaster sites. In addition, those accepted will work at Winnipeg hospitals, special needs schools, psychiatric hospitals and more. The open call listed where and when to apply.

Time passed slowly, finally, two full days later we were on our way to the interviews. When we arrived at the recreation centre, I was shocked. Waiting outside the program entrance door were 121 dogs, one cat and one rabbit. And, it was only ten in the morning. More would come over the next two hours. Groups of twenty-five at a time were allowed into the recreation centre. I was in the third group. There were five Search and Rescue Shepherds trying to control the crowd in the cramped lobby. More than a few dogfights had broken out. This was not a pack mentality, it was a mob scene. Dogs were barking and Shepherds were yelling! Leaning forward, tail high and body stiff, I sent out cold, hard stares.

"Back off, buddy. I want this job," was my message to any four-legged line jumper who crowded me. When I finally got into the inner room, Maxx greeted us. I was with the Producer. After saying hello, the Captain asked me to sit, stay, down and a few other basic commands. I did well except I popped up on the down stay when my stomach hit the icy gym floor. The next part was off leash, where I did a recall, fronting perfectly. The Captain made a few notes on his pad. While I waited for the Director to join us, I spoke with Maxx.

'How's the rib,' I asked?

'Not good,' Maxx said. 'I am retired. I will be working with the Captain in the Elite K-9 program. So far this morning, I have had twenty-two biters try to take a piece out of me and that's before my coffee break.'

'Wow, that must be tough. I am learning how not to be run over by a bicycle,' I said. He did not react.

Continuing, Maxx said, 'the Jack Russells fought with the leash, Shelties tripped their Shepherds, Beagles howled. The cocker spaniels could not sit still for more than thirty seconds. Frustrated, the Captain said 'Speak' to the bulldog named Ozzie-Ozzie right before you and he sat quietly. I guess he was the best of that bunch. Each one was nuttier than the last. The only one who I gave really high marks this morning was a rabbit named Smokey owned by Jill,' Maxx said.

'Were you scared of the biters?'

'No, I have been trained in avoidance. I back off when a dog gets aggressive, turning my head, deflecting the attitude,' Maxx said, stopping to rub his side. "I give biters no energy to react to. And, if necessary I will growl-lunge, letting him know I can go a few rounds if it comes to that. But it's my job to avoid conflict. One mean dog told me F-off. He said that the only thing that could make him cry was an onion.

'You should have hit him in the head with a coconut,' I offered.

The only one that nailed me was the cat,' Maxx said, turning to show me the scratch on his nose.

The Captain asked was my age?

'Almost one,' the Director said. 'But, he's very mature,' he said with a straight face. I decided to stop chewing on the leash.

We went home and waited.

Three days later, the letter came. In total, 227 dogs had applied for fifteen positions. The letter went on to say that although I was accepted into the training program there was no guarantee that I would graduate. In order insure the minimum of fifteen dogs will graduate, twenty-eight dogs had been invited to training camp. Everyone except the Director was thrilled.

"It looks like they expect approximately half the class to fail," he said.

The Producer responded with what I had waited a long time to hear. "Let's go shopping for new outfits and treats."

I was loaded in the car and we were off. When we arrived at Doggie Mart, I was disappointed to learn that they do not make Frye cowboy boots for dogs. However, they have a lovely assortment of coats with matching boots. First, I tried on a yellow rain jacket with matching rain boots and a wide-brimmed floppy hat that tied under my jaw. I looked stupid. . Had the Director not have been in the corner scowling, I am positive I would have gotten it. I would have liked to impress Mira with a leather coat.

After many failed sizing attempts, the Producer and I agreed on a dark green jacket with hunting dogs on it. My boots were black. On the way out, the Producer and I accessorised. I got dark blue collar and black leather leash. I was so happy to have a new outfit for school. She got an "I love poodles' pin.

Note to canine reader: Dog shoepacks come with six shoes. Regardless of what Ivan the stupid canine tells you, the extra two do not go on the dog's ears.

Blondie stopped by and we were off. Well, sort of. I realized that after a mile my paws were killing me. Salt, de-icer and other chemicals used to melt snow and ice, irritate my pads. I think the people who use these products on their sidewalks do not like dogs. Use kitty litter or sand as an environmentally friendly alternative to salt, while it will not melt ice, it will provide better traction for you and us. The problem for me today was ice balls. The change in weather made for the perfect ice ball forming conditions. For those of you who do not know, an ice ball is a mix of snow, ice, salt and gravel between the pads and toes of my feet. Once ice balls form, they are very painful. I was suffering. In this case, I was licking the ice when it formed which only helped it cement to my feet. Sensing my discomfort, the Producer and Blondie walked me home to change.

At first, when the Producer put my shoes on they were not what I expected. The leather bottoms were slippery on the hardwood floor. I had to think really hard which foot was which, when I moved. After a few minutes, I got the hang of it. Part of the reason I accepted the boots so easily was I did not want to break up a perfect set. For me, looking cool is everything! But, I have a curious side too.

I had stood perfectly still while the Producer put my shoes on, paying particular attention to the Velcro fasteners at the top. Fully dressed, I walked into the living room. When I returned, I had all four shoes in my mouth. The Producer laughed and dressed me again. This time, we exited as soon as I was dressed. Running with shoes is very stylish. Stopping is not possible. Any thoughts I had of being a runway model dog were gone. But my feet were warm and safe. For the balance of winter, I never went out for long runs without my coat and matching shoes on.

The Manitoba Search and Rescue Elite K-9 program initially was six months. Today, the course takes two years to complete. Dogs move up though a series of courses to attain the Elite K-9 status. This being the first time it was offered in Manitoba, the three levels were combined into one.

The class was divided into two groups of fourteen dogs, each grouping training on separate days. The format was like any other basic obedience class for the first month, boring sit-stays and mini treats. Then things changed in month two. Two dogs had left the program for reasons unknown to me. However, one did say if I was ever in Florida to stop by. This would have made our class of fourteen down to twelve had Binx not started a fight with Archie. They were shown the exit sign. Not all dogs like one another, sometimes there is no real reason. I could tell the Producer did not enjoy one Shepherd who was constantly bragging about all the jumps Magnificent Murphy, her dog, could do at agility class. Finally, unable to stand it any longer, the Producer asked how Murphy liked the weave poles. This is a series of 12 upright poles, each about 3 feet tall and spaced about 21 inches apart through which the dog weaves. The dog must always enter with the first pole to his left, and must not skip poles. For many dogs, weave poles are one of the most difficult obstacles to master in agility courses. "It is Friday's favourite. Learned it the first time out." the Producer said. The truth is that it took me 18 attempts with Auntie's help; weave poles make me nauseous. Murphy's Sheppard never bragged to us again.

On the agenda for today's class was 'leave it' and 'no take'. In 'leave it' the dog has to walk down a narrow path flanked by metal folding chairs. On every second chair is a dog treat. The Shepherd goes to the end of the walkway and calls his dog who is on a sit-wait. The first dog is Ozzie-Ozzie, the bulldog. His nose does not reach up to the chair height and therefore he has a distinct advantage. For him, the treat is on the barstool.

Only one other dog was flawless. His name was Rocket. The site of the metal chairs, ready to attack him, causes Rocket to sprint to his Shepherd where he does a perfect front followed by a get around which lands him alert at his Shepherd's left side. What a show off. I would have punched him. But, a red exit sign was flashing in my mind. Having missed lunch, I was scared. Determined to make it three perfect scores, I advanced. I made it past the first piece of hotdog, sweat oozed out of all my paws. My previous experience with hot dog pieces had not been a good one and I easily avoided it when the Producer yelled "leave it" from the end of the course. By the time I reached the nose height bacon strip, I was doomed. The smell was awesome! It was crisp just the way I like it. Ignoring the Producer's 'leave it', I snacked. I have always believed that if you are going to go down then do it in style. As good as the bacon was, the sausage, chicken, cheese, baloney and meatball further down the path were better. Arriving at the Producer's feet I asked. 'Don't you just love an "all you can eat" buffet?' She did not comment. Glaring at me, the Captain replaced the food. Most of the remaining dogs took one and, at most, two pieces of food on their journey. I was alone in the nine pieces category.

I had played 'no take' lots of times before with Auntie. Although when we played the game was called 'Mine' which simply meant 'hers'. In basic obedience, I do a sit-stay while she has the Shepherds walk around us, jump up and down and do all sorts of funny moves to the left and right of us. I really enjoyed that exercise. Later on at competition obedience, I had to stand-stay while she threw tennis balls and other toys. I had been proofed on my stand stay so I remained glued to my spot when she said mine. (For those of you who do not know, here is how I was proofed on a stand stay. At first there were short stand stays. The Director would count in "good dogs", "good dog one, good dog two, good dog three, etc." delaying the food reward longer each time until I could do a thirty second stand-stay, then one minute followed by three, five, ten minutes and more. Gradually and progressively, he increased his distance. After every successful short proofing episode, he always returned to the toe-to-toe position and praised me to "capture" the stay. Lastly, three weeks later, he had me stand-stay and pulled on my leash with constant pressure, not jerking. I did not move, I was proofed.

Positioned in a straight line, I really did not care what the Captain or other dogs did, I was not moving. When Rocket, the class alpha, broke the stay to chase one of the bouncing tennis balls, all hell broke loose, dogs running everywhere with toys in their mouths. For a moment, I thought I was back at puppy class. To be honest, I felt a little foolish being the only dog without a toy in his mouth.

By the end of month three, my class had dwindled to nine dogs. Unknown to me, the other class had dropped from fourteen to eight.

When I got home from my class SammyFarber was waiting.

'So, poodle brain, how was class?' he asked while snacking on a chicken drumstick that he had somehow freed from the fridge.

I explained what I knew, there are essentially three types of therapy dogs employed today. The first are Therapeutic Visitation Animals, these are the most commonly used therapy animals. Most often these animals are a family pet whose Shepherd has an interest in sharing the joy of animal companionship with those in hospitals, nursing homes and retirement homes who may otherwise not have that luxury. Seeing the dogs often lifts the spirits of residents who may have a pet waiting for them at home or they remember a long lost childhood companion. The second are Animal-Assisted Therapy Animals. These animals are specifically trained to support the efforts of physical rehabilitation and occupational therapists to meet the needs of a person's recovery program. The animals encourage patients to work on fine motor skills, range of motion, balance, and interactive skills. The third are Facility Therapy Animals, which as the name suggests, normally reside at the facility in which they are employed. Long-term care facilities, nursing homes, and psychiatric units are all examples of facilities that frequently benefit from the service of Facility Therapy Animals. These animals are unique in that they generally don't have one owner/handler but rather they work alongside facility staff working their magic every day.

Rambling on, I confessed that I was afraid of not making it as an Elite K-9 and, if I do succeed what job will I get. I like to sleep in my own bed at home. I may not be cut out to be a working dog. I guess I can only be myself.

SammyFarber replied, 'Anyone who told you to be yourself couldn't have given you any worse advice. Fake it till you make it,' he said.

'Hmm,' I said. 'Are you going to finish that last bite of chicken?'

Chapter 28

Help Her!

During the next few months my training was constantly interrupted by wheelchairs, walkers and metal tipped canes. The click, clank, clunk of the metal walker legs sent my feet in motion, running to the exit. It may have something to do with the goats' milk problem I had as puppy. And no, I do not blame all things on that. At one point, I thought walkers were either Godzilla or the Blob with metal legs. Oddly enough, wheelchairs, crutches and canes did not bother me.

Today, seated in a wheelchair, the Producer gave commands. If you think back to how I explained that dogs do not generalize and that is why they need to train in a variety of different locations then you know what happened next.

For the rest of you, I will explain. For my entire training career, the Producer was always standing. As odd as it may seem, the moment she sat down and barked out commands, I had no idea who she was? I thought someone had invented talking furniture on wheels. Finally, the rolling Producer asked me if I wanted a cheesy hound round. Amazingly, my head cleared and I recognized her. After that, I could respond regardless

ry11111111111

of posture.

The Shepherds had to complete CPR training and the Fire Department's 'Responding to Crisis, Disaster and Trauma' course. I went to one of the CPR classes. It was fun. Seated in a circle, the instructor told me to go phone 911. Much to her surprise, I ran to the phone. I knew the word, phone, because in our house we do not play board games, except cat checkers. Instead, most nights, we play find the cell phone, remote, and car keys. I usually win. (Secret to canine readers only: Do not look for the phone. Smell for the leather case. It is much easier to locate.)

I had done enough 'go to' exercises to put the pictures together in my mind. I thought I was doing very well as a new student till I got reprimanded for pounding on one of the flesh coloured rubber disaster dummies. What can I say, I like to mimic. I spent the rest of the class tied up in the corner.

With CPR and Trauma courses complete, I waited to be tested. Finally, the day came. An hour before the exam, the Director gave me a massage learned from a book he was reading. His whole hand massaged the mass of skin on my body in smooth circles using enough pressure so that his fingers moved the skin instead of just sliding over it. It was a non-invasive type of touch. He said the book called it the Abalone technique for stress and tension reduction. I felt a renewed sense of calm. As much as I enjoyed the massage, a vanilla-peppermint ice cream cake might have had the same effect. The day only got better. On the way to the final exam, the Producer fed me three whole chickens, eight burgers and a nine course turkey dinner, I was stuffed. In a calm clear and concise voice, the Producer informed me that she would be assisting me in my final test. At this point, I seriously considered that the Producer's neck blotch was in remission. Maybe, just maybe, the holiday they took involved a miracle drug cure. Life was looking up.

Arriving at the Rec centre, relaxed and stuffed, I waited my turn. The first dog through the ten sections of the exam was Magnificent Murphy. I thought he did well, except on Station two, the recall. I am sure he snatched a chicken strip off a chair, which is a seven point deduction. Daisy-May was next. Although breaking her three minutes down-stay to squeeze a stuffed cat toy, costing her five points, she finished strong. Bailey, the lab, was cruising along nicely till Station eight in the very far back of the course. Surrounded by Manitoba Search and Rescue staff with walkers, he freaked. Growl barked at everyone. I was next in line. The only event that threatened me was Station two, the recall past the bacon on the chairs. My full belly paid off, raising my head, holding my breath, I pranced to the Producer's arms without snacking.

I went thru all ten stations without any major error, I think? Hmm, except, at one point, backing through the metal rails on Station four, my big butt touched the cold rail and it rattled, scaring me. I might have bobbed and weaved, incurring a fifteen points deduction. The Producer calmed me from the sidelines. On the extended down stay, Section six, I was eyeing three tennis balls that had been rolled by. I geared down, challenging myself not to move. I could not afford a further seven point deduction. By station seven, the off leash figure eight, I could tell my puppy concentration was waning. The Producer tapped her side, refocusing me, but not before I grazed a folding chair on a wide turn. It cost me a penalty of three points. Okay, maybe it was less than a perfect day. However, I completed all ten sections of the course. My head throbbing from nerves, I was a wreck with sweat pouring from my paws. I was not sure if I had achieved the passing grade of eighty points. Having completed my exam, we left because the Shepherds had to go to work. I would have liked to have seen the others perform so I could gauge my place in the pack.

When we got home, SammyFarber was looking through the paper. I told him that I thought I had passed my exam. But I might have failed because of the goats' milk I had as a puppy.

'Doesn't goats' milk have an expiration date?' He asked.

'No, It's fresh from the goat teat.'

'No, he said. I meant doesn't your goat milk excuse being the root of all your problems have an expiration date?

'No friggin' way,' I said. I have a vault-like memory for every injustice I have ever suffered. However, I hated to admit it, possibly he was right. The excuse had expired. Nothing sucks more than the moment during an argument when you realize you are wrong.

The Producer told me the results from our test would be revealed in two more sleeps. I napped for ten minutes. Then again, for another five minutes. It did not work. No results were forthcoming.

Life, or lack thereof, is the way I perceive the world. The piece of evidence that I can smell death coming does not make me a genius. It makes me a dog. I see signs that are invisible to Shepherds. I am all about the details. Every minor change in one of my Shepherds creates a picture for me. I was seeing it. I will try to explain.

Her lack of appetite convinced me she was nervous, especially in the morning hours. Sometimes her eyes will tear, or I see just one or two tears waffling in an eye. She constantly looks in the mirror to see if there was any change to the small red patch on her neck.

'Help her! There must be a cure.' I pleaded.

Having not slept for two days, I asked Malibu, who I was playing cat checkers with, how he thought I might have done on section eight, the walker monsters, of the MSAR exam.

'I do not know. To the unsettling things in life, I close my eyes. The scariest being what is happening to the Producer. I cannot watch. I go in the closet and hide,' he said. Hmm, that explains how he got in there.

I am not surprised that he knows. Felines are not that different from canines in these matters. Often, I see Malibu sitting on her chest, kneading her like she was raw dough, pushing in and out with his paws, alternating between right and left paw. Sometimes, he kneads with claws completely retracted, while other times he will extend his claws, push in and retract as he pulls back. When I first saw it I was salivating. Because I thought he was "making biscuits." It's accompanied by contented purring, and from time to time even by drooling when Malibu relaxes his jaw. It's not uncommon for him to be in an almost trance-like state as he kneads with a steady, rhythmic motion. When asked, he tells me that he is trying to stimulate the flow of blood to her neck to reduce the redness. I am impressed.

'King me,' he said, returning to the game, flipping a checker over his shoulder and pouncing on it. After losing a few more games, I waited by the door.

Finally, I was off to the Rec centre. When I got to the training centre in the basement, there were 17 of us left from the original 227 dogs. The training equipment had been removed from the room. At the front was a large metal table with wooden plaques on it. We all had to sit-stay in a straight line. I wanted so much to succeed for the Producer. She had given one of her very precious life days to help me in my goal.

The Captain began. "Over the past six months, it is has been my privilege and honour to have worked with each and every one of you. You are all very special dogs in your own ways." Maxx, who stood by his side, smiled. "Although not all the 17 remaining canines achieved the minimum passing grade of 80, needed to graduate today, I want you to know that all of you have a very special gift that I hope you will share with the world. Keep in mind that 210 dogs have not reached this point. You should all be proud. Given the high failure rate, I have decided, in the future, to expand the course to two years. So, those of you that have passed should be very proud of your accomplishment, doing two years of work in six months is not easy. Those of you young ones who did not pass, you are still pups and there is time to grow and improve. You too did very well. It is okay to be scared of metal sounds and walkers. In time, you will learn. It comes with age."

Being the youngest in the class by far this age comment he made scared me. I thought back on station 4 with the walkers. Perhaps, a few more errors in performance.

"Judging by nervous shuffling paws, I know you are all anxious for your results. So, I will not keep you panting any longer."

"Scoring 98 at of a possible 100 points is our top dog, Scout. Having been trained by Manitoba's pinnacle horse trainer, he may have had a slight advantage. Will Scout, the border collie, please come up and get her award," the Captain said. Everyone clapped, while Scout and her Shepherd, went up to get her prize.

"In a very close second place, with 97 points, is border collie Rocket."

"Every dog has its day," I heard the Director whisper to the Producer.

'But, border collies definitely have the weekend,' I said.

After that, there were the obedience trained dogs, Kodiak, Randy, Abigail, and Molly scoring not less than 90 points.

The Captain stopped and looked over at us. After a brief pause, he continued. "The next dog I am about to call surprised me. I never thought at his young age that he would accomplish so much." (My nerves were frayed. I was sure he was going to call me.) "With 87 points, I give you the truly unique two year old, Ozzie-Ozzie." He went up with his Shepherd and received his plaque.

'Screw you Ozzie-Ozzie! You stupid bulldog,' I said under my breath. Yes, I am a sore loser. The last thing I really wanted to do was to insult any dog that scored higher than me. However, the truth is that it was how I felt.

There were only limited plaques left on the table. Certainly, less than there were dogs. The next two dogs called were the Magnificent Murphy and Hunter. I knew both of them. We had been through agility training together. These two speedsters excelled on the seesaw, tunnel, double and triple jump and weave poles. I sighed, realizing that it was no surprise that they had passed. I was feeling rejected.

'Looks like it's time to get the ark built Noah,' I said to no one in particular.

Following them were five year old dogs, Harper, Daisy-May, Duncan and more. I guess with age does come wisdom. With each name called, my heart sank a little deeper. I looked over at the Director. He smiled back, shoulders shrugged. The Producer was teary eyed. I knew she felt that she had failed me in my quest. In my heart, I knew I would return one day and pass.

The Captain paused, looked over the remaining dogs, and said. "If you chase two rabbits, both will escape. Remember puppies, self-determination is fine but it needs to be tempered with self-control if you are to succeed as an Elite K-9. With 80 points, the minimum acceptable level, is our last qualifier. In 15th place," the Captain paused and looked around the room again. From where I was standing, I could see where his eyes had stopped. I was thinking Bailey. He had been at canine good citizen with me. I had to admit, he was a hard worker. I had to give him that. Blue heelers tend to be that way. Lots of cattle for them to round up. Plus these pooches never take a vacation, they never ask for time off, they never call in sick. Then again, he did growl bark at the walkers.

"I give you the last member of this, the first team of the pilot program for Manitoba Search and Rescue Elite K-9 Therapy Dog division. This is a dog with a puppy body, canine mind and an attitude problem.

'Friday, Friday,' I whimpered, willing him to call me. 'I do not have an attitude problem. You Sir, have a perception problem.'

The One! The Only! Apricot Poodle, Friday." I was so keyed up that I ran over and jumped on the Producer. Energized, I did a victory lap around the room before going up for my plaque. I was jazzed.

The Captain told Bailey, who had herded the wheelchairs into a tight circle, refusing to let them out, and Riley who doubled my previous record of nine snacks on the recall, that they had scored 68 and 64 respectively. He felt with a bit more training, they would pass in the next class.

Hoping to lift their spirits, I suggested to both dogs that they take the year off and be house watchdogs. Seeing the puzzled look on their faces, I explained: a watchdog is one who guards the house by sleeping at the front door. If a burglar enters he falls over the dog alerting the household. It's a fun gig! You'll pass next year with honours.

On the way home, we stopped for celebratory ice cream. The Producer had a small chocolate sundae, the Director had a medium twist cone. I ordered the extra-large banana boat supreme with hot fudge and sprinkles. I got a small dish of vanilla. Oddly enough, although not what I ordered, it was delicious, the sweet taste of success.

The MSAR lady came the next day and measured me for my uniform. With a custom made jacket, my wardrobe was elevated. I was surprised to learn that my Elite K-9 black jacket made of PVC backed denier fabric with my name embroidered on it in gold leaf letters, did not come with matching shoes and a hat. During the final fitting, she said. "In the future dogs must be at least eighteen months old to start the first stage of the extensive two year Elite K-9 program. Your coat, Mr. Friday, looks more like a blanket. You will grow into it. Anyway, at slightly over one year of age, you will always be the youngest dog to have ever completed the program. You should be a very proud puppy. You are such a cutesy-wootsey dog. So, cutesy-wootsey I just wanna hug you."

I responded by barfing up my breakfast. 'Oh look, more food,' I said. She left quickly.

My first job was at the Children Rehabilitation Centre on Wellington Crescent. Since it was only a mile from my house, I told the Shepherds I would take the bus. They insisted on driving me.

Having completed nine different training programs, learned more than 75 commands, and fluent in three languages: Canine, English and Bleep, nothing in my past had prepared me what was about to happen.

My friend, Jasper, was waiting for me when I arrived. Jasper is an eight year old sheltie that went through competition obedience and agility with me. Her Shepherd brought along the scent items. The front row comprised of nine children in wheelchairs and their concerned parents. A dedicated group of therapy workers completed the anxious crowd. Talk about a high pressure performance moment.

"Jasper can read minds," her Shepherd told the audience. To prove this point, she had Jasper sit-wait facing a tree. The Sheppard showed the audience eight wooden dumbbells, each with a number on them. Placing the dumbbells on the ground in a random fashion, she asked the audience to pick a number. None of the kids responded. Finally, a staff member said five. Holding the number five dumbbell by the centre, she whispered to the crowd, "This one is it," before setting it back down.

Called, Jasper came running. I am thinking of a number from one to eight," she said, pressing her forehead. "Jasper, Go find! Go find," she repeated. Wanting to get a better view of the show, I went and sat in the front row. Wedged between two wheelchairs, I had a clear view of Jasper at work.

After passing her nose over each item, Jasper returned holding the number five dumbbell in her mouth. She had smelled out the correct one. I was impressed.

'What's your secret,' I asked.

'It is easier than it looks,' Jasper said. 'First, I was taught how to find a cheesy hound round that was hidden, then a toy. I use my sniffer. In this exercise, my Sheppard puts her scent on the correct numbered dumbbell by handling the centre of that one only. After that, I can easily sniff out the only dumbbell with the strong scent in the middle.

'Wow! I could learn that. I can sniff the right kitchen cupboard to open and take out the cheesy hound round container when no one is home. I mean if I did such a thing, which I do not do. No, never. Not me?'

The cheerful adult crowd applauded Jasper's find.

Realizing I was gone, the Producer looked around. Spotting me in the crowd, she called me over. I came, although I was reluctant to give up my good spot. I would have preferred to stay and watch the rest of Jasper's performance.

I was up next. I did Frisbee catches, ball runs, broad jump and variety of other tricks much to the delight of the crowd. Not everything was a crowd pleaser. How exciting is watching a down stay? When the high jump appeared, the crowd energized. It was set at the very high four foot mark. Checking the wind direction, backing up twenty feet, I sprinted full out, leaping at the exact right moment. The black and white bar wobbled, but did not fall. The adult crowd clapped in awe while the children remained silent. I was starting to realize that these children saw the world through different perspectives. Like chalk and cheese. For them, it is not about waiting for the storm to pass, it is about dancing in the rain.

I identified with the autistic children. It may be because their frontal lobes do not work same as normal people hence they are not big picture people. They see the world more like me, a connection of details forming a picture. The canine brain is the default brain for an autistic child. How cool is that I pondered?

Next was the meet and greet. In this exercise Jasper and I visited with kids in their wheelchairs in an effort to be patted. (Not as easy as I thought it would be.) The children's hands moved in a herky-jerky fashion that I was not used to. One child spooked me by pointing his stiff fingers at my eyes and jabbing. The simple act of petting a dog was extremely complex for these autistic children. In my canine world, when we learn a very difficult trick like 'bang, you are dead', we break it down to its smallest parts. For one week, we learn bang means down, week two down-rollover, week three down-rollover-head around. Sometimes, I do it with my feet pointed up because it gets a bigger laugh. Three weeks for one trick. It occurred to me these children had learned how to pet a dog the same way, small steps till they made contact with the desired object. As you know, I am a visual thinker. This does not mean that my non-linguistic thinking allows me to do a jigsaw puzzle. But, it does mean that pictures joined together form a language for me that I call canine. I suspect it was the same for these kids. I could see the picture of a patted doggie in their head when their hand moved toward me. Until I began to understand English, I thought everyone saw pictures in their head like I did. These kids certainly did. I am in no way implying that an autistic child and a canine think alike. What I am saying is that there is some similarity in thought process worth checking out.

This one child, Joey, who was having the most difficulty petting caught my interest for a number of reasons. I liked Joey's cowboy boots. Secondly, oddly enough, he and I were bonding.

I offered my canine words of wisdom: If at first you do not succeed Joey, then destroy any evidence that you even tried.

I considered he might understand my problem with walkers and light oscillating off them. There was a strange and beautiful kinship developing as I leaned into Joey. The cowboy tried again and achieved the petting goal.

Moving on to the next wheelchair, the little red headed girl, Cheyenne, age eight or nine, was staring at my furry apricot right paw. Looking down, I saw a fly had landed on it. Her clear blue eyes shifted to a nearby elm tree. The trunk was seven feet across. It was a vase-shaped silhouette soaring eighty feet in the air, gradually arching limbs pierced the sky. Turning, I saw a faded greenish yellow six inch long leaf was in free fall. For the next few minutes, I tracked her eye movements, seeing what Cheyenne saw. To my amazement, she saw the world as I do, as a combination of tiny movements making pictures. It was nice. I liked it. That's all. A surge of appreciation passed between us. Most, if not all Shepherds, see the big picture, missing the beauty that the red head saw in the details of the falling leaf.

She leaned over and asked me my secret for happiness. I told her, 'red meat is the one-way ticket to happiness. Fuzzy green meat is not so good.'

The next little boy would not touch me, deciding if I was friend or foe. 'If I do not know what something is or if it is foreign to me then I have the same problem,' I told him. Protecting my neck with my paw, I was hoping he did not see me as the snowman. Giving in to his fear, he did not touch me. His therapy worker asked me to bark. I found this a strange request. But, I obliged. Hearing me bark, the boy laughed. "Do it again, bark," the worker said and I did. The anxiety the kids were feeling not knowing if we were bad or good dissipated. All the kids were laughing. Who would have thought that barking, that every dog can do without training, would be the most effective. After about eight rounds, the Director said, "Enough. Enough with the barking Friday," I quieted. It was a moment of serenity, but within it was a spark of love not only for the moment, or the things held therein but for the value of every breath of life. I flashed back to the fire extinguisher. Briefly, I considered the possibility that the Director had made a huge mistake.

After saying goodbye to Jasper and waving to the appreciative crowd, we went home. All in all, it was a beautiful day!

When I got home, the Producer wanted to do more training in the basement before dinner. This was very odd since the Producer leaves my training to the Director.

I heard a noise, and I am ninety-eight percent sure it was bacon frying. 'Come find it with me,' I said to the Producer. 'Yup, it's bacon frying. Follow me. This way! It's bacon.'

"Stop pulling and pay attention, Friday," she said, trying to see her neck reflection in the window.

I knew this was not going to go end well. She had tied a new yellow and blue towel to the cord of an iron. I like yellow and blue, they stand out for me.

"Pull hard," she said.

Wanting to get back to the bacon search, I pulled on the yellow and blue cloth. The iron came flying off the table, bonking me on the head. Boy, did that hurt. Then, with the cloth tied to the radio cord, she was at it again.

"Have you hugged your poodle today,' I asked trying to distract her.

Ignoring me, she continued with my training.

"Pull hard, Friday!"

I pulled and ducked down, fearing the radio playing a country western tune would crush my skull. Luckily, only the cord released from the wall socket.

Repeating the same exercise, with the towel tied to the radio cord, five more times we practiced. I wanted to tell her that I already was trained on 'pull hard' but she seemed so happy with our progress.

Teeth clenched on the towel, legs braced for leverage, pull and duck, I repeated, wanting to please. After the seventh successful effort, she looked down and said, "I love you Friday". I looked up and told her 'I love you too, very much.' She said, "Let's go have cake. Worries go down better with cake."

'Yes, I agree. And, did you know stressed spelled backwards is desserts,' I added.

Now, some of you, I would guess 10 percent, already know what specific task I was being trained for. For the other 90 percent of you who have no idea, welcome to my world, I had no friggin' idea why the Producer was so adamant about teaching me to pull out a cord from a wall socket attached to a radio playing country western tunes.

Chapter 29

Pull Hard

It is written in their history. They came to teach. They came to heal. They came to comfort. Four intrepid French Canadian women came through the wilderness by canoe. The Grey Nuns stepped out of their canoe onto the shores of the Red River, and into the history of Canada, the province of Manitoba, the city of Winnipeg and my hospital. St. Boniface Hospital continues to lead by following in the footsteps of its indomitable founders. It was the first in Manitoba to conduct open-heart surgery in 1959. An advocate of innovation, it established a stand-alone research centre that has since become world renowned. Many lives have been saved.

St Boniface Hospital is continuing to break ground in quality of patient care, operational efficiency, and research discovery, improving the quality of life for all within reach of its open arms. It is in that spirit that they developed the canine program. Canines with proven skills, are welcome to visit patients. Their visitation program is administered by the Director of Volunteers, a woman named Karen. Many hospitals have yet to embrace the healing power of canines. If doing right means taking a different path, St Boniface Hospital is prepared to walk alone.

When I applied to work at St Boniface hospital I did not know what to expect. I was hoping for five dollars an hour and all the chicken wings you can eat.

At orientation, we learned the courses I would have to complete before joining the other seven working dogs. The first was confidentiality and hospital codes. Having been a proven Keeper of secrets, I did not have to attend. The blabber mouth Shepherds did. The next course was hand washing and bacteria control. Here again, only the Shepherds were forced to scrub in. The blood-workup, checking for a variety of diseases and current inoculations, was done at the lab in the basement of the hospital. Putting out my paw, I saw the Producer and Director roll up their sleeves. Checking for every disease known to mankind, four vials of blood were taken from each. The lab technician shook my paw. At that moment, I knew I was going to like this place. I only needed to show my veterinary immunization record. Lastly, I had to take the St Boniface Hospital Canine Good Citizen test. Having attended this class with Auntie on more than one occasion; I was not worried. I had earned my honourary good canine citizen certificate already. Dressed in my MSAR jackets, I readied for the test.

"Don't I know you from somewhere," the tester asked. "Of course," she said, twirling her long hair. "Of course, I do. You work at the Children's Rehab with autistic children. I saw your doggie show. My son Joey, loved it. Very impressive! There is no need for you to take the assessment," she said. "Go down to security on the main floor and get your ID and work clothes."

Work outfit? I was pleased. At security, they took my picture. The Shepherds got lanyards with laminated badges as well. The blue scarf with the St Boniface hospital emblem on it and the word 'volunteer' written in English and French was exquisite. I was to report to the sixth floor on Monday at one o'clock in my new outfit. The Director was given a parking pass and the code to the VDL (volunteer doggie lounge).

I spent the weekend listing to "Dr. Home Remedy" on the radio. I figured, in addition to my therapy job, I might as well dispense some medical advice. Hey, like you never played doctor?

On Monday, I reported to work half an hour early, hoping to make a good first impression. Pressing the code lock to my office, we entered. It was impressive, not that I had any other office with which to compare. There was a desk model HP touch screen sign-in computer, three snack trays (from left to right, potato chips, chocolate mint patties and cherry nib packages), locker keys, dining table with four chairs, and a floor model CQE-WC-00900 by Crystal Quest - 2 temperature ultra-filtration hybrid, hot and cold, in white with four filters water dispenser. Pressing the blue lever on the cooler, the Producer filled a paper cup with cold water. I watched and learned, wanting to know every aspect of my job. The next thing I remember was the cool sensation of cold water around my ankles.

"Please stop, right now, this very second, stop pressing that blue lever, Friday" the Director said.

Ten seconds into my first shift and I was going to get fired. I just knew it. The Director pulled me away and towel dried the floor. The Producer and I pawed us in on the computer touch screen.

The sixth floor is for medium stay patients. The hallways are bustling with wheelchairs, walkers and moving beds on wheels. There are no traffic lights or stop signs. I listened for bicycles. Not hearing any, I proceeded down the long hallway. I planned to start at the far end and work my way back to the nurse's desk. The smells in a hospital are very different than the dog park. At first, it smells like paper and ink, due to all the charts, pens, files and documents everywhere on the nurse's desk. Soon I picked up the lovely smell of body eliminations (poop, urine and vomit) coming from the first room. What can I say, I like the smell of poop. I am a dog. The next room had the metallic smell of blood, which can render the strongest stomachs like mine nauseous. I was holding my breath. We moved on. At the end of the hall, I entered the last room. The smell of newly cleaned sheets and hospital gowns assaulted my nose. Lemon fresh detergent, I think? All of these layered smells were masked by a heavy cloud of antiseptic lotion that floated around mid-high. Hospitals smell like the way sterilized plastic cups look to my eyes, dull and uninviting, but also efficient and clean.

At each room, the Producer asks if the patient would like a visit from the dog. We are invited in. I go first. The room has two beds separated by a curtain. I was surprised how compact the room was. Everything I had learned at Aunties Rally-O was put to the test. Sharp turns and staying tucked in tight to the Producer at all times, back-back and get around were common commands. Up-sit, which means to move up a few inches and then sit, is the Producer's favourite, allowing me to inch closer to the patient's bed. Since hospital beds have metal rails and thirty-inch frames, they are higher than most beds so it creates a problem for me. I have to extend my head to be patted. Looking over at bed two, I see a solution. No longer threatened by the rails, I back in nicely. Standing on my hind legs with my front paws on the bed rail, I smile at the bed two patient. We go room to room visiting with everyone. Each one has a dog or cat story to tell. In some of the rooms, there are visitors having awkward conversations about the cold weather. We were about halfway down the hall when something unfamiliar happened.

"Do you want a visit from the dog?" the Producer asked. The middle-aged guy in the bed turned around sharply and coughed. "No, no stupid disease carriers in here."

I have to admit that I thought he was talking about the Producer since I felt fine. I wondered how he knew of her illness. I was wrong again.

"Dogs are not allowed in the hospital. Call the police." Taking a deep breath from his puffer, he pressed his emergency call button and bells rang. The light outside his room flashed. I was confused. I did not know what to do.

The nurse came running down hall. "What's the problem Mr.

Smithers," she asked.

"Damn zoonose," he said, catching his breath. "I pay taxes and I pay your salary. You have savage beasts running around. I am Mr. Alfred Norman Smithers. What do you think my name means in this town?" he asked.

'Shithead,' I answered without thinking. The Nurse, who luckily did not speak dog, looked over at me and said, "It's okay puppy, not to worry. He is having an off day. It's very hard for him to keep air in his throat"

'Did he just call me zoonose?' The nurse did not respond. Before I moved on, I offered him free medical advice. Cause, that is what I do. 'Gargling is good way to see if your throat leaks.'

In the next room was the sweetest lady I ever met. Her name was Mildred. She was 92 or more. She knew a dog school word, 'hup'. Or, so I thought. At Auntie's, I was put on leash and sat next to the Director. When ready, he walked me quickly to the high bar, giving the command, 'hup'. I hesitated and he gently helped me over the very low bar. Once my confidence built, the bar was raised and each time he said, "hup", I cleared a new height, getting my treat or words of praise. Now, hearing the command and wanting to please, I leaped over the protective metal rail onto the bed. Landing perfectly, straddling the frail woman, she looked up at my furry white belly. "Woo-hoo," she said, clapping with joy. I could feel the Director's heavy eyes on me. Luckily, the Producer lifted me off the bed. When we were leaving, the lady with tear filled eyes told us that of all the things she missed, not being in company of her dog was the hardest. Mildred thanked us for coming and released the water in her eyes. I could see a small smile returning so I offered some medical advice, 'Laughter is medicine too.'

In the next room, there was a welcome mat laid out for me. Actually, it was apple sauce and blueberry muffin pieces on the floor. 'Finally, snack time,' I thought.

"Leave it," the Director barked. "It can have medicine hidden in it."

'Drugs hidden in apple sauce? Hmm, I wondered if that was what all the fuss at Elite K-9 food avoidance training was about?' Being at work, I obeyed. We had a nice visit with the young girl. Exiting the room, I thought I caught a glimpse of a familiar object in the corner. To me the command, leave it, meant anything on the floor or chairs was out of bounds. Moving closer, I realized that it was a little stuffed dog in the closet and therefore fair game. When we exited, everyone turned right except me, I bolted left. The Director caught up with me in Mildred's room where I dropped off the brown stuffed dog. Geez, the Director's face told me I was in trouble again. To this day, I do not know what I did wrong. Mildred said she missed her dog. And, I brought her one. That's my story and I'm sticking to it.

The rest of the floor went well. The second half of our shift was on the eighth floor.

Palliative care is a form of medical care, which concentrates on reducing the severity of disease symptoms, rather than striving to halt, delay, or reverse progression of the disease itself or provide a cure. No one goes home from palliative care. All possible cures have been exhausted if you are on this floor. The goals of palliative treatment are concrete, relief from suffering, treatment of pain, psychological and spiritual care, a support system to help the individual live as actively as possible, and a support system to sustain and rehabilitate the individual's family. Getting off the elevator, the first thing I noticed was the smell. When you walk by a room, there is a distinct smell, I don't know quite how to explain it in English. It is not like urine or stool. It is unique. Sometimes, on the eighth floor, sniffing at a room I know that a patient will not live long. I wonder if I am the only one who notices this. No one has been able to explain this odour to me. It does not seem to matter if the patient has cancer, heart disease or is dying from age related debility. It comes off the skin in the form of a gas. It was a sweet rather heavy odour, not unpleasant.

The wall colours are not neutral like on the lower floors, grays mixing with pinks and greens are everywhere. The floor is carpet, not vinyl, and the lighting is brighter. The Producer takes me down a long, wide hallway. The Director follows. There are no wheelchairs, walkers or moving beds. It is quiet, like the muted sounds of The Woods at night. I notice there are signs on the semi-closed doors of the patient rooms. And then it occurs to me, we are playing Rally-O. I wait for the Producer to read the first card.

"This one says, Stick Your Nose in the Door," she said. Had I known that it said, Immediate Family Only, I may have acted differently. Sticking my nose in the door, I saw a large room with a big bed, two lounge chairs and a river view. It was charming. The lone occupant, an elderly male, spotted me, his frail arm waving me forward. Dull brown eyes watched me as my pack advanced. I got close enough to be patted. He had a gentle touch and a warming smile. The brightness in his eyes had returned and for that patting moment, he was free from his disease, running in The Woods. At least, in his mind if not in his body. If you have never felt that you have found your place in life then I encourage you to sniff further. I had found mine.

In all the rooms we visited on the palliative floor, we were welcomed like long lost relatives. The Director believes that the quiet stroking of a pet, can significantly change your body's physiology, lowering your blood pressure and heart rate. The release of calming chemicals promotes a longer life. I do not know anything about that. But, I can tell you that on this floor, I get much more than I give. The sweet, heavy odour was strongest in this last room. The next patient, Dorothy, feeding me a vanilla cookie, said I reminded her of a childhood Corgi, not in looks, but in attitude. Moonbeam was her name. At her bedside was her seven year old great granddaughter. Sensing my sadness, the child patted me. With upturned lips, she said, "I love you doggie! You know, Grandma is going on a very long, wonderful car ride later tonight with her head out the window the whole way!"

I understood!

Over the next month, I worked nineteen shifts at the hospital, which took my mind off my secrets. It seemed apparent that the never to be found fire extinguisher was enough for the Director to be free to live a long healthy life. That only left two pressing issues. The red patch on the Producer's neck, and the location of a bone I had buried in the yard last week. Unlike Shepherds, when a dog gets a bone, he doesn't sell it and go out and make a down payment on a bigger bone. He buries the one he's got. But I could not remember where.

Being a workday, I looked forward to seeing my regulars. I had a slipper Rolodex in my brain. I knew exactly who everyone was. Shepherds try to memorize names or facial features which is not easy to do on an entire ward, moving from room to room. My 'slipper Rolodex' works every time. When I meet someone on the palliative floor I smell their slippers because there are always droplets of pee on them. Each one smells unique. So the next time you want to remember someone, smell their slippers. It's a secret. Cool, eh?

The Director was my only Shepherd at work that day. We visited every room on the ward. It was standing room only. On this particular day, existing the elevator, I noticed a red fire extinguisher in a glass case on the wall. Oh my god, not again I thought. My body froze.

Seeing the cause of my distress, the Director knelt down and whispered in my ear.

"It's gone for good. Not to worry," he said. "I love you and I will always be there for you, Malibu and Anna."

I relaxed.

I understood love. For a canine, love is like peeing on yourself, you get that warm feeling all over.

We moved on.

In my early shifts, the Shepherd would stand at my side in the room of the patient.

"How old is he?" The voice in the bed would ask.

"What does he eat?"

"How often does he take a bath?"

Many mundane questions, over and over again.

I passed the time by watching the EKG machine. It was much better than television. The arching and dipping line on the screen told me there was life. I loved watching it bounce. The Director would answer and we would be thanked for visiting. It was an empty experience.

I was sooooooo booooorrrreeeeeedddddd that I eventually fell asleep only to find someone's face glaring down at me.

'Geez, woman! Do you go up to every person you see and smother them like this? I didn't think so. I'm out of here. You're seriously watching me sleep? You realize how obviously creepy that is, right? I was having an off day.'

On my fourth or fifth visit that week, the Director could no longer bear to be in a room with a dying person, sending me in the room by myself for the first time. There is where my job changed. I had my 'Aha' moment, Oprah would be proud. The patients opened up to me, sharing their life, their picture albums. I learned the names of all their children, their dogs, their moments of joy and, most importantly, what they needed to discuss before they died. The Director stood guard outside the door because I was not supposed to be off leash.

Like all competencies, effective listening can be learned through focused practice. One such skill is the art of picturing what others are saying by turning words and phrases into concrete pictures. This is a very canine thing to do.

For me, being silent feels like being inactive. But, I learn that listening is the act of paying attention, the act of consideration. The silence is not suppression; it's where understanding begins. I do not try to judge, question or fix. I am that bouncing line on the computer screen. For that brief visit, I am part of their life experience. The screen is always more active when I am in the room. This touches me deeply. I make a difference.

Having learned 3 languages, 72 or more commands and more tricks than a circus pony, I am finally qualified to do what I was put on this earth to accomplish. My greatest gift was revealed; the ability to listen, comforting those who are dying. I have learned to be the silence that is needed when someone else speaks. It is how I connect with the patients in their final hours. Who would have thought that me, Friday Poodle, an Elite k-9 therapy dog would have such a gift. I mean I only scored 80 on the test. Not like I was top of the class. But, I was darn good at my job. I wrinkle or straighten my forehead to show confusion or determination. My eyes brighten when I hear their stories of a joy in their early days. My pupils dilate, showing the whites of my eyes, when they are scared. I comfort them, pulling my lips back and showing my teeth in what appears to be a smile. My tail is raised to show I am listening, my ears relaxed. Yes, I can be judgmental. If my tail wags more to the right, it is a sign of positive feelings; left-side wagging indicates negative feelings. These are gestures reserved only for my palliative patient communication; I will not do this with other dogs. I am honest with every patient. They deserve that.

Over the next week, I had a few days off because the Director had a cold and he did not want to infect anyone. I was feeling blue. Work energizes me.

Sniffles gone, the Director tells me that we are going to the hospital. I am so excited. Renewed bounce in my step. We arrived and pawing in on the computer I start my shift. The Palliative floor was eerie that day, more than usual. In some ways the process of dying is like the process of being born. Over sixty-one days on average, a canine goes through many stages of development that lead at last to labour and birth. In a similar way, a person with advanced illness goes through many changes over an extended period of time, with a set of clear changes occurring in the final stage, moving toward death. These are not signs of a medical emergency but parts of a natural process that does not need to be disturbed. Birth and death are very similar pictures to me.

The patients wait for the doctors to make their rounds, the x-rays, the technicians. The nurse who brings the medication. Anything different to stop the monotony of it all. There are the pregnant women waiting for new life to emerge. When I come I sit near the bed, I am not in a hurry. I am here to listen to them, straightforward, simple language about the things that are utmost in their mind when the drugs do not force those feelings down. I understand the concept of living on borrowed time. You may be surprised to learn this secret, all of the patients are aware of the seriousness of their illness. They are fully observant of how their loved ones are acting differently toward them. They have suddenly become like canines, understanding pictures more than words. They share it with me. Oddly enough, they do not share this knowing with their family and their doctors. They keep it secret. I think it may be because it is too painful for them. Telling me is the only outlet they have. They are okay that the doctors and staff do not always deal directly with them. As long as they are not made to feel like helpless children.

In one room, the grey haired frail woman explained.

"Hi Friday, I wondered where you have been. Were you ill? I missed you."

'The Director had a cold,' I explained.

I knew her from her slippers. She had been here for a long time. She went on to say, "I do not like people coming to see me, only canines because I look so awful. I do not like the way people look at me. I do not like the idea of a funeral, you know, maybe that is strange. I have a loathing for it. The thought of people looking at my body in a casket is a creepy."

Looking up, I heard two doctors on the other side of the curtain talking to each other.

"She will not see the morning, I suspect," the female doctor said.

"Hasn't eaten in four days," the male with the chart said. "And her feet are blue!"

"Is there a DNR? The morphine dose is very high and may not continue to work?"

"Yes," said the one with the chart.

"Godspeed," he said.

Oh, Hi Friday, the female said peeking around the curtain. We were just leaving, we did not see you."

I had heard the term DNR before. I thought it meant "Dignity N Respect" not Do Not Resuscitate. I like my version better.

I am keenly aware of her limited time. For many, there is no tomorrow. So I do not pass up any opportunity to listen.

I stayed till she fell asleep.

I had been to twelve rooms when we advanced toward the room on left at the end of the hall. Entering, I looked at the raised white bed. On it was a familiar face. Oh my god, I focused, it was the Producer. The Director leaned over the bed and kissed her on the forehead. She smiled.

We stayed for a short while. The Producer was very tired.

"We have to go now, love you," the Director said. "I will turn the radio to country music because I know how much you enjoy it."

Thank you. Love you too. Could I have a word with Friday alone?" She asked?

I wondered what she wanted to tell me, perhaps never walk by a pigeon coop with an owl in your pocket? Hmm, maybe not.

Sensing my presence was the only one in the room, slowly her eyes opened wider, a gentle smile followed. Eyes looking to the right; I followed. There, on the floor, was my yellow and blue towel lying on a cord coming from a socket on the wall. Scrunching her face, eyes tightening to slits, dry, cracked grayish lips pushing out her final muted words she said: "Please Friday. Pull hard."

I knew what she wanted. But, I could not react.

"Please Friday Poodle. Pull hard."

Reluctantly, I did what was asked and I left the room. The silence was eerie.

Chapter 30

Cow Cow Boggie

Stressed to the max, I did not sleep that night. In the morning, I admitted my crime. The Director drove me to a large white building. I knew what I had done. I had disconnected the life support tube from the Producer's life support machine and I had to pay for that. I had killed her. Having some understanding of the Shepherd world, I knew what was about to happen to me.

Today is my last day, Winnipeg, Manitoba, Canada, January 7th, my veterinarian is performing a two-stage process. There's an initial injection that simply renders me calm. It had been completed. A second shot to cause my death was eminent. This short break between shots allowed my surviving owner, Frank Richards, the chance to say goodbye to me without his emotions stressing me out. It also greatly mitigates any tendency toward spasm and other involuntary movement from me which might intensify the emotional upset that my owner would experience later on when he replayed the events of today.

I was not concerned about any frigging stress it might cause Frank, laying on that table, staring down a large needle filled with sodium thiopental. I thought he loved me? (What an idiot I am.) If I get out of this I am going to bark up one side of him and down the other. To think, geez, I never gave up Frank's secret. However, I pled guilty because I did it. Yes, I killed my mom, Frank's wife. Yes, I never denied that fact. I did what she asked of me. I will die with my head held high. Even if I have one hundred reasons to not do what you ask of me. If I love you, I will still look for that one reason to fight for what you want.

Frank cradled my head (so I didn't move while being injected or try to bite), while the doctor held a simple pump in his right arm consisting of a plunger that fit tightly in a tube above my muzzle. The plunger was pulled inside a cylindrical tube (called a barrel), allowing the syringe to take in the sodium thiopental at the open end fitted with a hypodermic needle that would eventually direct the flow out of the barrel and into my pumping puppy heart.

The nasal voice of the five o'clock news reporter on the lobby television cut through the tension.

Vancouver officers are mourning the loss of Zulu, a police dog who died Monday morning following a suspect pursuit. Zulu was allegedly stabbed by a suspect in the parking lot of the RCMP K Division in central Vancouver. "It's a tragic day here at VPSC," says Winston Dolman, spokesperson with the Vancouver Police Service Communications (VPSC). "I know both the handler and the dog myself. I was out training with that dog team earlier this month."

Zulu was a five-year-old German Shepherd who was a member of the VPSC for three years. The call started at around 5:15 a.m., when officers responded to a suspected stolen vehicle in the area of 725 Granville Street. There was a short pursuit that ended on 109 Market Street and Beach Avenue, where the suspect tried to escape on foot. Police say Zulu was deployed after the suspect was repeatedly told to halt and refused.

Police say Zulu was stabbed in the chest several times by the suspect.

He was taken to a nearby veterinarian, and passed away a short time later.

"There's no question that had he not been deployed to apprehend this subject, who was highly motivated to get away, we most likely would have seen one of our own members hurt or killed," says VPSC Acting Staff Sgt. Trevor Silken. "Zulu made the ultimate sacrifice and that was his job, and he did it well."

Although I had never met him, I felt very cheerless for Zulu. His job sucked. I speculate Zulu had been on this very table. I cried knowing I will see him soon.

I hoped that when the next batch of Delphinium flowers lost their petals that they float into the sky and band together to form arcs of coloured light. I loved the Director and the Producer and I wanted those arcs of light to forever bind me to them in the form of a rainbow.

The doctor was about to deliver the final blow when suddenly he stopped and excused himself. When he returned, SammyFarber was with him.

Knowing I needed to say goodbye to SammyFarber, the Director and the Doctor left the room.

'What are you doing here?' I asked.

'Getting medication to control my bladder. Last night I went on the paper four times, three of those times the Director was reading it.

'And you?' SammyFarber asked.

I told him what had happened. I told him about the special 'pull hard' training in the basement with the Producer. How I had disconnected the life support plug in the hospital and now they are going to end my life, I said. 'I confessed to my crime. I know, in the Shepherd world, what I did was wrong. But, I am a canine.' I said fighting back tears. 'I know if it had been me on that hospital bed, and I wanted to die rather than suffer with cancer then she would have pulled the plug for me.'

He asked me to repeat the part about the basement training again and what the cord was attached to. It seemed to matter to him? 'Iron? Radio?' Who cares, I thought. Plus, he wanted to know what I was hearing at all times in the hospital room. So, I told him 'Cow Cow Boggie' was playing in the background.'

SammyFarber had a sly look on his face. Remember the day they brought you home and you were filled with joy, go to that place while I explain. Every married couple has secrets. Did you know the Producer hates country music? Have you ever noticed that she turns off the radio the minute he leaves for work? She has never wanted to tell the Director because he likes it so much. Because when you love someone a whole lot you make those sacrifices. It's her secret. She is in the hospital for a very minor surgery. She will back at your house when you get there. From everything you told me, I think what you did, is unplug the radio for her. Geez poodle, you did not kill anyone except maybe a country western tune. Based on your age you are most likely here for a rabies vaccination. They probably gave you a preliminary shot to relax you. You being such a drama dog!

'Are you sure? Are you totally friggin' sure?' I asked SammyFarber.

'Given a choice between two theories, believe the one which is funnier, ' he said. 'And Poodle, let's keep what you thought you were doing just between us. Okay?'

'Swearsies,' I said, no longer feeling like the guy with the shovel walking behind the really big elephant.

After my rabies vaccination shot, the Director drove me home. In the morning, I had breakfast with the Producer, Director, SammyFarber and Malibu. She served bacon.

The End

Epitaph

It is with a heavy heart that I am tasked with informing you that Friday Poodle passed away suddenly on Sept 9, 2013 at 9:22 am. He was 8 years old. He suffered a massive heart attack, passing without pain or discomfort.

He will be remembered for his 5 years of service at the Saint Boniface Hospital in the palliative care ward.

In 2003, Friday Poodle received his Corporal stripes from Manitoba Search and Rescue for outstanding community work. And in 2011, was honoured with the rank of Lieutenant. In his lifetime, Friday Poodle achieved the highest level of Service dog status "Elite K-9". He overcame many obstacles to achieve this goal. Those of you who knew him well were aware that he had a very high-strung personality. However, Friday never gave up till he reached his goal.

Most of all, he will be remembered by his canine and human friends for his never ending smile. He left paw prints of love on many hearts. And, of course, he loved to play ball with everyone.

He will be missed deeply.

I love you Friday Poodle.

Purchase other Black Rose Writing titles at www.blackrosewriting.com/books
and use promo code PRINT to receive a 20% discount.

BLACK ROSE
writing™

Lightning Source UK Ltd.
Milton Keynes UK
UKOW06f1807060316

269703UK00006B/471/P